THE GRACE NOTE

BRIAN L. DOE

THE GRACE NOTE

ISBN: 0-9822056-7-8

ISBN 13: 978-09822056-7-9

LIBRARY OF CONGRESS NUMBER: 2008941894

COVER DESIGN BY ALL THINGS THAT MATTER PRESS

PUBLISHED IN 2008 BY ALL THINGS THAT MATTER PRESS

To Kelly,
Always…

To Billy, Bradley, Hayden, and Nathaniel,
Hitch your wagon to a star…

Acknowledgments

This book was not easy to write, nor was it effortless to conceive. Ideas are illusory little things floating in our heads, and with a monumental exertion of imagination, one might just have a story to tell. In the end, *The Grace Note* came from somewhere deep inside me, someplace real but perhaps forgotten. Yet, no storyteller is without the support of his family and friends, or of the experts and realists that are empowered enough to let him know when his facts are askew or almost ridiculous.

True friends and critics, editors and publishers, Philip and Debbi Harris, are responsible for reminding me of how powerful the mind can be, and of how special we all are. They stirred my muse more than once and never let up when she seemed confused. They are an ever-present aspect of my life and family, and I would be lost without them.

I owe a tremendous debt of gratitude to my friend and teacher, John Russell Lindsey—violinist, concertmaster, and professor at the Crane School of Music at Potsdam College. Not only has he inspired and carefully guided my own pursuit of playing the violin, but also he has been patient and informative. Without his willingness to discuss the more technical parts of the manuscript concerning strings, lessons, and technique, I would never have been able to present the reader with an accurate and true depiction of the craft.

Douglas Blackall, friend and music teacher, forever corrected my often erroneous wanderings through music theory. His perfect pitch continues to astound me, as does his fresh approach to the magic of music in general. It was he who first showed me how simple notes can mystify and amaze, making music for me an obsession that I will always have.

Jayne Roberts, longtime friend and colleague, set her critical eye on the manuscript in its early stages. I have often sought her advice and editorial prowess for my writing, and on every occasion she told me exactly what she thought. I value her analysis as much as I appreciate and fear her hard work and keen attention to detail.

My family suffered with me the most when new ideas died, and dead ideas haunted me. I thank my youngest sons, Hayden and Nathaniel, for loaning me their names, innocence, and hearts, and my oldest boys, Billy and Bradley, for giving me the drive and reason to reinvent the world, if only to convince them that dreaming makes us whole.

Of course, my heart and soul, Kelly, is not only my wife, but also my biggest fan. As a proofreader and brainstormer, she lent me her tears, her shoulder, and her unconquerable spirit. This story became as much a part of her as it is a part of me. She willingly poured her love all over this book, and she herself penned the words that would ultimately become Grace's note to Alex.

To all, thank you, even if I haven't mentioned you here. I am incomplete without you.

Table of Contents

PRELUDE 1
FIRST MOVEMENT 3
SECOND MOVEMENT 43
THIRD MOVEMENT 133
FOURTH MOVEMENT 251
CODA 295

Though tuneless, stringless, it lies there in dust,
Like some great thought on a forgotten page;
The soul of music cannot fade or rust,—
The voice within it stronger grows with age;
Its strings and bow are only trifling things—
A master-touch!—its sweet soul wakes and sings.

—Maurice Francis Egan, *The Old Violin*

And so, I lie beside you knowing that what began as a fairytale has unfolded our blanket of stars, the ones that we have wished upon all of our lives.

—July 2, 2004

"People ain't *was* anything in life....they're always who they were born to be...."

PRELUDE

Arms crossed, she stared up at a dozen stars strong enough to pierce the city's artificial glow with evanescent twinkles. From the fragile black void overhead she found a semblance of peace while all around her the earth shifted restlessly. A certain part of this woman did not belong here, hazy through magical fountain spray, teetering at the fringes of orange radiance casting pillar shadows across the segmented plaza. Yet, another fraction would live on in this space, entwined in the fragile melody of a thousand beautiful memories.

~

"I'll only be thirty miles from here," he whispered, crouched over the new grass with a hand on the stone to keep his balance. "If you need me…," but it hurt too much to say. Instead, he let the roses drop from his fingertips and onto the wet ground glistening in the morning rain. She had left the others to die already, the blood-red petals shriveling off the stems and falling away in brittle brown flecks and curled fragments. "I love you," he uttered, trying not to cry, not to allow that icy shudder to ripple up his spine and flutter into his chest again.

Once a week he returned to her. It never got any easier. He supposed he didn't want it to, because he feared losing her to the memories, to the intangible shadows of a dream that might someday become too distant to remember.

As late May's clouds rolled more thickly overhead, he swallowed the resentment that her silence bred in him.

If she would only answer.

Maybe then he would know just what to do.

FIRST MOVEMENT

"Do we have sex too much?" She had propped herself up on one elbow, the red satin sheets sliding off in the movement and exposing her bare upper body.

"I hope so," he whispered, kissing his fiancée's neck.

Her green eyes gleamed in the gray light smoking through the wooden blind slats. "Do you think it will ever get boring?"

Alex claimed to have won the most beautiful woman in the world. How and why she had come to him was anyone's guess. One day she was just there, and he had been drawn into her like violin strings winding on tuning pegs. Over time, he came to realize that when he had first met her on the side of a quiet street in a small town upstate, she hadn't been at her social best. Since then, he had witnessed her in gowns and dress suits, all made up and shining like a princess. And of course he'd seen her in far fewer pieces of clothing.

Nonetheless, the first time, in that initial instance of contact three years ago, she had been at her most beautiful. Cropped amber hair shining in the sunlight, her purple T-shirt fit snugly over her breasts and flat stomach. Those dusty blue jeans that she still owned hugged her hips and defined her in subtle curves and long legs. There were no airs, no diamonds or pearls, with the exception of a thin gold ring that shimmered in the summer sun from the middle toe of her right foot. No eyeliner obscured the natural glow in her crystal eyes; no foundation masked her creamy, unblemished face. Charlotte had been caught in her most perfect form, and the unpainted, unpolished image of the young woman had definitely piqued his interest.

Their first date had been in a diner called *Giovanni's*, though most of the townspeople insisted that it was a restaurant. He had a different idea of what constituted a restaurant. The upscale grooming of Manhattan surely played a role in shaping his thoughts of the outside world, seeing in it an appropriate model for the rest of humanity that might not have been quite as "civilized."

He remembered how badly he had wanted to kiss her that evening, but he had to settle for walking her to her car and watching her drive away. He did have her phone number in hand, however, scrawled on a small paper napkin that he'd carefully folded and slipped into his front pocket. A day later, from his small apartment in the city, he'd called and asked her out to dinner, this time at a real restaurant. She accepted, perhaps more willingly than he anticipated she would. There was something guarded about her, he'd thought. Mostly playful and maybe a little seductive, a greater part of herself always managed to rein her in; she grew somewhat more aloof and sassy the longer he was with her. Oddly, the defensive part of her personality had a greater appeal to him than the whimsical side. He had noticed the subtle vacillation of her demeanor on their first date, and it was what had left him on the curb watching her vehicle slide away from *Giovanni's*. Not until later would he discover what Chicago had done to her.

On a Friday afternoon, he left the city and drove north to meet her. From there, he took her back to the city, to a fancy Italian restaurant with red carpet and elaborately draped windows, called *Giovanni's*. The joke was worth it; she seemed to lose her edginess that night. She wore a lavender silk dress with spaghetti straps that Alex had been quick to incorporate into a corny pun. He loved the lines of her collar bones and the rounded squareness of her shoulders that the dress revealed. Her laugh lulled him into an easiness he had never felt before.

He still wasn't quite sure how one thing had led to the next, but what he did know was that he didn't bring her home until Sunday evening. He had gotten the first kiss on their second date, and their lips touching on the corner of two colliding city streets brought him to an ecstasy whose memory ached in his ankles. The relationship spiraled from there, and soon he spent every moment that he could with her.

"Do you love me today?" she asked softly at his ear.

"Yes."

"And tomorrow?"

"Even more." He pulled her toward him and squeezed her in his arms, brushing a hand through her tangled strands of hair. She nestled so peacefully in his hold that he thought she had fallen asleep again. "Are you getting bored?"

Suddenly alive, she sat up and looked down at him. She smiled. "Of course I'm not getting bored," she said friskily. "I was talking about you, Mr. Brogan."

Alex laughed at her and she let her naked body slump against him. "Believe me," he answered, "I am certainly not bored. You don't know how times a day I'm amazed at how much passion you still have. You overwhelm me."

She frowned. "Is that a bad thing?"

"No. You've latched onto every part of who I am. I couldn't imagine my life without you."

Charlotte kissed him. "I wish you could know how much I love you, Alex."

The moment grew ever more serious, and for only an instant, a heartbeat, he felt something ominous in the air. His stomach growled and he shucked the notion.

"I know how much you love me," he assured her. "But I love you more." He grinned at her.

"I'm serious," she continued unaffected. "I'm not talking about you knowing how much I love you. I wish you could *feel* how much I love you, the way it tingles through my body."

He touched her lips with a single finger. "I tingle, too," he said quietly.

Charlotte studied his face for a second before she spun away from him and bounded out of bed. She moved quickly, nakedly into the shadows of the room and abruptly reappeared with a violin pressed between her chin and shoulder, and a loose bow screeching across its strings.

"I am Mr. Alexander Brogan!" she announced. "Concertmaster of the New York Philharmonic Orchestra, and—"

"Tonight," he interrupted her speech, rolling out of bed, "I will play solely for the Princess of Manhattan."

He slid on his bathrobe and took the instrument from her. He tightened the bow hair as she climbed beneath the bed sheets and supported her back with a mound of thick pillows. Eyes sparkling, she waited patiently for him to raise the violin and begin to play for her, and only her. She loved these private concerts.

From memory, he glided the bow over the strings lightly then forcefully, back and forth, piecing together a movement made of all the little sounds and melodies he knew that she adored, that she often hummed in the stillness of the apartment as she read or cooked or watched television. He sometimes plucked the strings in *pizzicato* with the pointer finger of his bow hand; other times he colored the tones of notes with his left hand, with the quick and short maneuvering of his wrist in *vibrato*. No matter the technique, Charlotte beamed at the sacred expression of sound rising all around her as he played for her like a knight serenading a maiden.

If Alex had known that someday he would captivate the heart and soul of such a stunning girl with his violin, perhaps he would never have struggled so vehemently with his mother whenever she insisted that he practice or go to a lesson. Oftentimes, his sisters begged their parents to make him stop, to deliver them from the singular hell with which that scratching and screeching tormented them. He would have gladly obliged had his mother told him to put down the violin and go out and play with his friends. He would have sold his own family into slavery if it had meant freedom from violin lessons with Mrs. Jacoby on Mill Street. But Mom never told him to join the game of stickball unfolding in the road or to have a seat on the couch and watch MTV. Instead, every Wednesday after school he arrived at the old lady's house with violin case and music binder in hand. As an adult and a strings teacher himself, Alex eventually came to realize that Mrs. Jacoby was a kind woman with solid skills and teaching methods. But to a seven- and eight-year-old boy, she was a menace; the devil that robbed him of his childhood.

For a time in high school, he attempted to appeal to his mother's emotional side by persisting in the argument that honing his advanced violin skills was harming his chances of playing professional football. Regardless of his mother's apparent amusement, the logic didn't sound at all ridiculous to him at the age of fifteen, and he knew that his father had always wanted a son who played for the New England Patriots. In the end, the man only got half of his dream, and the fact that his father still considered Alex his "son" had astounded the self-conscious teenager for years afterward.

As a high school senior, and later as a college freshman at the Berklee College of Music, he had abandoned all tricks and manipulations and had settled himself into the perfection of his craft. He practiced more and longer, becoming a serious music student. He joined quartets, sat for the school's student orchestra, and attended concerts and events all around his college in the heart of Boston. Soon he was giving lessons to lower classmen and absorbing the praises and admiration of his professors. At twenty-one, with a year of college left to complete, he auditioned for an open violin position with the New York Philharmonic Orchestra. It was a second section position, but a position nonetheless. He won the appointment and later struggled to complete his college obligations while participating in Philharmonic events.

As a twenty-two-year-old college graduate, Alex moved to a first section position in the organization, which was one of the proudest moments of his life. Forever after, however, he sought the concertmaster's seat. The completion of a master's degree ultimately garnered him a teaching job at Juilliard, yet he still maintained his dream of someday becoming concertmaster.

And if he "played his cards right," as a colleague had intimated only a few days ago, he would be made concertmaster within the year, upon the retirement of the current one. Excited and hopeful, he planned to devote himself even more to the school and to the orchestra, proving above all else that he was a true leader and a talented musician.

Charlotte, as was to be expected, always contended that he was the best she had ever heard. He, consequently, continually reminded her that her sexual relationship with him mattered little in the classically-minded world of old men in tuxedos.

Alex bowed at the conclusion of his masterfully worked tapestry, and Charlotte clapped and whistled like a dazzled groupie at a *Def Leppard* concert. Her cheeks flushed red as he approached her and laid the violin across her lap.

"My lady," he breathed, and she wrapped her arms around his neck.

"Perfect," she said, "like always."

Standing, he tied the robe at the waist. "I'll make breakfast," he offered. "Stay right where you are."

After he had left the room, Charlotte plucked the strings of the violin on her lap. The sound made her giggle, and she took up the instrument and pressed her fingers on the fingerboard, all the while continuing to pluck the strings and to make shaky notes of varying pitch echo out of the f-holes.

He had told her two years ago, when he first played for her in the living room of their new apartment in a kind of christening ceremony, that the violin was a "Strad." Later, when trying to decide on an appropriate Christmas gift, a man in a music store had asked Charlotte what kind of violin her fiancé owned. When she told him, he asked how old it was. She wasn't quite sure, but she was certain that it was not a copy. The man had chuckled, obviously doubtful of her story. On New Year's Eve, while they rubbed shoulders with faculty from Juilliard and members of the music community, just before they had snuck off and had sex on the tiled sink of his administrator's guest bathroom, she told Alex what had happened. He had become mildly irritated, not with the man's questioning of the story, but rather with the insult Charlotte had been made to feel.

In a taxicab on the way back to their apartment, Alex, slightly off kilter with Chardonnay, explained to Charlotte—though she had heard the story a dozen times before—that a "Strad" was a Stradivarius violin. Antonio Stradivari made violins in Cremona, Italy from the latter half of the 15th century until the 1730s. The master violinmaker's design was said to be the most perfect a violin could ever be made, and historically became the model and standard by which all future violins would be crafted. Owning a genuine Stradivarius, he explained, was rare, since so few were known to be in existence, and those that were could sell for millions of dollars.

He had purchased the Strad at an auction in Prague, where he had once played in a summer music festival. It had been disguised in rags and twine and most likely passed off as an instrument of lesser quality. He had intended to have it repaired and hung in his study as a work of art; that is, until the man restoring the violin, after a careful inspection of it, called him one evening in disbelief at the fortunate find. Like the repairman, Alex kept the faith that it was genuine, pointing out to Charlotte the label affixed inside the body of the instrument that read: *Antonius Stradivarius Cremonensis Faciebat Anno 1722.* Moreover, he showed her how the f-holes in the body of his violin were slightly offset, affecting the symmetrical appearance of the instrument. This intentional discrepancy, though it was hardly noticeable from any distance, not only solidified the violin's authenticity, but also, Alex claimed, proved that the distinguished and gifted luthier had truly viewed his art from a progressive and aesthetic vantage point that had yet to be resurrected among modern violin makers.

The story made little sense to Charlotte; it didn't impress her beyond the woman's limited understanding of violins, bows, or music scores. She didn't care that her fiancé's violin was probably worth a few million dollars, sought after by the Smithsonian, or what kind of instrument it truly was or might be. If he was convinced, so was she, reverberating the simplicity of her trust and absolute belief in him. He only had to play for her, to make the pretty music, whether it be from a Stradivarius or an empty shoebox strapped with rubber bands.

She could hear that he had put on a CD of the London Symphony Orchestra's rendition of Mozart, Bach, and Beethoven's greatest works, the music whispering from the speakers of the stereo in the living room. Closing her eyes, Charlotte laid her head back and slowly drifted off to a dream of castles full of princes and white horses.

Twenty minutes later, Alex set a tray on her stomach and gently roused Charlotte from sleep.

"I have to get ready," he said softly. "I'm supposed to be at Lincoln Center by five."

She rubbed her eyes and focused on the scrambled eggs and toast on the tray before taking up the glass of orange juice and drinking from it. "By five?" she uttered, still groggy. "What time is it now?"

"Just after three," he answered, having left her side to dig through his dresser drawers.

"Just after three?" she squeaked. "I can't believe I'm still in bed."

"Think of the eggs and toast as a late lunch, then," he commented. "I have to get into the shower." He glanced at her, clean boxer shorts wadded in his hand. "We're always going," he said. "It doesn't bother me in the least that we've been in bed all day. There are some weeks that I don't spend half that time in here."

"Things slow down in the summer," she reminded him, chewing on a crust of toast. "Besides, this time of year is so depressing it's good to be busy."

"Summer is months away," he replied from the bathroom doorway. "Someday we'll give up this lifestyle and take it easy for a while."

Charlotte pushed out her bottom lip in an attempt to look especially sad. "But I love this life," she pouted.

"I know you do," he said. Alex considered her contorted face for a moment, and then laughed as he disappeared into the bathroom.

~

He stood in front of the full-length mirror and straightened his bowtie. Turning sideways, he ran his hands down the front of the white tuxedo shirt and glowered.

"Have I gained weight?"

Charlotte, wrapped only in a bath towel, sat at the vanity and brushed her short damp locks of hair. "You look great," she answered. "Sexy. You always look sexy in that tuxedo."

He wasted a few more seconds examining himself in the formal attire before conceding to the idea that it didn't matter. After all, the slacks were adjustable to one size larger in the event of an emergency.

"Okay, beautiful," he said at last. He had double checked his cuff links and pulled the tuxedo jacket from its thick plastic hanger, folding the coat on his left arm. "I'll see you after the concert." He leaned over to peck her cheek, but she turned her head and engaged his lips in a suspended kiss that could have easily stopped time.

"Bye," she whispered coyly, releasing him.

Alex stared into her eyes, absorbed the reflections dancing in the shimmering green irises. "Wow," he uttered, "you sure know how to make a man not want to leave the house."

She smiled widely and pushed him away in an easy gesture. "You're going to be late," she warned him. She glanced down at the crotch of his slacks. "We'll take care of that later."

"I'll remember you said that," he replied, going for the bedroom doorway.

"You won't have to," she called after him.

He stopped in the doorway. "Don't forget to call Monique."

"Talked to her last Thursday," Charlotte said. She was brushing her hair again. "We decided that we'd just meet in the plaza this time. Will's got some dinner meeting or something with politicians from City Hall. It must be so much fun being an assistant district attorney and a real estate lawyer, and kissing ass all the time," she quipped. "Anyway…"

Alex tapped his fingers on the door casing as he waited patiently for the woman's signature digression to end. He tried not to look at the digital clock on the nightstand, though the blazing red numbers continually gathered his attention and teased him with minutes slipping by dangerously. He was expected backstage at Avery Fisher Hall in the Lincoln Center complex by five o'clock. If he didn't catch a cab quickly, at least within the next three minutes, he'd be late. And potential concertmasters were never late.

"Monique said she'd call when they were on Broadway," she continued. "They shouldn't be late; we're just going to have to skip the usual dinner tonight, that's all."

"We'll eat together afterward," he offered, violin case now in his grip as he maintained a respectful composure in the face of a rapidly weakening patience. "I'll send a car over for you around 6:15, then."

"Okay."

He stepped into the hallway to leave, but—

"Alex?"

He reappeared, growing visibly harried. "Yes, honey?"

"I love you," she said softly.

Alex had to go, but he lingered just a second longer to smile at her, to let her eyes shine over him. "I love you more." He had to go, but the vibration of her soul streaming across the room toward him and rushing up his body kept him there for an extra moment.

"Be careful," he spoke finally, and then he hurried off to catch a cab.

~

Alex dialed Charlotte's cell phone number into his own for the third time as he paced up and down the tiled floor of a private warm-up room backstage. Again, he reached her voice mail and left another message for her to be careful, to call him as usual when she got to her seat.

"Don't bother getting back to me now. It's almost time to start. Just let me know when you're here…Sometimes I wonder why you even own a cell phone."

He knew that she either had the phone shut off or that she was gabbing with someone. It was true that he often mused over why she owned a cell phone when he'd always had issues with contacting her. Sometimes she forgot it at the apartment, other times she couldn't find it at all, and most often she turned it entirely off, or just the ringer, and let it fall to the bottom of her purse. She returned the majority of his calls—eventually. But on concert nights, no matter what, she never ever failed to have her cell phone on, available, and with her. It was the rule.

Always anxious about her safety, Alex had worked out a system with Charlotte months ago. Just before going onstage to perform, he would put his cell phone set on "vibrate" in his breast pocket, under the tuxedo jacket. Charlotte knew to call him when she had finally made it into the hall and had taken her reserved seat. Neither would say a word; the plan was only intended to assure Alex that she had made it to the concert safely by way of a silent signal. Of course, the entire plan had to be completed in secret if they were to have any success in thwarting the policy strictly prohibiting the use of cellular telephones in the building.

After the day he'd had with her, he wanted to hear her voice once more before facing the audience. Since the cab ride, he hadn't been feeling right. The pit in his stomach he usually attributed to pre-performance jitters had turned sour, slightly nauseating him. Charlotte's voice would relax him, and she would say something funny, suggestive, irrelevant that would ease the tension a little. However, she hadn't answered her phone, so the prospect of feeling any better disappeared. He would have to settle for knowing that she had made it safely into the tier box. Having her only yards away would be enough to get him through.

~

The metropolitan air felt ironically fresh and tasted pure. In the glare of a city whose burning lights could be seen from space, she might have actually detected a star or two in the clear sky if she squinted and concentrated on that dark spot churning above her. In the black evening gown running cleanly below her satin shoulders, and in the sparkle of her hanging diamonds, she was a perfectly beautiful reflection of the night.

Charlotte stood beside the fountain in the Josie Robertson Plaza of Avery Fisher Hall on the north side of Lincoln Center in Manhattan. Glancing back toward Broadway, she thought about whether she should have stayed in the limousine, like Gerald—the driver—had suggested. But she assumed that her friends would have an easier time finding her if she stood near the fountain instead of having them guess which of the thirty identical black limousines idling at the curb of the drop-off area, she was in. This was the first time she had ever had to meet them at a performance; they usually had dinner uptown then took the limo over to Lincoln Center together. Regardless, the warm orange light glowing through the columns of Avery Fisher relaxed her, and she absorbed a tingling exhilaration from the crystal light bubbling out of the gushing fountain. The plaza, sprawled out before her in segmented glimpses of concentric circles like ripples in a pool, put her on the edge of a vast and wonderful universe. She felt so tiny, yet so majestic—a princess wavering delicately in the rings of a spiraling, breathtaking royal court.

Moreover, she swelled with pride simply because she had become an intimate part of the tradition and the honor. Her fiancé, Mr. Alexander Brogan, was a distinguished member of the New York Philharmonic Orchestra, occupying a chair in the first violin section, and she had come again, like always, to see him play. Most of all, she loved to watch the players bounce the bows across the strings, barely understanding the technique as *sautille*, but always having to stifle the giggle in her throat whenever it happened. And the violinists' bows sliding straight up and off the strings so that their nimble fingers could pluck in *pizzicato* brought a smile to her face.

Though she and Alex had been together for three years, Charlotte never lost the wonder for the orchestra. In her mind, there was no experience equal to hearing strings played live, except for sex with Alex. And to her good fortune, she was able to hear that single violin weeping, laughing, and singing in the study of their 18th floor studio apartment each evening as Alex tip-toed through the stacked scores balancing tenuously on the Georgian stand they had haggled over at an antiques market years earlier.

The plaza grew steadily quieter. She glanced at her watch in fear that the overture would be starting soon. She couldn't very well forsake performance etiquette to enter the hall while the musicians were playing; there were very strict rules governing that kind of "rude" behavior.

Snatching the cellular phone from her diamond handbag, she dialed her friends, a young lawyer couple with whom they had become acquainted some time ago through Alex's position as a violin teacher at Juilliard. Their daughter, Natalie, was a pupil of his, and over the course of time, after the acceptance of an obligatory dinner invitation from the couple, they had become good friends. In fact, Alex held the husband, Will, to be one of his best friends in the city, not to mention a great contact to the District Attorney's Office for the occasional parking or speeding ticket. Eventually, it became customary for Charlotte to accompany Will and Monique to the orchestra in Alex's absence, and in their history of attendance together the lawyers had never been late or failed to call her if the plans had even remotely changed.

The overture would begin any minute and no one was answering on the other end. Slapping the cell phone shut, Charlotte became painfully aware that she was the last person left in the plaza now. Even the limousines had one by one rolled off to the parking garages. Only the noise of vehicles from Broadway and West 62nd and 65th Streets remained behind to wait with her in the open air of Josie Robertson.

"Damn it," she breathed, pulling the shawl tightly around her bare shoulders.

Charlotte gazed toward Avery Fisher Hall, fully resigned to going in alone and waiting at the hall doors until the overture was finished. Then she would sneak in quietly and take her reserved seat in the 1st Tier Box. She could not believe that Will and Monique would stand her up like this. She grew increasingly anxious the more she thought of it. After all, she was in the city. Manhattan or no Manhattan, the city was city—*everywhere.*

She was sure that Alex had already begun to sweat because she hadn't signaled him, and when he was nervous, he worried about missing notes, jumping strings, and other things that could only be important to a professional violinist. Though she felt uncomfortable with bending their trust just a tiny bit, she opened her cell phone again and dialed his number. After three rings, which was the customary length of time to wait, she hung up and dropped the phone into her handbag, certain that Alex's cell phone had begun to vibrate in his breast pocket and that the man could clear his mind of fretting over her and focus on the concert instead.

The fuzzy feeling against his chest made him smile. The orchestra was seated and had just tuned to the concertmaster's direction. He could do what that old man did, he thought—effortlessly. He could mark scores and manipulate time signatures, bowings, whatever. He felt his body start to relax since he knew Charlotte was in the tier box though the bright lights kept him from seeing her. He was more than ready to begin.

Charlotte counted the clicks of her heels on the segmented plaza stone as she made her way around the fountain and toward the hall, the ginger light of the building washing over her slight body. In the vast silence of the place, the simple ticking of her shoes almost annoyed her. Or was it because she was now officially late, or that Will and Monique never showed? Whatever it was that ate at her she tried to quell as she breathed deeply and held the air in her lungs in an effort to steady her nerves.

The conductor raised the baton and at once violins came up to shoulders, violas readied, cellos and double basses stood at attention. The baton dropped and in one swift movement violin and viola bows came down in unison and the concert hall filled with the opening notes of a building masterpiece. Quickly and loudly the overture swelled into the tier boxes and vibrated along the walls and through the floors, rushing into the audience. Alex plunged into the notes, consumed by their power and arrangement. From the elbow, he maneuvered the bow over the strings, jumping and shifting fluently as his other hand ran up and down the ebony fingerboard. He played higher in the middle measures until the piercing sounds screamed into the curves and angles of Avery Fisher Hall and the entire orchestra swooned like a swarm of bees changing direction and scattering off to their own rhythms.

Mind preoccupied, she never saw him approaching from the direction of the opera house. Unknowingly, she was far too removed from the building's entrance to have any hope of finding safety within it. And because the performance had already begun, security was undoubtedly concentrated at the hall entrances and at the back of the tier boxes. She remained ignorantly encapsulated in the empty plaza, and the city that moved carelessly and constantly all around the square—on Broadway, on West 62nd and 65th Streets, on all the streets all over Manhattan—was indifferently unaware of the danger approaching her.

The first violins culminated in a tumultuous vibrato as the second violins and violas fell beside them an octave lower. Cello strings groaned and the basses thumped over the score. Soon the orchestra hung suspended in a handful of notes, teetering on the edge of a maddening dénouement. The conductor jerked his arms, pulling the movement into a cascading finale that reverberated in Alex's ears, spinning and whirling all around him.

He had her by the arm before she had time to turn toward him. Opening her mouth to scream, he drove a gloved fist into her face, splitting her lip and reducing the noise in her throat to a whimper.

Coiled in nickel and brass, echoing from hollow wooden bodies, the sound rattled through the music stands and twisted out over the audience, breaking into fragments of melody and ringing harmonics.

"Don't scream or I'll kill you."

Double basses marched on in deeply pounding triplets. The violins delivered their song in soprano alto—higher, higher, threatening to shake the plaster from the ceilings, shatter the awestruck crowd into bits of rapture.

Charlotte fell forward, pain blitzing through the muscles of her face, but he held her up. She felt the chain of diamonds torn from her neck, and her handbag fall to the ground. He yanked her toward him, but she couldn't see his face. Her eyes had filled with tears and her head swam in a throbbing ache.

Bouncing down the fingerboards, the music rolled back and unwound itself, turning around the orchestra, settling over them.

"Come with me."

A sudden skip and the first violins flared again, burning the air in fifth position and trilling to the cellos' extinguishing hum.

A fire blazed up her spine and she fought against him. He wouldn't take her out of the plaza; she wouldn't let him take her. She laid an open hand powerfully across his slick face, and the fingers around her fragile arm dug into her skin. She yelped and writhed against him. He was angry. With her free hand, she clawed at his cheeks, his eyes. Someone yelled into the thick night air. Footsteps—

A half rest dumped silence into the hall. For a moment nothing moved, nothing but a quiet pulse of breath escaping the collapsing lungs of the musicians.

She felt the searing in her side; the sting in her chest. Suddenly she was free and falling to the cold earth. She screamed once and rolled onto her back, kicking her legs into the air.

An explosion of the final dozen notes tore open the silence and the Philharmonic crashed into the end of the overture and rose up again to the fevered applause of the audience.

It was over.

And he was gone—gone with her diamonds, handbag, cell phone. He stole away into the night having taken everything away from them.

~

The New York Times reported the loss soberly in a brief article of the *Arts* section. It frustrated Alex to know that the newspaper seemed to be making more of the idea that a prominent member of the Philharmonic had suffered a bizarre tragedy and less of the fact that Charlotte had been an actual person whom he loved so much. Though he'd rather have not read about it at all, any report of her death belonged in the obituaries and should have been only about her and the celebration of her brief, but passionate life. Yet apparently it was newsworthy that no official leads had been secured in discovering who had killed Charlotte, and that heavy reprimands had been handed down to Lincoln Center's security force. Besides, who killed people in the open air of a complex as public and majestic as Lincoln Center? What strange twist of fate had allowed one of "them" to infiltrate the diamonds and dollars of lower Manhattan? Alex was not only grieving, but also disgusted with what he thought he knew—the city, its institutions of music and art, its public servants. On and on the list in his head ran while a brooding resentment painted him in hueless shades that fell brusquely on the walls of his numb existence.

He had met her at an antiques market in Sleepy Hollow, New York. He hadn't been doing anything, really, but driving back from Ottawa on that warm, sunny afternoon in mid-September three years ago. But a music stand leaning against the casing of a broad flea market doorway had caught his attention, and he parked the car and made his way to it. The dealer, a middle-aged man with fading red hair and a strained smile, watched him closely as Alex lifted the stand and examined its condition. Immediately he realized that it was a Georgian, more than likely a replica, but nonetheless an old one.

The Georgian Period in England lasted from the reign of George III in the early 1700s through that of George IV who died in 1830. During this time there had been a revolution in art and architecture, one that Alex had always found fascinating. Burned into the wooden base of the stand was a seal bearing the calligraphic inscription, *Roberts & Langley of Hamptonshire, 1747*.

The stand had no doubt been used and thrown around somewhat as was evidenced by the patches of worn varnish and the chips in the feet and legs. There was a slight crack and a stray drop of red paint in the upper right corner of the shelf, but overall the music stand was in excellent shape.

"No shit," Alex had whispered, knowing that he held an authentic piece of Georgian history after all, no matter how—

"Can I help you, sir?" The dealer's shadow rolled up his blindside.

"This stand," he answered, "how much?"

The dealer showed his crooked teeth in an open grin. "I can't sell it to you."

Alex returned the smile, assuming an impending punch line. "Just tell me what it's worth and I'll pay you."

"Fact of the matter is," the dealer rejoined easily, "it's already been sold."

The man with the red hair nodded toward a young lady standing only a few feet away from them. Alex hadn't seen her approach, and the sudden awareness of her presence sucked any thoughts of the antique Georgian music stand temporarily out of his mind. He felt his consciousness falling into the sparkle of her crystal eyes, and a tingling sensation prickled his cheeks.

"You're five minutes too late," she quipped.

He glanced at the stand in his loose grip; had he stared at her a moment longer, he might have dropped it altogether. The afternoon sun strained itself in shimmering flickers through her short amber hair and outlined her thin features in a hazy aura. He swallowed once to ease the dryness spreading over the roof of his mouth.

"Why would you want this old thing?" he asked smoothly, though he struggled against his thickening tongue.

She stepped near him and took the stand from his sweaty hands. "I happen to be a music fan." Hesitating a moment as if trying to remember who he was, Charlotte turned away.

He touched her bare elbow. "Wait," he uttered. "What kind of music?"

Charlotte considered him playfully, the obviousness of her attraction to him dancing in the lenses of her eyes. "Is there a right answer to that question?"

He laughed. "There is an answer I'd like to hear."

"Then I refuse to answer you." She said goodbye to the antiques dealer who had stood back long enough to watch the interplay of the two strangers, then she briskly made her way to the sidewalk.

Alex hurried after her. "I'll double whatever you paid."

She halted and met his eager face. "No."

"Double and I take you out to dinner."

Now it was her turn to laugh. "Do you want me or the music stand?"

Good question, and he hardly had any difficulty answering it. "Okay," he said, "you're beautiful. Will you go out to dinner with me?"

In a word, she appeared shocked. Then the twisting ends of a subtle smile curled in the corners of her thin pink lips. She turned on the balls of her feet and continued down the sidewalk, leaving him in her wake to watch the movement of her hips. Her purple T-shirt fit snugly to the curves of her torso and had crept up enough above her waistline for him to notice the flaring points of a sun tattoo on her tanned lower back. He must have awoken in a dream to find this singular goddess plucking at his heart, for only in his wildest visions would such a beauty also be cradling a vintage music stand.

"Wait!" He strode up beside her. "Okay, forget about the music stand. Go out with me…just once."

"I guess *somebody* didn't want a music stand that badly, after all," she commented.

Alex enjoyed her wit and the way the words floated off her tongue. "I have a feeling that going on a date with you would prove far more valuable than some antique."

She stopped again and held out the stand to him. "You win," she said simply.

"What?" He took a step away from her.

"If harassing me about a date is your way of getting this old thing, then you can have it. You win."

He considered the offer. "How much did you pay for it?"

She set the stand on the sidewalk and threw back her head. "Unbelievable!" she exclaimed. "You're serious."

Alex watched the color flush into her brown cheeks and he smiled. She was gorgeous.

A flame burned in her eyes. "Fifteen," she said at last.

"Fifteen what?"

"Hello, dollars."

"Are you kidding me?"

"No." Her hands moved to her hips. "Fifteen dollars. And to think, it would have cost you more to take me to dinner." She flicked out her right hand. "Double," Charlotte demanded.

"Thirty dollars?"

Grinning sarcastically, she cocked her head to one side and nodded sassily.

He studied the music stand: Tarnished, chipped a little, small crack, red drop of paint. "It's got to be worth at least five hundred dollars."

"Forget it." She scooped up the music stand and marched down the sidewalk.

"I don't want the damn thing," he called after her. "I want to go out with you, really."

"Cheap bastard," she answered back.

"I'll give you a thousand dollars *and* take you to dinner," he added. "That should prove to you that I'm not joking."

Twenty yards away, she was at the side of a silver SUV, yanking the back door open. "Who do I look like to you, Pretty Woman?" she huffed, sliding the music stand onto the bench seat. She took a deep breath and held it in her lungs for a second. "Fine, meet me at *Giovanni's* at seven o'clock."

He only dared to close the distance between them by a dozen feet or so. "I don't know where that is," he admitted. "I'm only passing through."

She shook her head and slammed the vehicle door shut. "Well, that's a promising relationship waiting to happen. It's just down this street, at the end, past the cemetery. I won't be surprised if you don't show up."

"See you at seven," he said.

She looked him over one last time, and he was sure that she had that playful grin on her face again. But in a moment, she was gone, evaporating into the liquid ripples of heat rising from the pavement, abandoning him to the proverbial butterflies fluttering in his gut…

The telephone rang on the kitchen wall beside him, the sound screeching into his ears. Instantly irritated, he yanked the receiver from its cradle.

"What?" he asked hotly.

"Alex, it's Will."

"Hi," he breathed into the phone. Where were they? Where had they been?

"How you doing, buddy?"

Alex thought about the question. "I'll get through it," he answered at last.

"It was a beautiful service," Will continued solemnly.

"As funerals go, it was perfect."

"I wish you'd come to the house afterwards. I don't know if it's a good idea that you be alone today."

He smiled. His friend's words were almost ridiculous. "Being alone is exactly what I need right now, Will. I think I have to make some changes in my life. There are some things that I have to clear off my plate."

"Like what?"

He hesitated. "Just give me some time." He hung up the telephone and pulled the black tie from his neck. His head felt swollen with pressure and he could feel the blood pounding through his temples.

Weakly, he made his way down the hallway and into the study. In the middle of the room, draped in pages of music, the Georgian stand stood like a reprimanded child, still and mute, as if humiliated at its own existence. A practice violin rested quietly against the arm of a chair. He slid off his suit coat and dropped it to the floor, then reached for the violin. In one quick sweep of his free hand, he cleared the sheet music from the stand. Plucking a bow from a hook in the shelf, he tightened the horsehair and then set the instrument on his shoulder. He cried, but he could not feel the tears in the valleys of his face. Instead, he began to play, to rip out the third movement of Vivaldi's *Concerto No. 2, Summer*. In the rising and falling notes, his emotion crackled through the left hand and sprinted up and down the fingerboard. The passion overwhelmed him and he clenched his teeth. But it was all so perfect—the intonation, the power, the unadulterated hatred for the arrangement. He played on and on, pronating his bow hand so forcefully that the strings seemed to be fighting against the horsehair, wailing, threatening to break beneath the pressure. Louder and louder still the notes screamed out of the body of the violin, and he remembered, remembered…

Giovanni's was not at all what he had anticipated. *Diner* was closer to the truth than *restaurant,* but he found her nonetheless, in a booth at the rear of the establishment. She smiled widely at him as he maneuvered his body through the people and the chairs to get to her.

"I figured that since you were just passing through, my chances of you actually changing into something more decent were slim," she said as he slid in across from her.

"Something more decent?" he repeated. "What's wrong with what I'm wearing?"

"For a guy, you're dressed pretty well, actually," she confessed.

He checked over his attire just to make sure he hadn't missed anything—light green polo shirt, khakis, brown shoes. If anything, he presented himself more like a nerd than a professional musician, if any difference truly existed between the two.

"It's the shoes, right?" he asked timidly. "I always wear—"

"It's not the shoes," she assured him, smiling again. "It's nothing. Really, you're fine."

He gazed at her until he thought he had made her feel uncomfortable. "So, what's your name?"

"Charlotte. Yours?"

"Alex."

The way she peered at him through those sparkling green eyes captivated something deep inside his body. His heart beat quickly and his palms grew slick. Silence spread between them as *Giovanni's* patrons jabbered and shifted their bodies around the room, though the two strangers remained cushioned within their infant bubble. Alex glanced down at the table, trying to think of the next step. It had been quite some time since he'd last had a date, or rather since he'd last stopped running, playing, teaching long enough to go out on one. And the weight of loneliness had certainly settled on him over the years. But each minute seemed to align itself ever so rightly on that day, and without a sound the pieces fell flawlessly into place.

"You never answered my question," he said.

She grinned and looked away, pretended to notice something at the front of the restaurant. "Why does this whole relationship feel like some scene in a movie?" Her eyes were on him again.

"Maybe it's more a like a dream than a movie."

"You're good," she said, exposing her glossy white teeth.

She considered him for a moment and he thought he would stumble into those eyes.

"Do you even remember the question?"

"Rock, blues, a little classical—"

"A little classical?" he interrupted. "That's a great start."

"Why do you want to know so badly?" Charlotte put her elbows on the table and leaned toward him.

"I'm a musician."

"So what do musicians eat?" The round waitress stood over them, having come on the pair like a stealth bomber.

"Jesus," Charlotte gasped, a hand going to her chest. "You scared the shit out of me, Wanda."

With a husky chortle, the waitress pulled a pad from her apron and made her pen ready. "What'll it be?"

"Do you have menus?"

Wanda's cheeks jiggled in the tremor of another chortle and she touched Charlotte's shoulder. "Where'd ya get this guy?"

Charlotte tried not to laugh at Wanda or at Alex's building chagrin. "He's not from around here," she answered. "But you know, Wanda, only *Giovanni's* makes you read the board on the way in. It's probably the only restaurant in New York State without menus, so I think we can give him a break." She winked at him.

"Say," Wanda responded, "you really takin' off and gettin' outta this place?"

"Maybe. I haven't decided yet. You'll be the first to know if I do. How about two chef salads with grilled chicken and ranch, and a bottle of white?"

"Want the whole bottle?"

"Whatever you have."

As Wanda rolled away from them, he cleared his throat. "Where are you going?"

She picked at the corner of a paper napkin lying folded on the table. "Don't know. I haven't made up my mind."

"What do you for a living?"

"I have an engineering degree, and I've spent the last few years working for a surveying company. We're on a contract for the new high school in town. It's too slow for me, though. I suppose I could go to the city, but the thought of that scares me. I don't want to end up dead or something."

I don't want to end up dead or something…

"Engineering, impressive."

"Let me guess," she was watching him again, smiling, "you're a doctor or a lawyer or something?"

He smirked. "Now, that would be too slow for *me*." He paused. "Actually, I'm a violinist. I play for the New York Philharmonic and I teach at Juilliard."

Charlotte's mouth dropped open in pleasant surprise. "Wow, *that's* impressive. It's not every day that a girl meets someone with such an interesting occupation."

"It sounds more glamorous than it is, I think."

"I doubt it." She was leaning toward him again. "Will you play for me sometime?"

At the instant the E string snapped, Alex threw the bow across the room and snatched the violin from his shoulder. Enraged, at the apex of his grief, he swung the instrument over his head by the neck, and brought it down smashing onto the desk. The instrument cracked, split, exploded into pieces, leaving only the head and a few thrashing strings in his trembling hands…

In the next moment, he was moving slowly over Charlotte, her legs wrapped around his waist as he made love to her. Deeply, absolutely they consumed each other on the dining room table of her tiny cottage. And he played for her as she lay naked, nestled in the folds of a satin bed sheet. He drew out the peaceful notes of Pachelbel's *Serenade,* the passion of Massenet's *Meditation,* of Saint-Saëns' *The Swan*—easing each vibration, every melody and tone, into her quivering soul. And they had danced like children to Mozart's *Rondo in B-flat major* as the new sun snuck soundlessly into the living room.

Shortly after he had met her, in the swirling excitement of early autumn, she arrived at his Manhattan apartment with a special gift for him in a long box.

"What is it?" he had asked eagerly.

She curled up on the cushions of his leather couch. "Open it," she answered.

He tore through the paper and pulled open the flaps of the box to find the antique Georgian stand refinished and carefully packed in gold tissue paper.

"It's perfect," he said in an easy breath.

"Funny how things happen for a reason," she uttered, closing her eyes as his lips met hers…

"And what was the reason for this?" he spit through clenched teeth. Grasping the empty music stand he swung it into the air, his every thought intent on destroying it. But he stopped and lowered the gift to the floor. He slid down next to it, falling to his knees. Eyes blurred in the pain, in the wet doom of a broken heart, he collapsed onto the cold hardwood floor, embracing himself and the haunting memories in the dying seconds of the day.

~

Seated in a corner café, Alex watched the taxicabs scramble over the filthy pavement as pedestrians moved in unison up and down the sidewalks, mindlessly carrying their briefcases, purses, closed umbrellas. No one spoke to each other. Instead, they merely floated here and there past the window like lifeless images on a television screen. He was numb to their existence, and living among them was growing evermore bothersome. He had to get away from the city, its smell and noise. Too many faces reminded him of the past, of what his life had become. A collision of passion had buckled to violence, and he wanted nothing more to do with this metropolitan lifestyle, this perpetually running charade of smiles and sycophancy.

"Been here long?" Will stood beside him, silver tie flashing beneath the florescent lights of the café. He dropped into the chair across from Alex and unbuttoned his suit coat.

"A few minutes."

Will signaled to a waitress, who promptly approached and filled the empty coffee mug on the placemat in front of him. He nodded and she moved away from them. "Glad to see that you've gotten out of the apartment today. It's been a little while, hasn't it?" He studied his friend's face as Alex continued to mind the human migration on the other side of the glass. "Natalie tells me that you're not going back to Juilliard."

"No, I'm not."

"The Philharmonic?"

Alex met his dark eyes. "I spoke to the conductor yesterday. My tenure there is about up. I don't want to do it anymore."

"What are you going to do, Alex? Monique and I have been worrying about you for weeks. Natalie asks every day when she's going to see you again. You've got to let us know how we can help. There must be something that we can do."

Alex smiled half-heartedly and looked into his coffee cup. "If I'd had any problems breaking my contracts, I might have needed a lawyer." He paused, filling the hesitation with the gibberish of the café.

He hadn't had any trouble at all stepping away from his professional obligations, primarily because everyone felt sorry for him. He resented the pity. He could see it in their eyes and in the way they handled him, as if he were too fragile to touch. Will looked at him the same way, tip-toeing delicately through a conversation that Alex only partially believed.

In the end, his contribution and importance to the Philharmonic and Juilliard seemed so easy for them to release. The lack of contention from his colleagues and administrators toward his desire to quit the only profession he had ever known mildly irritated him. Regardless, it was over.

"I wanted to see you today because I have something to tell you," he continued. "I'm leaving, going north to teach."

"Teach?"

"Music, in a public high school. I start in the fall."

Will frowned, the idea perplexing him. "That's months away. What are you going to do in the meantime?"

The herd had commanded his attention again. Was it so hard to believe that he wanted out, that he needed to go away?

"I've got some money saved, some severance pay. I have to find a place to live, get myself acquainted with the area."

"Where are you going?"

"It doesn't matter." He set his jaw and let the lawyer's question ride up his spine in a warm tingle. He wanted nothing to do with any part of this careless existence, but apparently no one understood, no matter how much they expressed their sympathy or feigned concern. Unfortunately, he would have to completely dissociate himself from even those whom he'd called friends because he couldn't risk any intrusion on his new life. He needed to recreate the confines of that bubble he once felt himself inside when he'd first sat with Charlotte in *Giovanni's.*

Leaning toward him, Will shook his head. "This doesn't make any sense. You can't stop living, Alex; you've got to—"

"Start over." Alex gazed into the lawyer's face. "Start over," he repeated evenly. "I'm getting out of the city, Will. Consider it already done. Tell Monique and Natalie that I just had to go. I can't stay here any longer. I don't want to play the violin anymore, or cater to the crowds and the elite. No more perfect students and self-important prodigies. It's not in me anymore. It died with Charlotte. She kept me alive. You should have seen how she watched me play, how she giggled and smiled at the sounds and techniques. And she didn't know anything except that it filled her with so much joy. That's all she ever wanted, and she never asked me for anything else. The thought of her innocence still amazes me."

Will sat back in the chair and took a deep breath. Soon he, too, watched the apathetic New Yorkers scramble futilely to work. "Maybe it's the best thing," he said softly. "If it's what you really want." As if suddenly ashamed, he looked into his lap. "About that night, Alex—"

"I don't want to talk about that night."

"We should have called earlier. She never would have left without us if we'd only called to let her know that Natalie was sick, that we had to—"

"It was no one's fault," he said sternly, the muscles in his face twitching. "It was no one's fault." He rose abruptly from the table and stared down at the lawyer. "Goodbye, Will."

Will reached out and took Alex's forearm. "Please call. Let us know where you are and what you're doing."

"I might," he answered. And with that he made his way out of the café and into the pulsing streets.

~

He passed the next few months preparing to leave the city. He put a down payment on a house up north, and had arranged for his personal belongings to be trucked there. Now, he moved cautiously through the empty apartment, absorbing the echo of his shoes on the hardwood floors. In the study doorway, he took in the hollowness. A few splinters of the smashed violin remained, covered in tiny shrouds of dust. He had packed away the music stand, placing it carefully into the box that Charlotte had wrapped it in. It still contained the gold tissue paper.

Spring had crept up on him again, and he recalled the uncomfortable heat of summer to come that always suffocated them when the central air system randomly quit and they had to wait for the serviceman to deliver them from the hell. He remembered a poem that he had memorized in grade school for no particular reason other than because he liked the way it sounded. Strangely, the words came back to him in a different light as he stood staring into the voiceless spaces of the apartment.

Slate gray and silent,
Green pines hold the day;
Transient Summer
Has chosen to stay
At some later date
Far from here, now,
And Autumn moves in
With suitcases of clouds.
October's phantoms

Squander the night,
Then men who know nothing
Follow the light
That leads them to snowstorms
In Winter's frail clutches,
A manger, a fable—
He knows that so much is
Illusion and shadow,
Right down to Spring melting,
When cold rolls to nothing
And Summer is waiting,
Pretentious and smiling,
So silently gloating,
Striding toward heaven
With dreams he's stolen.

It would be better where he was going. Quieter, more open. No dreams to have stolen through the remaining seasons of his life. And there it could all go away—finally. He had decided not to destroy the music stand, but to bring it with him if only to remember Charlotte. He could never shatter anything about her. She had, after all, refinished the stand herself, meticulously sanding and preserving its detail. And she had done it all for him. Just him. The moment had been perfect, he remembered. Flawless.

The scene before him reflected the corrupted emptiness that haunted his every thought, and he turned from the doorway and moved soundlessly through the apartment. There was nothing left to consider; no pressing need to make sure he hadn't left anything behind. After all, only that piece of him he no longer desired to be remained. It was time to start over in a new place with new people. He would never forget what he had once been, nor would he soon lose that feeling of it all falling to pieces.

The sooner he left, the sooner he could begin again.

SECOND MOVEMENT

His big city mentality struggled to wrap itself around the lower standard of living he discovered in small town upstate New York. His apartment in Manhattan had cost him more to rent in a single year than what people were asking here to own an entire house.

On a whim, he bid low—very low. Whereas he half expected to find a decent house running somewhere in the hundreds of thousands of dollars, he in fact secured a Victorian for less than seventy-five thousand. From flashy, ultra-modern metropolitan style rimmed in slate and stainless steel, he found himself settling into old and plain, into wallpaper and oak, on a quiet street shaded by scarlet maples. In fact, all the houses on the street looked relatively the same, though some of his neighbors took better care of their property than others. His house was the only white one on the block, and the one that appeared to be most in need of repair. But he wasn't interested in repairing or remodeling anything at the moment. The roof didn't leak and all the windows opened and closed. There was a paved driveway, but no garage. Inside, the wooden floors were intact though worn, and there were not enough cracks in the walls to warrant concern. Overall, the dwelling was adequate for a man who still had no idea where he would be in a year.

By the time Alex made his final trip to the house from the city, the movers had already filled the lower rooms with his belongings and had vanished. Address changed and finances in order, he had no reason now to return to Manhattan. His new life began at this place, in the form of cardboard boxes and a large house that enveloped him in a new kind of emptiness. He refused to consider loneliness; enough minutiae flitted through his brain on a daily basis to reinforce the denial of his physical and emotional self. Instead, he passed the hours unpacking, ensuring that the process consumed ridiculous amounts of time and attention. He had shifted a set of six glasses from one cupboard to three others until deciding where they would be most accessible to himself and the phantoms in his head if the issue of needing a drink arose. Once inside the proper cupboard, there came the compulsion to choose the most logical shelf on which they would live.

Later, the excruciating time it him took to arrange a bathroom doubled with the fact that there were two of them, one upstairs and one down, and neither had a shower. He had sat on the toilet in one of the bathrooms and studied the cast iron tub and its clawed legs. No shower, but he could get used to it, he concluded. He no longer had to worry, after all, about having to fly into the bathroom and then bolt out again clean and fresh because he was crunching minutes between rehearsals, teaching, and performances. The pace of his life had slowed dramatically and he presently had the time and patience to think about things that never occurred to him before, like where to put the soap dish.

A temporary fascination he acquired—and yet another medium by which to avoid the dangerous emotions frothing in his stomach—had manifested itself in a television station solely devoted to interior design and renovation. He watched it continuously, or, rather, listened as he puttered here and there about the house. He even tried some of the suggestions, like laying out his oriental rug on the living room floor diagonally from the couch. But the idea soon struck him as absurd and he followed the more conventional means of decorating by positioning furniture and rugs in perpendicular and parallel lines, regardless of the network's criticism of how boring and unimaginative such tactics were.

Ultimately, he could not prescribe to the modern science of interior decorating and abandoned the television shows altogether. After all, very little of his old apartment had been designed by himself. If it hadn't been for Charlotte's touch and the advice of their interior decorator, the apartment layout would have screamed minimalist and unexciting. Alex would have never placed a single daisy purloined from the park down the street into a crystal vase and set it in the middle of the kitchen table "just because." Nor would he have spent the time to dump potpourri into a ceramic dish or deliberately lace back curtains so as to create symmetrical folds and creases in the fabric of the window treatments. Only Charlotte did such things, and only Charlotte could make it all make sense to him simply in the name of beauty. Without her, he preferred boring and uneventful.

He moved laboriously through each room, emptying boxes and restacking others into which he wasn't quite ready to delve. Couch, chairs, tables, lamps were all set out and carefully placed. Everything was almost in order. Across the foyer from the living room was an open space most likely used at some distant point in history as a parlor or den. Here, he put any box that held some connection to his musical existence, save for the CD player on a side table in the living room. He didn't unpack any of these items; even the Georgian stand remained concealed in cardboard leaning against a wall. He moved a rocking chair that he'd found in the basement beside the washer and dryer the previous owners had abandoned there into a corner of the room. Behind it, just out of sight, rested a black, hard plastic violin case containing a Stradivarius violin almost three hundred years old.

He had thought about putting it all into storage, but something kept him from doing so. Perhaps that lingering presence of Charlotte he was convinced he regularly felt caused him to hang onto the things. Then again, his life, since the age of seven, had revolved around music and the perfection of playing the violin. It was as much a part of him as his own heart, and letting go completely proved impossible. Alex convinced himself that by keeping the music scores, the rare violin, the Georgian stand, he maintained some certain element of sanity and identity. He was who he was, though there was nothing requiring him to act as he used to be. Many times, in his lowest moments of reflection and memory in the new house, he wondered if his decision was all an illusion, if he would eventually realize the idiocy of his resolution and turn once more to that ingrained desire to play. He supposed that either keeping true to his promise never to return the city or resigning to the only life he'd ever known would be as easy as cutting off a hand.

He had resolved to work through the house in silence. The façade of unshakable determination grew to nearly manic proportions, and he feared that listening to the radio, some classical piece, or even a *Bon Jovi* album would tempt him or depress him beyond control. He didn't like being out of control. But he wasn't so consumed that he didn't realize how illogically he might be acting. Someday, he told himself, it wouldn't be such a big deal; time would heal him. The problem was knowing how many days, weeks, months had to pass before he let himself be at least human, and, at most, normal again.

The greatest confusion that plagued him, however, was the population's apparent inability to understand how deeply the pain had embedded itself into his gut. No one could feel it burning as much as he could. Instead, he'd been viewed as depressed, maybe unstable. But he was neither; he had been in love and that precious gift had been torn away from him. In a horrible instant she was gone, and he felt as if he had been robbed of everything. Why then would he continue to add beauty to the world when all it had given him was darkness? And he didn't care if this belief was unfair or if it was the mark of a madman. Who were they—that ship of fools—to judge him? They didn't understand how happy he had been.

On his knees in the living room, he dug through a shoebox of business cards, ticket stubs, and general memorabilia of good times with Charlotte; memories he didn't have the strength to relive. Then he uncovered a photograph of the two of them entwined in each other's arms, beaming into the camera. In the background, the Eiffel Tower stretched into the cold, wet afternoon. He remembered the old man whom Charlotte had accosted in broken French to take their picture. As soon as the flash had gone off, she turned in his arms and kissed him so intensely that he felt the earth shift beneath his shoes. If he had allowed himself to get caught up in her lips any longer, he never would have stopped the old man from moving stealthily into the crowd, disappearing with their camera.

Later that evening, he made up for the abrupt reconnaissance mission that had pulled him away from her in the square. First dinner in one of the ritziest establishments in Paris, then candles and a hot tub in their hotel suite just minutes before midnight. He closed his eyes as the blood rushed into his head. He could still recall the feeling, the passion as he made love to her like he had never made love to anyone. Inside of her, warmth gave way to a release so complete that the heat of their bodies threatened to fuse them together for all of eternity. And perhaps they had sparked the last strong weld of their relationship that night. She had felt it, too; he knew she had. Afterward, he proposed. She cried so hard that he wasn't sure if she would say yes, or if he had upset her. As a matter of fact, she never did say anything; she only cried, slipped on the diamond engagement ring, then buried her head into his chest. He held her for a long time, until she reached for his face and kissed him softly. In the next moment they had rolled into the fire again, their bodies moving so synergistically that maybe they had at last become one being.

He wiped the tears from his face and dropped the photograph back into the box. Something about her had latched onto him from the instant he had met her, and though the days crawled forward without her, that something had not yet released him. He could still see her face as clearly as if she were just now sitting across from him, smiling, wondering what he would surprise her with next. He could taste her lips, feel her breath on his face and the curves of her body in his hands. In the creation of his own reality, he could resurrect her at will, but when he reached for her, Charlotte was merely what she had become—a figment of his imagination and the illusory world he continued to stitch together from the tattered weave of a thousand broken memories.

Only a single picture had been placed out in the house. On the side table, near the CD player, he had set a photograph framed in black of Charlotte sitting at a table in a dark gray evening gown. Pearls sparkled around her neck as she tilted her head toward him and grinned. In fact, the image was so perfect that he used to tease her about how it wasn't really her, but the advertisement picture that came with the frame when he'd bought it from Wal-Mart. Alex had snapped the photo at a friend's wedding reception, and there was little doubt in the subtle glaze of her eyes that Charlotte had been having a grand time amidst the elegance of the day. He wanted to remember her this way, as a princess in a great and wonderful world, because he knew that was how she had always felt, despite the energy he'd expended trying to get her actually to believe that she was a princess.

The look on her face in that photograph reflected the most captivating part of her personality. Kind and passionate, she had known no love as intense as theirs, and she was finally, truly happy. From a disturbed and troubled childhood, she had overcome obstacles by the time she was twelve that no kid should ever have had to face. Her father, a fireman and an abusive alcoholic, committed suicide days before her ninth birthday. On Christmas morning when she was twelve years old, she woke up in the family's run-down south side apartment in Chicago to find only a note from her mother under the Christmas tree, feebly rationalizing why she had decided to abandon Charlotte and her older sister the night before. Rural Illinois framed the boundaries of the remainder of her high school days. She had been sent to live with her father's parents on a dairy farm where she finally received the love that she had been denied since the moment of her conception.

Alex met her on the streets of Sleepy Hollow, New York over fifteen years after, unaware that the chance encounter had occurred during one of the few breaks she ever took from her job as a surveyor. Yet even before he would discover the unsettling details of her childhood, he had already fallen deeply in love with her, and she had embraced the attention and affection with every drop of her soul. His blood pressure rose with the thought of how completely and unconditionally she loved him. In the three years that they had been together, he had endured with her the death of her grandparents and the unexpected passing of her sister to ovarian cancer. And though the notion tore at him from the inside out, when Charlotte was killed, it seemed that the family curse had come full circle and closed on itself. If her mother was still out there somewhere, she would represent the last remaining element of the family. But, like Charlotte had in life, Alex didn't care if the woman was dead or alive. It didn't matter anymore; his only concern had ever been Charlotte.

On the first ring, he scooped the cordless phone from the coffee and table and pressed it to his ear.

"Hey, Alex, it's Dad."

His father, Reggie, was a retired machinist from the highway department in his hometown of Foxboro, Massachusetts. Shortly after he'd left the department with little more than a gold watch and a monogrammed pen, he and Alex's mother Janet, a school nurse, moved to Florida. He hadn't seen them since Charlotte's funeral, though Reggie called once or twice a month.

"How's the weather down there?"

"Warm and sunny," Reggie answered lightly. "How's the new house? You getting along all right?"

Unlike Charlotte, Alex had always had his parents supporting him. Though his father would have rather seen his only non-athletic son play professional football, he nonetheless accepted the boy's decision to go to college for music. And when Alex had been chosen to play for the New York Philharmonic, Reggie and Janet couldn't have been prouder of their son, though the atmosphere and pace of the lifestyle was tremendously beyond their grasp. His sisters, both older, had done well for themselves over the years. Marcia had married a dentist and Camille, the oldest, had finally made it through law school and was employed at a firm just outside Washington, DC. They had all rushed away from their hectic lives to be with him from shortly after Charlotte had been killed to the close of her burial ceremony.

"I finally got all my stuff from the apartment moved in. I'm trying to sort through everything now and get it into some kind of order."

"Your mother and I were talking about you this morning," his father said, "wondering how you were doing. She's at the store now. I just thought I'd give you a ring."

Alex smiled to himself. "Are you taking care of yourself, Dad?"

Reggie laughed into the phone. "You know me, always doing my own thing—"

"Even if it kills you. You've got to keep an eye on your blood pressure," Alex reminded him. "And stop annoying Mom so much," he kidded.

"I don't annoy your mother," Reggie responded. There was an easiness in his voice, a kind of reassurance that some folks just didn't let life take them seriously. "You know her, she's set in her ways and the world be damned."

"That's Mom," he said.

"You're all set with the new job and all that?"

He nodded. "Yes, everything's set. I just have to wait until September rolls around and I can start."

"What are you doing in the meantime?"

"Like I said, getting the house in order, trying to settle in. That's all." He paused, catching sight of the picture of Charlotte on the side table across the room. "Just trying to move on, Dad."

A moment of silence, then: "I know it's hard, son. And I know that only you can feel the real pain of the whole thing, but you've always had dreams and ambitions. Don't let go of who you are so soon. The more you let yourself sit alone thinking, the less likely you are to come out of all this stronger. You know what I mean?"

"Yes," he said softly, though he didn't really know what his father meant. It was still far too soon to let the pain go entirely. And the hope that once fueled his every move had dissipated months ago. Alex had no idea when he would be ready to live again, though he was growing tired of considering the point.

"Look, Dad, tell Mom that I said hello."

"I will, Alex."

"I love you guys," he added.

"We love you, too," Reggie said.

"I'll talk to you soon."

"Think about what I said, son," his father gently insisted. "You have a way of shutting me down every time I bring it up."

"I will, Dad," he answered, though he knew that the chances of trying to break out into a new mode of thought free of grief and confusion were slim.

He turned off the phone and stared across the room at the picture of Charlotte. Maybe he would put it away, pack it into the shoebox and hide it on the top shelf of a closet. But he wouldn't. Being able to look at her face whenever he wanted to offered some small comfort to him. Though he could no longer touch her cheek or listen to the sound of her voice as she tried to squeak out a recognizable note, she was there with him. And sometimes it crossed his mind that perhaps as she stood over him in the silent night or sat across from him at the dining room table she wondered why he continued to torture himself. No doubt, Charlotte would be angry at him for having seemingly given up. His dreams, after all, had been hers, and if from beyond the grave she still had some investment in them, he had no right to abandon what had made them happy, what had made them who they were together, without first securing her opinion in the matter.

Then again, there was no longer anyone to negotiate with, or to consult. The love of his life was gone, and he had sold his stock in faith and life to some darker part of the world.

~

"Hi."

Head ducked under the open trunk lid of his Volkswagen, he stared disgustedly at the piles of sheet music that had shifted sometime during the last trip up from the city, and now lay completely unorganized in a thick and heavy sea of paper. It wasn't that he hadn't heard the tiny voice; instead, he ignored it. He'd seen the little girl sitting on the front step of the house next to his when he had pulled into the driveway, and in light of the present task spread out before him in utter disarray, he was anything but feeling friendly.

"Hi."

He closed his eyes for a second, just to make the mess and the irritating pitch of her voice go away—if only for an instant. Then, out of the subtlest sense of guilt, he backed away from the trunk and glanced over at her with a forced smile that she returned in a toothy grin.

"I'm Kelly."

Nodding politely, he considered the catastrophe in the trunk again.

"I'm ten. They say I'm a prodigy."

Ten? Bone-thin, she didn't look ten. For some reason he expected a ten-year-old to be taller. Of course, she was sitting. Maybe standing she would be longer. No matter, it was obvious that she was lonely and just a little too congenial to be a normal kid. Straightening his cramped back, he laid his open hands on the trunk lid and slammed it shut.

"Prodigy of what?"

She twirled a brown curl in her pointer finger and rolled her big eyes. "Math, science, music. Things like that."

"Things like that," he repeated evenly. There was nothing in the world that he really wanted to talk to Kelly about, and he knew that if he didn't turn from her and go into the house now, he'd be unwillingly sucked into some prepubescent prattle about dolls and boy germs—

"What's your name?"

And it was beginning already.

The screen door of the porch swung open behind the girl and a fat old woman in an offensively flowered muumuu appeared. With a paisley handkerchief, she patted the sweat that continued to form below the silver bangs of her perm while she pushed the eyeglasses back up her greasy nose with a single, pudgy finger of her other hand.

"Kelly Jean," the woman commanded, "you get your bottom in this house right this instant. Mr. Grady will be here any minute and you've yet to change those dirty clothes. And there best not be anymore frogs in my laundry basket, either." She became suddenly aware of Alex blankly watching her. "And who are you, and why are you bothering my granddaughter?"

"He's our new neighbor," Kelly chirped. She frowned and put her chin into her hands. "But I don't know his name yet."

"Well, welcome to the neighborhood, mister," the grandmother offered indifferently. "Now, if you don't mind, my Kelly's got to change those clothes."

Before he could blink, the large old lady and her skinny little granddaughter were gone and he was left staring at the chipped and faded green paint of his neighbors' front step.

An hour later, Alex had managed to siphon the trunk of its paper ocean and transfer the scores to the living room floor. Amidst the boxes and crates he had yet to unpack stacks were slowly taking shape again. One for Bach, one for Beethoven; here a few sheets for Ernst, and there some for Kreisler, Bruch, Paganini. And as he meticulously sorted each masterful piece, he grew ever more keenly aware of how much he had come to resent these composers. What did they know about human emotion—about life and death? He hated the very notes that she had loved, that he had loved playing for her. Now Vivaldi's second movement of *Winter* was as inspiring as any cold, dark moment of the real season. What *nocturne* was it that had made her cry? How she would laugh at the bouncing bow in *Joy to the World*. Perhaps these were the reasons he held onto the music. It had given her life, and at last it had become her memory.

The crunching tires of a station wagon pulling to the curb drew him curiously to the front window. Absently, he watched as an elderly man in a white button-collar dress shirt, corduroy blazer, and khakis climbed unsteadily out of the vehicle, wisps of thin, gray hair scattering incorrigibly over his bald forehead. Reaching back into the car, the man produced an instrument case, rectangular and leather-clad. Instinctively, Alex recognized it as a violin case.

"Musical prodigy," he mumbled, suddenly uneasy. "What are the chances, Mr. Grady?"

As the old man set off slowly and stiffly toward the neighbors' house, Alex retreated to the kitchen; more pointedly, to the refrigerator from which he took a cold beer, twisted it open, and consumed a quarter of the bottle in a single gulp. The occasional "shot" calmed his nerves. And when there were no shots of hard liquor to be had, a good slug of malted barley flavored with hops was a sufficient substitute. After all, he often mused, the calming of his nerves was more in the action than the alcohol. It wasn't an excuse, he told himself. In reality, if he had a single beer or shot more than twice a week he was doing something. The world was not yet ready to label him an alcoholic; he didn't have the habitual nature to enslave him as such.

Another swig of beer convinced him that he would rather have the coffee he'd brewed at dawn, still warm in the pot of the coffee maker. Mug in hand, he grabbed the *Times* from the counter and went out onto the deck to relax in the late morning sun. He didn't miss the metallic view of steel and glass from the rooftop veranda of his Manhattan apartment. He would never trade the fresh, clean air of his new backyard for the polluted, petroleum based sounds and smells of New York City. If anything, Alex spent more time gazing into the flawless blue sky, imagining the shapes in fragmented puffs of clouds than he probably should have. But he could hear birds singing—never out of tune or blaring like taxi cab horns. The light summer air rustled ever so gently in soft vibrations through the trees here; the rain brought a freshness and relief no open fire hydrant could fake. Besides, in about two months he would be officially a new member of the music staff in the local district, and he would never again know the stress and heart-taxing pace of professional musician or respected academic. As a regular public school teacher, he would finally take it easy for a while.

Avery Fisher Hall had become only a shade in his subconscious, and Lincoln Center's sprawling plaza a scarlet stain on his soul; so much the less for Juilliard. He'd made a new commitment between soul and mind, and no matter if the gates of heaven groaned open and God himself gave the order, he would never return to that poison bubble, raise his strings to eager students or pretentious concert guests and their glittering façades. Not again—that nightmare was over and only its ghosts continued to harass him. Big and small, those phantoms were constantly there, and he never quite knew when they would pop up or in what form they might manifest themselves. He decided that nothing good would ever come to him in the years ahead, for his God had so ruthlessly seized all he had held sacred.

His body sunk into the canvas mesh of the reclining patio chair. He had set the empty coffee mug on the weathered planks of the deck and, with the newspaper folded neatly on his lap, he thought that he would close his eyes for just a minute. The noonday sun wetly traced the subtle lines and angles of his aging face, and its warmth spread sleepily through his chest and legs. Not so long ago, he was nine years old and playing his first concerto in front of an audience of parents, teachers, and friends. Not so long ago, the precious life in a young man gained decades in a single tragedy. He was tired now, and apathetic.

"The tone is off because the right hand technique is atrocious today!"

Alex turned his head to one side, toward the back of the neighbors' house in response to the sudden voice. His eyes remained closed, but he felt the consciousness rising in him from the threshold of a colorless sleep.

"You will do it my way or no way—"

Lids flickering open, he peered with foggy eyes at an open window—

"Play it again."

Mellow sounds of half-notes bowed from lower strings settled on him, urging the awakening. His eyes began to clear and he sat up, rolling his head to loosen the stiffness in his neck and shoulders. Violin tones vibrated at his temples.

Through the open window of the house next door, he caught glimpses of the little girl and the old man each time summer inhaled and drew the lace curtains toward him. Stiffly, at an iron music stand, she carefully pushed and pulled the bow over the strings of her violin while Mr. Grady loomed crookedly near her, tapping out the time signature on her shoulder with the eraser end of a pencil.

"Now faster," the old man insisted, "and mind the slurs."

He could not see her fingers working over the ebony fingerboard, but the sound alone of the mundane scale scratching out of the room and into his backyard convinced him that she was nervous. If only the old man would step away from her and let Kelly move through the notes uninhibited…but he shouldn't care about the notes or the little girl. He didn't teach violin anymore; he had no right to comment, mentally or verbally. Instead, he closed his eyes again and tried to ignore the whole affair, like he'd tried to ignore the skinny ten-year-old on the porch steps two hours ago—

"No, no, no…if you can't feel the progression, you'll never play at Juilliard."

The word stung him and he found himself staring through the window one more time. Rising from the patio chair, he moved to the railing and leaned toward the house to get a better look at the practice session. Mr. Grady had relocated his ancient form to the other side of the music stand so that he could glare at the girl over the top of the sheet music.

"You've got to get away from her," Alex breathed. "Let her play the damn thing."

Finally exasperated, Kelly dropped her bow arm to her side and glanced up at the old man sheepishly. "I can't—"

"Then you have no desire to learn, young lady. I'll spend my time with those more suited for the solo stage." Mr. Grady hastily gathered his violin case and sheet music and marched past the window as Kelly's glassy eyes followed him.

"You can't teach like that," Alex said aloud. He shoved himself away from the railing and moved quickly through the house. By the time the old man was a few feet from his station wagon, Alex had already stepped out onto the front porch.

"Excuse me, Mr. Grady?"

At the bumper of the station wagon, the old man halted and turned toward him. "Do I know you, sir?"

Alex smiled weakly. "I doubt it," he said. "I just wanted to remind you that a good strings teacher never sacrifices the student's individuality for the sake of the art. You must know that. Hartmann, Auer, Heifetz, they all believed in the idea."

Mr. Grady stepped toward the curb, clutching his violin case. "And I suppose you're somewhat of an authority on teaching violin. What are the odds you'd be living here, next to this aspiring young lady? My God, if you're so well versed in the art, you teach her."

Alex considered the gray face for a moment. "My intention is not to teach her, I only—"

"Sir," Mr. Grady huffed on, "I am a graduate of Berklee and an accomplished violinist. What dribble graces your resume, young man? When did you play your first piece before the wondering eyes of a full house?"

"I was nine," he answered.

The old man hesitated. "And I suppose it was something worthy of being played even wet behind the ears."

"Actually, it was Mendelssohn's *Concerto in E minor*, 2nd movement. It was my first solo appearance."

"How impressive. So that validates you as—"

"By the time I was twenty-one, I had a chair in the second section of the New York Philharmonic Orchestra. Less than a year later I sat beside the concertmaster. At twenty-three, I saw my first student in a classroom at Juilliard. That validates me as an authority on teaching violin. But all the while I maintained my individuality. The best teachers in the world never threatened to take that from me. If you rob her of who she is, you're right, she'll never make it into Juilliard. And my suspicion is that she'll only have you to thank."

"Good day, sir," the old man said with finality and with a certain pallor in his brow. He turned unevenly on his heels and got into his car.

In the den, Alex pulled his violin case from behind the rocking chair and brushed the dust from it. He laid the case on the desk, the tips of his fingers lightly tracing the plastic lines and aluminum trim. He didn't need the instrument on his shoulder to remember the feel of it, to recall the bow balanced in his hand. It was instinct, and his perfect pitch could make the notes in his throat without strings or keys. In effect, there was no need for the violin at all, save the magic of its voice.

The nostalgia waning and the weakness passing allowed him to hold fast to his resolution. Grasping the handle, he yanked the case from the desktop and placed it again behind the rocking chair.

~

A dozen times a month he would dream about her and the black butterfly. At first the images were strange to him, but gradually he found some subconscious element of Self interacting in the fantasy. He could project himself at will into the illusion of Charlotte and her butterfly, but he seemed prohibited from making the dream happen. Instead, he often wondered when it would come again. He would see her sometimes for nights in a row, and at other times not for days. But as the moments gained clarity with each passing occurrence, he saw her there in a black dress, sitting on a patchwork blanket beneath a flowering tree. In an instant she'd be naked and he was over her, then he'd be stretched out beside her, brilliant sunlight shining at her hips. And she whispered to him—*Alex, Alex*...Smiling, hair tangled in the clean sunshine—*Alex, I love you*...A black butterfly, gliding gracefully through calm blue air, forever fluttered to a landing on her bare shoulder. His hand, as if extending from some invisible point behind a camera, would come out to brush the butterfly away, but she'd touch his forearm, stopping him. He could feel her cold fingers on his skin, and always when he awoke, the sensation lingered for minutes afterward.

He had never been able to move past that spot in the dream. As soon as she touched him the illusion would end, black butterfly on her shoulder. He eventually came to his own interpretation of the dream: The butterfly was his personal metaphor of death, and Charlotte not only appeared to him wearing the last piece of clothing he'd seen on her, but also in the form in which he loved her most.

Alex had watched from the edge of a sterile curtain as they cut off her evening gown in the emergency department. The baton had been raised for the first movement when his chest began to vibrate and his heart dropped into his stomach. Without reaching for the phone hidden in the inside pocket of his tuxedo coat, he stood, his eyes catching the astonished expression on the conductor's face, the disgust in the concertmaster's frown, and hurried off the stage to the warm-up room. Will gave him the grim news; the lawyers had arrived only seconds after the attacker fled. Monique held the dying woman while Will futilely pursued the murderer to the fringes of Lincoln Center. In the next breath, Alex was racing down the hallway of New York–Presbyterian Hospital, screaming for Charlotte.

Maybe then, watching on in horror as the doctors and nurses quickly prepared her for surgery, he had seen that black butterfly weaving like a shadow through the room on currents of fear. Surely, it had finally found its resting place somewhere on her body when she died on the gurney just as the doors of the operating room swung open to receive her.

Mid-afternoon lulled him into sleep as he laid himself back on the living room couch. He'd never been as lazy in his life as he had been for the last week. He lived in a small town now, with no professional engagements to attend. She greeted him quietly beneath the tree, warm smile exposing glistening teeth. The sun glowed white in the branches of the tree whose pink blossoms fell all around her like delicate snowflakes. He moved toward her, reaching for her, until at last—

The telephone rang beside him and his body jerked to consciousness. Sitting up, he rubbed his temples, suddenly irritated.

"Could I please speak to Mr. Alexander Brogan?"

He squeezed the phone in his right hand as hard as he could, wishing he could crush it. "This is him."

"Hello, Mr. Brogan, my name is Cynthia and I'm calling on behalf of Nationwide Telephone Company. This month Nationwide is offering—"

Whatever the telephone company's deal of the month might have been, it was lost in the explosion of plastic and low voltage wiring as the cordless phone burst against the wall on the far side of the living room.

~

He had discovered that a person could *feel* death. The ordeal was more than waking a body, attending a funeral, and witnessing a burial. For the living, there was a branded sensation in accord with dying; a surreal uneasiness that could be stirred at will and let to creep into the bloodstream of a still-beating heart. Perhaps the inevitability of death brought people into kinship with it, he mused, and as family and friends passed on first, the feeling came to remind us that we are all waiting in line to die, despite bets wagered on everlasting life in a place called heaven.

A thin band of sunlight filtering through the bedroom blinds streaked warmly over his face, waking him to the morning symphony of birds in the red maples outside his window. For a moment, he listened, counting the time, naming the notes, watching them suspend on imaginary staff lines and compose themselves into invisible sheet music. But the abrupt noise of the old lady's voice interrupted the score, and it fizzled into his subconscious mind.

Beside the nightstand, he peered through the blinds as the woman emerged from the front of the house, pulling Kelly by the hand alongside of her.

"The service starts at ten," she barked. "We're going to be late if you don't get your bottom in gear. And we will *not* disrespect the man's soul that way, missy."

Kelly followed obediently, head down and black velvet dress flowing at the ankles, as her grandmother whisked her around the house. In an instant they were gone, and a minute later the lady carelessly maneuvered a vintage silver Plymouth Duster out of the driveway and down the street.

Hot water flowed soothingly over his shoulders. He lay in the bathtub and stared blankly at the steam forming white images of Charlotte that in the end were still only steam, formless and intangible. The morning of her funeral played out freshly in his head; the little girl's black velvet had resurrected the memory of those hours before he'd destroyed the study in their studio apartment.

Monique had planned most of it, sparing him the agony of completing such a task on his own. The service had taken place at St. Patrick's Cathedral on Madison Avenue so as to accommodate the anticipated overflow of mourners who would come to pretend, to pay their respects because they knew *him,* or because they felt obliged to honor the illusory camaraderie of the professional musical bond. Securing the gothic facility of vaulting stone and stained glass had no doubt been made easier by the fact that the archbishop was a patron of the New York Philharmonic

Orchestra and was in some fashion related to a well-known cellist back in the old country, wherever that had been. He had sent his condolences through the lips of a groundling priest: *Godspeed to the soul of such a wonderful musician whose talent will sing eternal in the Kingdom of Heaven.* The archbishop obviously had no idea who had died, choosing only to hear the words that might fall favorably onto the collection plate.

On a bright Tuesday morning, Juilliard's faculty arrived in force. Even Doug, a custodian at the school, had taken half the day off to don his best shirt and tie and attend the funeral of a woman he had never even met. Members of the Philharmonic solemnly filed into the pews. Among them was the hoary concertmaster, Stephen Winslow, whose eyes betrayed a true sadness that shamed Alex for having in the past wished for his demise. After all, he occupied a station that Alex had coveted. The old man's leathery face had worn the ugly mask of disgust the last time Alex had seen it, on that horrible night when he had abruptly departed from Avery Fisher Hall's stage, abandoning its audience and its orchestra. When the news had finally surfaced about the tragedy in the plaza and their ears had been stung by the gruesome details, maybe all of them forgave him in some small way for tarnishing the Philharmonic's stellar reputation. Maybe then, the embarrassment that each member had felt seemed trivial in the loss of a human life. The conductor made a vain attempt at approaching his grieving colleague, but seemed to reconsider in the weight of the moment. He slipped into the shadows of the rear pews and disappeared among the others.

Alex weakly shook the hand of Lincoln Center's chief of security, numbly absorbed the apologies that a week later would be formally delivered in writing, via the United States Postal Service, on heavy cotton bond paper complete with an elegant water seal. He had opened the letter, scanned the apparently sincere words and then mailed it back in a new envelope without so much as an acknowledgement. He supposed that ultimately people were sorry, maybe even genuinely so, but it didn't make the loss any easier to endure. Letters, cards, flowers, words came from all over the city and from some parts of the state, country, and Europe. Regardless, they hardly filled the churning void only Charlotte could satisfy.

Students arrived with their parents and sat quietly in awe of St. Patrick's soaring arches and its gaping vastness. And relatives came—aunts, uncles, cousins he had never met and others he could do without. Many of them had flown into the city from other states and rented rooms in Manhattan hotels that surely taxed their budgets. Still, they had come for him, for the mysterious girl that had sadly died. They were confident that she had been good for him, though they didn't know her name, and they never had. But Monique and his parents had not been remiss in any way with letting the family know what had happened. He supposed it had to be that way in order to affirm the value of having relatives.

One person hadn't come, however. At least he didn't know if she'd been there. He wouldn't know, he was sure, even if he had seen her. Charlotte had had so few photographs of her family, and the ones that had been framed and displayed in the small cottage she used to own were mostly of her grandparents and her sister who'd died of ovarian cancer. He remembered a small picture of a middle-aged man in a fireman's coat and helmet, her father. It sat nearly concealed on the mantle of the fireplace by a bouquet of silk flowers. She had only kept a single photograph of her mother, and it was the woman's high school senior picture. Though he remembered the large dark eyes, the angled chin, and the same inherent beauty with which Charlotte had glowed, he wondered if her most striking traits would reveal themselves to him if he ever saw her. But she hadn't come. He was sure that he hadn't seen her, no matter how much he doubted he would even recognize her.

His parents and sisters had been the first to arrive. He smiled even now thinking about them. Somehow, his sisters bitching about a scratching violin in the living room, his mother barring a young boy from the life of a "normal" kid, and his father's failed dreams of being an NFL dad proved totally insignificant in the light of what each had become. They had all grown up and settled into the commitment of leaning on each other, for better or worse. And he loved them for it.

Mom and Dad sat on either side of him in the first pew, holding his hands as his body trembled and he fought to keep his eyes dry. Behind him sat his sisters and their husbands, and from time to time he felt the girls' hands on his shoulders, on the back of his neck. He couldn't look at the white casket accented in gold and draped in the cloth of St. Patrick. He couldn't do it, and he didn't want to remember it. Instead, he stared at the hundreds of flowers that crowded the altar, stared into the ruffled and fluted petals of red, white, yellow, purple until his eyes felt like they would bleed. Voices echoed in the ceiling; a string quartet sounded from some alcove hidden above him. Prayers and blessings. So many tears…

Alex and his family, along with Will, Monique, and Natalie quietly accompanied the explicitly private funeral procession thirty miles north to Sleepy Hollow Cemetery, not far from where he and Charlotte had met only a few years before. He'd thought about taking the group to *Giovanni's* for lunch, but, nausea aside, he suddenly resented himself for having considered the notion. That had been their special place, and he wouldn't unbalance its sacredness by going there without her.

In the bedroom, he pulled an olive green golf shirt over his head. Collar up on one side and down on the other, dark brown hair a thick, wet, incorrigible mess, he stared at himself in the mirror for a long time.

The sensation had started almost as soon as he had gotten into the bathtub. Now he could feel it aching in his knees and crawling through his lower back. A sadness had come over him; a knot had formed in his stomach. The sunshine outside his window no longer lingered in the bedroom. Shadows had already begun to form in the far corners, and the muted light reflecting back at him from the crystal surface of the mirror painted his face in pale tones.

Mr. Grady was dead.

He could feel it, just like he could the night Charlotte died. Different people, same sensation. He felt as if the universal soul had shifted, and the energy had subsided for only a moment. A single heartbeat. Then the machine had come to life again and the earth moved on without them.

~

Four *Tylenol* later, he could still hear the monotonous exercise echoing out of the neighbors' house over and over, no matter where he retreated to in his Victorian. His head pounded with the notes, and it was becoming unbearable. Alone in her practice room, the little girl stroked out an elementary étude, a short piece of music intended for the practice of technique. It was something from Suzuki, he gathered, a kind of method for playing the violin developed in the mid 20th century by a Japanese violinist named Shin'ichi Suzuki. The method had become the most popular form of teaching violin in the world, and one that even Juilliard had embraced. Needless to say, he had gotten very familiar with the method over the years, but he never thought that he would have to hear any of its lessons tortuously repeated throughout the course of an hour.

She played it well, he admitted with an ice pack on his forehead as he lay prostrate on the couch in the living room. Her intonation was perfect, as each note rang true and exact, and whether she played it slowly or quickly, she never missed a beat or scratched out some random sound. Just by listening to her play for the first few minutes after she'd begun, he could tell that she had an uncanny command of the bow and that the fingers of her left hand were strong and nimble. He only wished that she would stop playing, or at least do something else. But she had kept the damn window open and had set herself to performing the same piece dozens and dozens of times. He had closed his own windows, at least the ones on that side of the house, forty-five minutes ago, but the sound seemed to be leaking through the clapboards.

Eventually, as if herself tiring of the tedious exercise, he began to notice that an occasional note was off or dropped altogether. She would suddenly play perfectly again for a series of measures, then the mistakes would repeat themselves.

It was finally too much. He threw the ice pack across the room and marched through the house to the back deck. He yelled her name once, hoping that he had remembered it correctly. But *Kelly* stuck in his head. Yes, he was sure it was Kelly. Her name could have been anything at that point, because she was so entranced in her activity that she didn't respond anyway. Though he was growing ever more angry, the sight of her gave him pause. He had never seen a student as young as the little girl stand with such a clean posture or hold the instrument like she was part of it and not separate from it. In the comfort of her own home and in the solace of her imagination, her body swayed in time to the music, as if the whole piece had transported her to some other dimension.

Regardless, he yelled her name again and still got no response.

Alex made his way down the steps and around the house to the driveway. He approached the open window of the neighbors' house and gripped the sill. "Hey," he snapped.

Kelly halted in mid-stroke of the bow and lifted her chin from the violin. She turned toward the window and smiled, not the slightest trace of surprise or shock on her face. Something told him that he had entered into a rouse.

"It only took you an hour to come over," she said, sounding far too smart for her age.

"Will you please stop playing that same thing over and over?" he asked slowly.

"This?" And she continued the étude, grinning wildly.

He stared at the gravel below the window and gritted his teeth. "Kelly," he huffed, "*please*!"

She stopped again and stared at him. She wasn't smiling anymore. "Tell me what I'm doing wrong," she said directly, her large, brown eyes shining.

He took in a long breath and held it in his lungs for a moment. "You keep playing the same thing over and over. You're annoying everyone on the block."

"Tell me what I'm doing wrong."

He glared at her. "I just told you. Play something else or close this window."

"You don't like my playing?"

His patience was thinning faster than she realized. "That's not the point. I'm only asking you to—"

"And I'm asking you to tell me what's wrong with my playing," she insisted.

He considered her round face, the brown curls twitching over her temples. She wanted something else from him, he thought, something other than a reprimand or the repetition of his forceful request. Running his tongue over the fronts of his top teeth, he waited for her to blink. But she wouldn't. Instead, she gawked an answer out of him.

"Your G's a little flat," he muttered at last.

"Then my F-sharp's off, too," she said.

"No," he answered. "Your fingers are small enough that F is right where it's supposed to be."

"Thank you." She smiled at him once more. Setting the violin on its stand and laying the bow across her sheet music, she reached for the window to pull down the sash, but he stopped her.

"You wanted me to come over here, didn't you?" he interrogated, narrowing his eyes.

"Yes," she answered simply.

He stepped away from the window. "Why?"

"I heard you talking to Mr. Grady last week."

He waited for her to finish the thought, though he guessed what was coming next. The reservations he'd had about mentioning the old man's style of teaching were coming back to him again. If he had only kept his mouth shut like his mind had told him to, he wouldn't have run the risk of anyone, especially Kelly, discovering that he—

"You used to teach violin," she announced, shattering his reflections.

He looked away from her and into the maples across the street.

"So I thought that maybe you could be my new teacher."

Alex met her swirling irises. "Your *new* teacher?"

Kelly nodded, and her smile drooped into a puckered brow. "Mr. Grady's dead," she said.

He put a hand to his forehead. "What are the chances?" he mumbled, though he'd already felt the death. The scenario was developing into a nightmare. "Listen, Kelly," he said, approaching the window again, "I don't teach violin anymore, okay? I haven't taught in a long time and I don't intend to start again. I'm not sure what you think you heard, but Mr. Grady and I were simply having a friendly conversation about theory…or something like that, and—"

"Actually," she interrupted, shaking a tiny finger at him, "you said that a good strings teacher never sacrifices the student's individuality for the sake of the art." She crossed her arms and peered down at him. "I believe you were criticizing the way that he was teaching me. And that tells me," she continued with exaggerated gestures, "that you were watching me, Mr..."

"Alex," he said, exasperated. "My name's Alex."

"You were watching me, Alex," she discerned proudly. "I need a new teacher and you can teach me."

Absolutely not. And he certainly would not allow the ploys of a ten-year-old girl thwart his commitment to refrain from teaching violin at all costs. Throughout his career, he had gone toe-to-toe with some of the pushiest conductors and musicians ever born, and the majority that had devoted their lives to the pursuit of a musical agenda were usually elitist and aggressive, to say the least. This girl was no great match for him. Yet, her mannerisms reminded him of a girl he once loved, a girl who had been horrible at taking no for an answer. Inappropriate as it was for the moment, he smiled, and he immediately feared that the facial expression might have signaled a weakness in him and a potential victory for her.

"No," he replied. "I don't teach anymore."

She leaned out the window, her face inches from his. "I need a new teacher," she said frankly. "You can teach me. It'll be easy; I'm a prodigy."

He grinned at the absurdity of her words. She was too young to be so delusional. "I'm sorry, Kelly, I just can't. If we had met at any other point in my life, I might—"

Suddenly, a large wrinkled hand wrapped itself around the little girl's arm and yanked her into the house. In a heartbeat, the fat old woman had poured herself into the open window and glared out at him.

"What are you, some kind of pedophile, mister?" she demanded, face jiggling and flushing red.

Alex stumbled backward in dismay. "No," he defended, speaking quickly, "I was only talking to her about—"

"About what?" the old woman yelped. "Are you some kind of hippie or something that come to take advantage of my little granddaughter?"

He could hear Kelly in the background calling for her deranged grandmother to stop questioning him because she could explain. The old woman swung her bovine figure toward the little girl. "Why, did you meet him on the Internet or something?" She turned on Alex again. "I've seen stories about men like you on Dateline NBC. You're not fooling me, mister!"

Alex shook his head and walked away from the house, returning to the deck as the old lady yelled something about Chris Hansen and cybersex, then slammed the window sash shut.

~

On her birthday, he lit candles and set the dining room table for two.

He made her favorite, salmon, in the hopes that some more natural part of her soul might return for just a little while. If he could have a single wish—one final grace from God—she would come back and have dinner with him tonight. And he would say all the things that he should have said, do all the things that he should have done when he'd had the chance months ago. But his life had stolen the moments away, the opportunities when he might have stopped long enough to look at her a second longer, to tell her how much he loved her, how beautiful she was, again and again. It would have cost him nothing but time, yet apparently the minutes had moved more freely over nickel-wound gut strings than in the currents of his heart.

Suddenly, the idea was ridiculous, and he quietly chastised himself for being so morbid. At his end of the table, he stared at a prescription bottle of *Xanax* that a psychiatrist in the city had prescribed to him. Months old, he had yet to swallow a single one of the pills, but in his present state of weakness, he entertained the thought of finally medicating the growing instability.

"What am I doing?"

Defeated, his head swimming in a surreal uneasiness, he stood and collected his plate and silverware from the table.

No C-scale had ever taught him anything about life; no minuet had ever offered a plan for survival. Only Charlotte had given him the inspiration to move on, to be better, to love with everything he had inside his body. Lately, he was disgusted with who he was and what he was becoming. Like the scroll of a violin, he was going in circles and arriving at nowhere. He traveled on a continuous path of grief and disappointment; the art that had for so long sustained him now seemed to be mocking him. Every memory, each thought, framed itself in the haunting notes of a forgotten sonata, a concerto, a symphony. He couldn't get the music out of his head, nor the feeling of the strings under his fingers or the bow in his hand. The movements, the playing, Charlotte, had all combined to become one great specter possessing the wilder regions of his mind.

Leaning over to blow out the candles, he thought he caught a glimpse of a tiny shadow fluttering through the orange light. For an instant he saw clearly the black butterfly, but then it was gone, flaking to dust and dissipating into nothingness. He began to tremble, and, dropping the plate and silverware to the floor, he braced himself against the table. The emotion swirled from his ankles and raced up his spine, culminating behind his eyes. As he began to cry, his body lost its composure and he fell to his knees, shuddering.

The night moved forward without him, and eventually he curled up on the hardwood floor and fell asleep, cheeks wet with the pain of remembering Charlotte, her smile, her laugh, the wonder in her eyes. He awoke beneath the tree again. She lay on the patchwork blanket, waiting for him, her shining eyes drawing him into the dream as the sun burned white in shattered bursts through the branches of the flowering tree. In a heartbeat he was beside her, reaching for her, but in that moment he faltered, looking away in dread of the black butterfly appearing. When he turned back to her, she was gone. Fear settled on him. She had never left him in the illusion. Then he was laying on his back, staring up through the branches of the tree as pink blossoms fell over him. The mellow notes of music surrounded him, and he turned his head to see Charlotte standing next to him with the violin. Sitting up, he stared at her, and she offered the instrument to him…*Play for me.* With shaking hands he took it…*Play for me again.* Laying the violin on his shoulder, it began to play itself, to sing out a tune that he barely recognized. Then it was gone and he lay beside her once more. She touched his face with her hand as the black butterfly finally came, beating through the crystal air, landing on her shoulder as always…

His eyes opened with the pain in his neck and the stiffness spreading through his shoulders. He forced himself to stand as the morning sunlight landed rudely on the table. The broken plate and the silverware were on the floor, the candles had burned down to stubs and extinguished themselves, and a pair of flies had found their salvation on the filet of salmon he had set out for Charlotte the night before. Charlotte. What was that music? He could feel the urge to recreate the sound pulsing on the tips of his fingers; he could see the mysterious notes taking form in his head.

Stumbling into the living room, he dug through the CDs on the rack next to the stereo. In a search that grew more desperate with each passing second, he suddenly thought he felt Charlotte standing behind him. His heart beat quickly and he turned instinctively to embrace her, only to be reminded that he was alone in the room. He shook off the vision.

"You've got to get a grip on yourself," he muttered.

A CD case fell from the rack and slapped against the hardwood floor. Startled, he picked it up and read the cover: *Kreisler*. Fritz Kreisler? He was familiar with the violinist and composer, but he couldn't recall ever having played any of his works for her. Loading the CD into the stereo, he listened to the first few seconds of each track as he skipped through the recording until at last he heard the music from the dream. It was a piece entitled, *Liebesleid*. Translated from German, it meant *Love's Sorrow*. As he absorbed the notes rising and falling in slow waltz tempo, a coldness prickled in his backbone. He could play this piece; he knew he could. But instead, he pushed the repeat button and turned up the volume, filling the house with the music, and denying that fraction of himself that might be weak enough to reach again for the violin.

In the dining room, Alex gathered together the silverware and the fragments of the broken plate from the floor. He dumped the shards of porcelain and the salmon from Charlotte's plate into the garbage can and then filled the sink with soapy water and began to do the dishes. As he rinsed the suds from a fork, a variation of sound threading through the music whispered in his ear. He listened, hot water running over his hands, until at last he realized that someone was playing along with the recording, just out of tune enough to be detected by his trained ear.

Dropping the fork into the sink, he turned off the water and walked slowly into the living room. Whoever was playing was close, somewhere in the house—in *his* house. He pressed his open hands to his ears and closed his eyes.

You're hearing things, he thought.

But when he uncovered his ears, the sound was still there. It was coming from the parlor, where he had abandoned his identity and left it to hide beneath the dust of the old Victorian.

"Charlotte?" he choked.

Alex stepped into the parlor doorway and halted in shock. The blood rushed into his face and he watched on with simmering irritation as Kelly, her back to him, bowed the *Liebesleid* in controlled and precise movements over the strings of his Stradivarius. He noticed a slice of cake on a small paper plate on the seat of the rocking chair, and backed quietly into the living room. He didn't want her to know that he was there. Instead, he felt the sudden compulsion to test this little prodigy, and perhaps to humiliate her, just to see how good she was.

When Alex stopped the CD, Kelly stopped playing and the house went mute. He waited to hear movement from the parlor, to hear the girl try hurriedly to return the violin to its case and appear at the front door as if nothing had happened. A minute passed, and when no noise came from the room, he lowered a recording of Williams' *The Lark Ascending* into the stereo to tempt her to play again. He knew this piece included notes in upper positions that only truly gifted players could hit repeatedly with unfaltering accuracy. This would prove her talented, but not a prodigy, and he could relax in the idea that no bizarre twist of fate had delivered the little girl to him. It was only a coincidence, though he had never really believed in them.

As he hoped, the first few notes that she played were off, and he expected her to break down into bow scratches and inferior technique, altogether rendering her attempt to imitate Williams' masterpiece an embarrassing fiasco. But without warning, she fell into the movement, following the notes as if they were her own. She played it by ear, and he was astonished.

He had failed to make her fail, and the amazement of the situation that so obviously struck him did little to quell the annoyance that rose against him. Abruptly, he turned off the stereo and marched into the parlor.

"What the hell are you doing?"

Kelly turned to him, violin under her chin and bow raised. A trace of fear crept into her shiny face, and her mouth dropped open.

"Where did you get the audacity just to walk into my house and help yourself to my things?"

She lowered her arms to her sides and looked away from him. "I knocked, but—"

"But what?" He was yelling at her. "You just thought you'd break in and touch things that don't belong to you?"

Her slight form drooped in the reprimand. "I brought you a piece of cake because I—"

"Because why?"

"Yesterday was my birthday, and, well, I only wanted to—"

The coincidence belted him in the stomach. "Your birthday?" He'd begun to sweat and shake. He stepped toward the girl, his shadow falling over her. "Get the hell out of here," he commanded.

Kelly's glassy eyes flared with intensity and she suddenly pushed the violin at him. "Why do you hate me so much?"

Alex clasped the instrument and the bow as she brushed by him and ran out of the house, leaving him angry, the emotion trembling through every fiber of his body.

He returned the violin to the case that Kelly had lain open beside the rocking chair, and then took the paper plate and its cake into the kitchen and threw it away. Why wouldn't she leave him alone? Why did the music haunt him? He couldn't get away from it, and as he stared down at the cake in the garbage can, he felt ashamed of himself for having yelled at her, for having tried to belittle her, if only to the private audience in his mind. Yet he refused to acknowledge any form of perfection, any mercy for the expression of life in the notes of passion that the world still held onto, despite the poisonous vacuum of his own hollowness. She shouldn't have come into his house without permission. She shouldn't have—

"God damn it!" he breathed hotly, driving his fist into a cupboard door.

From across the room he saw her standing there, tears in her eyes.

"It was the only thing you ever wanted," he uttered to the stillness. "You only ever wanted me to make the pretty music…"

And when her image had faded away into the sunlight, he slid down onto the floor, back against a cabinet, and let the birdsong flittering through the windows consume the bitter remnants of his anger.

~

Alex hadn't experienced this much stress since high school physics. Not even Charlotte's death had put him into such a muddled predicament. Grief was a single-sided feeling for him that had over time mutated into fear, anger, depression. But it didn't compound itself like this had. She had broken into his house, hadn't she? It was her birthday…she had no right to play his Strad—and she only wanted to learn. She wanted him to teach her. The hardest part for him was the notion that maybe Charlotte would have wanted him to teach her…and she and the little girl were so much alike—persistent, stubborn, suddenly emotional. He shouldn't have yelled at her, and the cake, smashed into the garbage can…definitely his lowest point.

He remained at a loss for action. Uncertain, frustrated, if he could work it out in his head. If she would only answer. Maybe then he would know just what to do. She had, hadn't she? The dream. The music…*love's sorrow.* She had brought to him the violin; Charlotte had wanted him to play again.

Play for me…

He supposed he could interpret it as a sign or an excuse. Did her spirit bring him strength or an avenue by which to let the weakness win?

Play for me again…

Yes, solely for her—or some part of her, reflected in the large eyes of a ten-year-old prodigy. In an exasperated breath, he resigned himself to the idea that there was only one action he could rightfully take, if only for Charlotte. He wondered if his concession would push away the ghosts and give him back his sanity. If so, perhaps there would be some salvation in it after all.

At last he would lay down his sword; or at least he would try.

The large old lady in the flowered muumuu answered the front door, or rather yanked it open and stared him down with fiery eyes. If he had been Kelly's age, the sudden and aggressive appearance of the woman certainly would have been enough to compel him to dash frantically away from the house and down the street. But he wasn't a ten-year-old boy anymore. Nevertheless, he thought about running like a scared child; she terrified him to the core. He felt the springs loading in his ankles and his body tensing, preparing him for a potentially necessary flight if the viper chose to wage an all-out attack on him.

"Well, well, well," she declared, "if it ain't the big, bad wolf."

He dropped his shoulders as the shame burned in his cheeks. Lifting his chin, Alex quickly salvaged the remaining fragments of his dignity and pretended to be brave.

"I've come to apologize to the girl," he said resolutely, as if in his faked gentility he would nobly coax the dragon from its lair and gain the precious treasure of the beast. Instantly, he felt absurd.

"I wanted to tell Kelly that I'm sorry," he said, reconsidering the words.

"She's in her bedroom, quite upset," the woman answered sourly. "You've made her cry."

He looked away from her, wounded. "I didn't mean to—"

"You may not have, sir, but you did."

"Would you mind telling her that I'm—"

"No. You'll do it yourself." She turned sideways and pointed into the shadows of the house, the gesture commanding him to enter at once.

Anxiously, he stepped past her and into the foyer. At the bottom of the stairs to his right, the grandmother called up to Kelly, telling her to come down because someone had arrived to see her. Then he was ushered into a sitting room to wait.

"Sit your bottom there," she grumbled. "My Kelly will be down in a minute."

Alex sat on the edge of a couch cushion, hands on his knees. The old woman poured herself into a rocking chair by the window and picked up her knitting. The only sound in the room was the quiet ticking of a clock somewhere near him, working in disjointed rhythm with the occasional click of knitting needles. She wouldn't speak to him, and he didn't have the nerve to say anything; he just wanted the whole ordeal to be over.

Then he would consider teaching the little girl.

On the opposite wall hung a framed photograph of an attractive young woman from the waist up, with long, sandy hair and beautiful brown eyes. She held a violin. It was a professional shot, one staged purposely to showcase the performer and her instrument. He had posed for dozens of them in his lifetime, for concert programs, school catalogues, special events. Slowly, he attempted to rise in an effort to get a closer look at the picture on the wall, but—

"Sit," the woman ordered again, and obediently he sat like a well trained dog.

"Who's in that photograph on the wall there? The woman with the violin—"

He noticed the child in the archway and stood. His palms sweat and he found himself uncommonly nervous in the face of such a tiny adversary. Her eyes were swollen from crying, and she stood with her skinny arms crossed. Her dejection stung him. He had never wanted to hurt her, only to make her accountable, to make her understand that…

"I'm sorry, Kelly," he uttered almost automatically. "I shouldn't have spoken to you the way I did."

She looked up at him, tear streaks glistening on the rounds of her cheeks.

"Surely you should have," the old woman interjected.

Alex gazed at her incredulously, but she never wavered from her knitting.

"She knows better than to waltz into someone's house and mess with their stuff. Her Great Uncle Timmy was a thief. Went to prison for taking things that didn't belong to him. My Kelly won't grow up like that. She knows better."

Kelly let her arms collapse lifelessly to her sides and sniffled. "I'm sorry, Alex," she whispered. "I shouldn't have done it."

"Go back upstairs," her grandmother charged.

The little girl lingered for a moment, as if there was something else she wanted to say to the man. Alex held his breath and waited for the words, but they never came. Instead, Kelly turned from the grown-ups and raced back upstairs, her feet pounding angrily on the staircase.

"Have a seat," the old woman said to him. Her voice, though still above a normal volume, had softened, and the surprise of it sunk him into the end cushion of the couch.

"My name's Luella," she said, calmly detached. She began to rock in the chair, spindles and braces groaning, and her fingers continued to work the knitting needles through pastel colored yarn.

He sat quietly and listened. He would know when she would want him to speak; that much had become clear to him in his brief but bitter relationship with the aged grandmother.

"Kelly's my granddaughter," she continued matter-of-factly, "and I've raised her up myself. She was born in Alabama, started school in Georgia, and ended up in this place just before her mama passed away. My husband and I relocated here from New Orleans some time back, and he died seven years ago last Tuesday. He was a powerful man with a big heart. Kelly's got his heart. Unfortunately, she's got my Cajun black pepper disposition. Her mama had it, too—"

"Ma'am—"

"Call me Miss Luella," she insisted, and for the first time in minutes she made eye contact with him, her irises a stony gray. "Make no mistake about it," she continued, back to her knitting and rocking, "I'm old, overweight, and I suppose a bit paranoid. How my day goes depends on which one of my personalities wakes up in the morning."

He smiled at her Southern candor, and the muscles along his spine began to relax.

"Mr. Grady was a miserable old turnip," Miss Luella went on, "but he knew that hurt little girl upstairs had a gift.

She's certainly not perfect, but she understands things that we don't. It's like she's got a sixth sense about the world. And, my Lord, can she play the fiddle."

"I know," he breathed, remembering how the child had played by ear, decently bowing out the notes of a masterpiece. His eyes wandered to the woman in the photograph, holding the violin.

"God rest his soul, Mr. Grady's gone, and so is my Kelly's guide through this music business. You're a man of music, aren't you Mr…"

"Brogan."

"Mr. Brogan? You play the strings, as they say?"

He nodded. "Yes, I'm a violinist…or at least I was."

She peered at him over the heads of her knitting needles. "You *was*? What, are you a horse whisperer now?" She grinned at him and he chuckled. "People ain't *was* anything in life, Mr. Brogan. They're always who they were born to be, no matter how it comes out in work and play."

"I lost somebody very close to me," he answered soberly, "and it changed my life. I don't play the violin anymore, Miss Luella."

Abruptly, the old woman stopped knitting and dropped the project into a basket beside the rocking chair. "Mr. Brogan," she said in a long, easy breath, "by the time you're my age, loss is a way of life. My husband's gone, and what mother wants to bury her child long before her own death? Loss happens, sir. How you grow from that's the test. What matters is how you live, not how others die. If that was the case, you might as well have died with them. There's no point in *not doing*."

"What do you want from me?" he asked. A sudden sense of resentment tingled through his shoulders.

"You know what I want, Mr. Brogan," she countered. "I want it for you *and* her."

"And what would be the point?"

Miss Luella smiled sadly. "You're like pepper on a boll weevil, Mr. Brogan. One might think you were a relation of mine, a Bayou rat with a chip on his shoulder. Thinks the world owes him something, or should at least stop and waste away the minutes crying with him." She shook her head and turned her face into the sunlight on the windowpanes.

Alex looked into his lap, feeling somewhat self-conscious. Was it that obvious? Could she stare into his eyes and see the pain, the loss…and the selfish denial of his talent and purpose in life?

Play for me again…

"She wants to go to Juilliard." Miss Luella's eyes were on him once more. "You'll be paid, Mr. Brogan, and well, too. It'll be the going rate for private lessons."

The woman in the photograph seemed to be watching him.

"Why does it have to be me?" he questioned. "There have got to be string teachers around that would work better with her than me. You're an hour from the city."

"Work better with her than you?" She frowned. "I don't know what that means, Mr. Brogan, but I can tell you this: You're the answer to my prayers, sir. But the devil comes in many forms to tempt us. I just had to make sure that you weren't the devil."

"What makes you so sure?"

"The devil shows no humility," she explained. "And he certainly wouldn't show up here to apologize to some little snot that most of the time isn't worth the apology."

He smiled again and rose from the couch. "Let me think about it," he said.

"There's nothing to think about, Mr. Brogan." She tried to wiggle herself out of the rocking chair.

"Don't get up," Alex said. "I can show myself out."

Miss Luella considered his face for a moment. "I can see the darkness in your eyes," she commented. "Perhaps you chose us, Mr. Brogan. This whole affair seems too good to be true, doesn't it?"

The picture on the wall waited for his response.

"Yes, Miss Luella, it surely does." He extended a hand to her, and she took it weakly. "I just need some time to think about it," he repeated. "I have to clear my mind first."

"Suit yourself, sir."

He backed away from her and pivoted into the foyer.

"Mr. Brogan," the old woman called after him.

Alex stepped into the archway of the room. "Yes?"

"That's my Clarice there on the wall."

He stared at the photograph.

"That's my Kelly's mama."

He blinked once and nodded, then lowered his eyes to the worn hardwood floor. A heartbeat later, he had turned again, showing himself out of the house as the sun rolled slowly through gathering rain clouds, and the wind played softly in the trees.

~

In the closing paragraph of an 1849 letter to a friend, Washington Irving wrote: "I hope as the spring opens you will accompany me in one of my brief visits to Sunnyside, when we will make another trip to Sleepy Hollow, and have a colloquy among the tombs."

Alex knew well of visits to Sleepy Hollow Cemetery, that sprawling historical city of the dead where Irving himself had lain for a century and a half. The graveyard bordered Broadway—North Broadway to be exact, where Route 9 entered the village—and the irony had never escaped him. Laying her to rest here made sense after all. He had met her at the other end of the street a few blocks away, while the flea market man with the red hair and freckles and crooked smile watched on in opportunistic glee as she rolled her big eyes and scoffed at the young musician's vain attempts at persuasion. She'd been finalizing surveyor data for the construction of a new high school during the week in which they had first locked eyes, but her transit and calculator had instead formulated a quirk of destiny to a power more intense than she could ever have imagined, he thought. Their love, unbeknownst to either of them regardless of Alex's initial fantasies of her, had been planted on a road in Sleepy Hollow, germinated in a booth at *Giovanni's,* and left to blossom in Charlotte's cottage, all under the guise of a mundane existence swollen with measurements, numbers, music notes, and strings. As far as he was concerned, her only connection to any place was to the tiny village and its haunted past. Chicago had been her private nightmare, an area to which she would never return. The city had come later, but he wouldn't have reminded himself of the glittering life he had abandoned by burying her any closer to Manhattan. The nearest he came to the suffocating madness of metropolitan life now was congestion on the Tappan Zee Bridge spanning the Hudson River, or the chaotic racing to toll booths on the New York State Thruway that always raised his blood pressure. Otherwise, the wind brought him north to a more secluded existence amidst scarlet maples that only recently had begun to challenge him.

Once a week he came to lay roses on Charlotte's grave, to talk to her while all around them spirits whispered in their crypts and birds shielded the private conversations with their own sweet song. Sometimes he would stop at the Old Dutch Church in an attempt to commune with God, to pray, perhaps out of guilt, or fear, or hope. Most often, he found himself staring absently at the ornately carved pulpit and its circular staircase, or fixating on the small wooden cross at the back of the altar table. Gazing through the wavy glass of the ancient house of worship, he saw only the mutated images of crumbling, historic tombstones in the original churchyard, sticking out of the earth like the twisted and rotting teeth of an old man.

Sometimes, before going to Charlotte, he would wander across the old churchyard to Hillside Avenue and visit the Irving family plot framed in a waist-high rod iron fence. In the center of a dozen or more thin, gray stones, Washington Irving's large white marker with the rounded top and edges stood out like a pearl among rubble. Famous as the author had become with his tales of headless horsemen and sleeping Dutchmen, Alex had expected more when he first visited the location. In the background all around the plot stood mausoleums and monuments emblazoned with family names that only relatives would recognize. In its simplicity, Irving's headstone proved far more impressive than columns, arches, and colored glass.

One of his more frequent stops, however, was to the Witherby mausoleum on a rise of land between Dingle Bank and Hemlock Grove. He had discovered it by accident on an overcast morning only days after Charlotte's burial. A massive white stone structure, it had narrow, horizontal stained glass windows in the upper part of the north, east, and west walls depicting the New York City skyline, complete with obvious icons of the Empire State Building. But the size and grandeur of the columned tomb was not what so often drew him to that peaceful spot. Rather, peering through the clear glass of its double golden doors in the south face, he could see the urn-flanked crypts of a husband and wife within, side by side. On the left lay the husband, the glassy stone bearing the inscription:

I wait for the time
When we can soar
Together again,
Both aware of each other.

His wife lay to the right, their crypts sharing a wall. Her tomb read:

I never knew
A day
I did not
Love you.

The verses alone kept him coming back to read them over and over again. Perhaps if Charlotte had lived, if they had married and spent the rest of their days together, the foot of their tombs would have born similar epitaphs. But she had died unexpectedly, and he hadn't been the same since. Maybe soon all that would change.

With the sun hanging low in the east, he stood at the edge of her grave, hands in his pockets. He'd brought no roses. Anxiously, he shifted from one foot to the other as he organized the words in his head so he'd get it right the first time. He held his breath; let it out in a puff. He hadn't been this nervous since he had proposed to her in Paris. Now he felt a little ridiculous worrying about possibly offending the dead. She was dead, wasn't she? He often wondered if she was, or if she had simply shuffled off her mortal coil, as Hamlet once said, and lived in the silent places where time pushed no one and pain had no sword. There was little doubt that she was with him, day in and day out. Like death itself, he could feel her there, and if he listened closely enough, he could hear the subtle nuances of her voice whispering in tones just below the ticking of the clock, the hum of the refrigerator, or the beating of his heart.

A long time ago, he had read a poem about the dead, and pieces of it sifted through his mind as he stared at her headstone, traced the elegant letters of her name with his eyes:

Never gone unless
We push them there;
Ask quietly enough,
And they'll answer you.

*They'll answer you...*Alex held his breath again; held it until the pressure behind his eyes retreated and he regained control of his trembling limbs. The physical response to her memory had become nothing less than involuntary—an overwhelmingly charged reaction that he neither dictated nor expected, no matter how often it happened. But above all else, what attacked him when he remembered Charlotte had become welcome, undisputable proof that he had truly, deeply, madly loved her to the core of his being. He would never love that completely again.

A warm breeze brushed quietly through his hair and he eased his tired body into an old depression of clover beside the headstone. He laid an open hand on the smooth face of the simple granite marker, felt the engraved script of her name under his fingertips. He closed his eyes and searched for her face, her smile. But he couldn't see her as clearly as he had days ago, weeks ago. Nonetheless, he conjured a hazy image of her, a blurred photograph of a great smile, shining eyes, flushed cheeks. He could see the pink sunlight glowing on his eyelids and he opened them as the words formed.

"I don't want to dream about you anymore," he said. "I only want to remember us and the way it used to be. I draw all my strength from those memories—"

Emotion interrupted him, coming on so suddenly, and he tried not to cry.

"I can still smell your hairspray on our pillow cases..."

Holding his breath, he struggled to gather everything he wanted to say, attempted to order each thought as it raced through him.

"You're everywhere I look, everywhere I turn. I think I see you on the street, in the grocery store, and—I'll never lose you, Charlotte. You're too much a part of me. I only want to stop dreaming about you and the tree and the butterfly."

Alex turned his face into the moving air, felt the tears begin to dry tightly on his cheeks.

"I made dinner for you on your birthday." He started to laugh. "How demented is that? I have to get a grip on myself. In a few months, it'll be a year since you died, and I'm acting like it was just yesterday. Should it hurt this much?"

He listened to the finches squeak and twitter in the willows behind him.

"When is it supposed to get easier?" he asked. "I'm always reliving it. I have to stop doing this to myself, and you have to help me."

In a strange mix of feelings, he cried and smiled, laughed and sighed, while his whole body shook. So much confusion welled up from somewhere deep inside; at last it was just beginning to froth over and bleed off his soul.

Alex, Alex…

"I hear your voice, I swear I do, but then it turns out to be a bird singing, the leaves rustling, the telephone ringing. What is it you want to tell me? I'm listening, I really am. I just don't know what to do with myself, with us. Just tell me what to do."

He sobbed, buried his face in his hands as if ashamed the world would witness him so completely undone. Wiping his swollen eyes with the back of his hand, he drew the summer air into his chest and held it there until his heartbeat slowed.

The question, already hours old, had formed in his mind long before the words made it real: "Should I play again?" He'd thought about it on the drive to the cemetery, had rehearsed it.

"You brought the violin to me; you put it into my hands and I played it."

Desperately, he wanted Charlotte's approval, though his rational mind fought to ignore the truth, the excuse, of wanting to play again.

"Should I make the pretty music that always made you smile? Should I give it to her, the little girl? Tell me…"

In the corner of his eye he caught a glimpse of color and turned his face to see it fluttering over the gravestone—big and beautiful, the monarch lighted on the opposite corner of the stone and laid its wings wide open, displaying twin brilliant orange surfaces traced in black veins and satin accents dimpled with specks of pure white. An instant after, it came to life again, popping from the edge of the granite and ascending zigzaggedly into the clean air. Then the butterfly was gone, floating off to visit the countless other souls whose energy seemed to draw it there.

Alex watched her flutter away, lips parted and heart racing.

"Thank you," he breathed, though the fragile monarch had become too small to see. "Thank you," he repeated. He pulled himself to his feet as a twinge of immediacy, a pulse of newly charged energy, spurred him.

"I guess I've got something to do," he said, "something much larger than myself."

He stepped off the grave, turned, but came back to her.

"No matter what happens, Charlotte, I'll show her how to make the air stir, how to make God Himself pay attention."

He bent to touch her name again.

Alex, I…

"I know," he answered to the stillness. "I only wish I'd had the courage earlier to see my way through this. I guess I just wanted a simple sign, an answer that would let me know what to do. I thought myself lost without you, and I suppose I never stopped feeling sorry for myself long enough to realize that I'm not alone. You wouldn't leave me like that. Not you."

A tenderness came over him with the recollection. "I miss touching your body, kissing you, hearing your heart beat, feeling your breath on my face. I was never bored. We never had too much sex. There was never a single problem, not a single thing wrong with us but fate."

He stepped back from the headstone and looked into the clear blue sky. He smiled to himself, lighter, relieved.

"I'll see you again, soon."

He walked slowly away, down the hill and onto the uneven road, sun warm on his cheeks and neck. He could have driven to Hillside, the part of the cemetery where Charlotte lay, instead of parking just inside the South Gate. But he never did, no matter how often he had come to visit her, because he always had the time to take his time. Alex walked so he could absorb the spiritual force of the place, ground his own soul, and initiate himself again into the secret world of the dead, so that each time he came back, he felt welcome to visit the daughter of their dreams.

His return to the car brought him over Headless Horseman Bridge suspended above the Pocantico River whose peaceful meandering through the rocks and fallen limbs cluttering its bed had become the beauty of its existence. He continued down Sleepy Hollow Avenue, crowded on the river side with tree branches hanging heavily over the road, keeping the sun from reaching the soft, moist earth. On the hill across the road, retained by stone walls and stairways, iron fences and railings, tombstones and mausoleums centuries old watched him pass, the souls of Van Tassels, Benedicts, Oldmsteads, Angels, and a thousand others mutely embracing him, yet ushering him from their sacred solitude with cool, shady fingers of summer air.

Charlotte had released him, but, more importantly, he had allowed part of himself to be let go. One step at a time, each day, he would be better than before. Perhaps his prison had been an illusion, his sentence self-imposed. Regardless, his world would be different now, though no less darkened by her absence. The pain of his loss would not quickly dissolve, nor would it ever altogether leave him. He would carry her memory to his own grave. He supposed that he could only try to prepare himself ahead of time for setbacks, surprises, twists of fate that he would not see coming, like a blind man looking for light.

Near the end of his walk, he passed by the juncture where Sleepy Hollow and Hillside Avenues met, a place where an ancient oak had been recently felled, its trunk cut into sections and laying among the headstones. An old man in a lawn chair sat in quiet prayer, arms and open hands held up to the heavens, communing with the spirit of a loved one Alex didn't know, and conversing silently with a god whom Alex had not yet fully forgiven.

He found his car in the shadow of the Old Dutch Church, spent a moment in the driver's seat staring at the old man. He was not the only one lonely in this world, Alex realized. Everybody missed someone, spent the remainder of their lives waiting for that time of reunion in death, if such an event really occurred. No, he was not alone and his pain was not unique. Alex wondered if the old man in the white T-shirt and blue suspenders had received his sign, or if by faith alone he had come to the cemetery to pray for other things. Maybe he had already figured it out, or maybe he was still trying to understand.

There remained plenty left for him to accept and comprehend. For now, he had a new direction in which to grow. He would be lying to himself if he didn't admit that he was looking forward to feeling the violin on his shoulder again, bow in hand and strings beneath his fingers; this time, for a renewed purpose—for redemption from some illusory sin of being the one who had lived—for himself, for Charlotte.

This time, for the little girl and the pretty music.

~

He carefully removed everything from the desktop—pens, pencils, stapler, calendar, dictionaries, assorted papers and magazines—and set the items on the bookshelves wherever he found space, or dropped them into a drawer. His movements were deliberate, as if preparing a table for surgery. Even the sunlight, invading the space in a thick white band, seemed to be watching with bated breath.

Satisfied that he had thoroughly cleaned the desktop, he considered the boxes stacked in the corners of the parlor and decided he would not venture to unpack them just yet. Instead, he reached for only one, tall and thin against the opposite wall, and carried it into the center of the room. He remembered each and every time he had handled this box, especially the first time when Charlotte had wrapped it in gold paper and laid it on the living room floor, daring him to guess what was inside.

Opening the folded box flaps, he pulled the tissue paper away from the Georgian stand and lifted the antique from its cardboard coffin. He placed the stand at the corner of the desk, to the left of the window. Running a finger over the lip of the shelf, he seemed to draw the sunlight into the scrolls and fine rounded details of its face. Her soul lived inside the Georgian, existing in every fibrous cell, absorbed at the moment she laid her hands on its surface and began to reclaim its original beauty. In the process, she had left her own beauty behind, a fragment of herself that would remain forever. And so he had kept the stand; he'd stored it in the box she'd chosen and left it just out of reach, but close enough to remember.

Resurrecting a centuries-old Georgian music stand was a miracle far less formidable than the more crucial wonder of reviving his soul. Now the case lay open on the bare desk and he gazed down anxiously at the sleeping Strad. He could not recall having ever seen it so beautiful, the ambient light of the room shimmering over its curved body and inlaid purfling. Instinct told him that the lower two strings would soon need to be replaced, their coils separating so slightly at the nut that only a trained eye would notice. He had not lost the gut feeling of, or the union with, the violin after all. Alex smiled, carefully tracing an f-hole with the tip of his finger.

The instrument came to rest on his left shoulder in a single deft movement, canceling out any lag time for reconsideration. He plucked a bow from its holder in the top of the case and, pressing the violin between his chin and shoulder, tightened the horsehair.

His system for tuning hadn't changed since he had been a child learning for the first time how to equalize the sound of his student violin. The process worked for him, so he'd never abandoned it. First the open A for reference, his ear humming pleasantly as he turned the fine tuner in the tailpiece and the string at last settled into its perfect pitch. A and D together, working the D string until the wavering stopped. Now D and G, same thing. Lastly, the bow returned to the A and made it sing out against the highest of them all, E, until the two achieved just the right harmonic union.

The easy part was over; tuning a violin was not the same as playing it. His palms had begun to sweat, and he fumbled a moment as he adjusted his hold on the bow in order to achieve the correct form. Taut horsehair lying exactly perpendicular across the four strings, he dug through his mental repertoire as the fingers of his left hand, in first position, felt for the notes at the lower end of the ebony fingerboard.

Whatever he had finally begun to play, his mind didn't register titles or movements; only the notes mattered at first. His eardrums buzzed with the slightest error of intonation, with every note that vibrated off the strings even minutely out of tune. He had to hear the notes, each one, in every octave and scale, ring out purely and perfectly. And, like pieces of himself, they all came back to him again the way the working universal chimes had intended them to sound. He closed his eyes and let his body collect the tones, mellow and piercing, fast and slow—whole, half, quarter time.

As the sun began to set and crimson shadows stretched across the room, he continued to play until at last he felt one with the violin, the way it used to be. The reconciliation fulfilled itself, and he thought of nothing but the music, the sound, and the technique. And as darkness fell, he still kept true to his practice. He didn't need light to see because his eyes had been closed anyway throughout much of the extended practice session. His instincts honed themselves again; like a blind man knowing his path by touch alone, he walked the fingerboard sightlessly, familiarly, and absolutely. Everything soon became perfect once more.

Dawn woke him from his trance. He took a deep breath and finally laid the instrument and bow back into its case. The tips of his fingers, calluses softened by the months they had been allowed to heal, hurt, tingled as if they had fallen asleep though their master had not. He considered the empty music stand for a moment, thought about the pieces he would eventually put on it, and then walked through the house and out onto the deck. The sky greeted him warmly in tones of pink and blue—a new day. He glanced at the house next door and wondered if the little girl had heard him playing all through the night; if she, like he not so long ago, had become irritated with the repetition and subtle mistakes. Smiling in satisfaction, he left the blossoming morning to its own design and sought the comfort of his bed, heeding his body's aching need to sleep.

~

Years ago, shortly after Charlotte and Alex had begun dating, and more specifically, minutes after they'd had an explosive bout of sex, a brief discussion occurred concerning children. The subject was one about which Alex had very little to say, not because kids in general scared him, but because the thought of having his own kids terrified him. He remembered clearly the kind of rambunctious children he and his sisters had been, though he admitted perhaps too quickly that the girls were worse. His parents, he'd contended, would undoubtedly spoil their grandchildren, and with the lifestyle he'd planned to have, he couldn't imagine caring for babies and dealing with attitudes, wants, and attention deficit/hyperactivity disorders. After all, the children he made contact with everyday were disciplined or else, since Juilliard and its reputation had no tolerance for incorrigibility. His strongest argument was that those kids went home after an hour to torture someone else. As soon as the lesson concluded, his responsibility as teacher and babysitter thankfully ended and he was alone again to worry only about himself.

Charlotte, on the other hand, had a family plan nicely and neatly drawn in her mind. There would be at least one child, and she would have to be a girl. Maybe later a little brother would be necessary, but she left no doubts about the girl.

"A princess," she'd commented. "And her father could dote on her as much as he would dote on her mother."

"Then there'd be two brats in the house," he'd said lightly.

Her nickname would be cute, like Maggie or Abby, but her full name beautiful, like Elizabeth or Victoria. Maybe she would have two names, like Ellie Mae. And her bedroom would be pink with a sign on the door that read, "I'm the Princess." And her tricycle would have frilly ribbons dangling from the handle grips, and she would wear lacey dresses and wide-brimmed hats with flowers on them. And she would be the perfect mix of her mother and father, with curls and ringlets, big hazel or brown eyes, daddy's smile and mommy's heart. She would be theirs and live for them and through them. It all had made complete sense to Charlotte, giggling with the thought, though it hardly alleviated any of Alex's reservations.

Yet the chances or transient dreams of reproducing with the love his life had been torn away from him, and at last he was left to worry only about himself. The reality of it sickened him, and if he could go back in time, he would have said everything on the subject that she had wanted to hear.

Appropriately, Kelly's name meant *war, strife,* and *bright-headed,* and she made no bones about it, ringlets, big eyes, and all. If anything, Alex was sure that she was not exactly the little girl that Charlotte had had in mind, though she was probably the more realistic manifestation of what a child of theirs would be like. Moreover, he didn't find himself thinking "princess" in any sense of the word.

The two girls shared the same strong-willed, stubborn personality, one drawing on the hardships of inner-city life, and the other on what may have been a raw, unscrupulous Southern upbringing. Alex knew from the start that he would have to tame the young one if she were ever to be a successful student. Charlotte, as an adult and the fiancée of an apparently cultured and elite violinist, had learned to temper her disposition. Her saving grace many times had been her heart, which she left exposed for some to hurt and few to protect. Kelly, on the other hand, lived somewhat through fear, and he knew that he could scare her into submission. Consequently, she also was controlled by emotion, and often fear turned to crying and dejection, things that challenged Alex's inexperience with children. Ultimately, he found himself damned either way, so instead he sought a balance between a structured, demanding system of instruction, and the open-ended possibility of self-expression in the same forum. He had, unfortunately, made a powerful comment about individuality during the confrontation with Mr. Grady, and Kelly showed no signs of having forgotten his words.

But, above all, the girl also possessed an unguarded heart like Charlotte had, and he felt it his duty to at least protect it. Besides, he continually worried about being accosted by Miss Kelly's grandmother, Luella, who had been almost completely responsible for her granddaughter's demeanor, as far as he was concerned.

He and Kelly had their first official meeting on a Monday. At 11 a.m., Kelly appeared on his front porch, pink and silver soft violin case in hand. She'd brought no binder, nor lesson books or sheet music. Instead, she had arrived with only the necessary tools to begin her instruction under a new teacher, and that was the way he'd wanted it.

A day earlier he had knocked on her grandmother's front door and presented his plan to the old woman: He would teach Kelly three times a week—Monday, Wednesday, and Friday—and she would not miss a single lesson no matter what; Luella would ensure that Kelly practiced every day for at least an hour and maybe two; he would be paid thirty dollars an hour, which was well below the going rate for the area, and the lessons would last two hours; he would be free to take the girl's instruction in any direction that he wanted, even if it was not the direction into which her grandmother wanted her to go; and, Kelly would never be late, unruly, or, under any circumstances, *cry*.

"Well, now, Mr. Brogan," Luella had replied, "you've spent some time thinking about this, haven't you?"

"That's all I've done for a week," he said dryly.

The old woman tapped her fingers on the arms of her navy blue recliner as she rocked the bulky piece of furniture back and forth. "I'm still not entirely sure that you're not a weirdo," she muttered.

He glanced at the picture on the wall of the woman with the violin—*Clarice,* he remembered. He smiled, actually amused.

"The choice is yours," he said. "If you agree to the terms, then send her over to my house tomorrow morning at eleven o'clock. She only needs to bring her violin and bow. I'm not interested in what she's already learned or what she's been practicing. I have my own course of study that she'll follow."

Luella sat forward in the recliner, the movement an obvious physical strain for a woman of her size. "Your house? You'll teach her here in the dining room where she's always had her lessons."

He stepped toward her, pretentiously valiant. "Absolutely not," he answered. "I don't teach that way; I don't want any outside influences during the lessons. You'll be free to review with her what she's learned each day. I could even videotape the sessions if you have any concerns."

A moment of silence came down on them as Luella glared at Alex. Then the large old lady erupted into laughter and slapped her hands against her thighs.

"My, you're a stickler," she cackled. "I might like you yet. Okay, then, Mr. Brogan. You go on home and get yourself ready. Miss Kelly'll be over in the morning."

And here she was, hair in pigtails, and beaming from one ear to the other.

"Good morning," he said warmly. He gestured her into the house. "We'll work in the parlor. We both know that you're already familiar with that room."

Sheepishly, she nodded.

He had set out two chairs in the parlor and had placed half a dozen pieces of sheet music on the Georgian, purposely chosen to challenge the girl's self-proclaimed prodigal ability.

If she can play these, he had thought, *she'll be well on her way to Juilliard.*

For a professional concert violinist like himself, his approach to discerning whether the little girl was in any way a prodigy, or at least truly gifted, would be simple. First, he would listen. Much could be gathered from allowing the ear to hear what was on or off, what was good and what was exceptional. He would have her play scales, successions of notes ascending and descending according to fixed intervals, and arpeggios, notes of chords played in rapid succession instead of simultaneously, each meant to determine dexterity and intonation. Next, she would be asked to play a slow piece and then a fast piece of classical music. Here, he would test her knowledge of solo Bach, with which students of her purported ability should be familiar, and perhaps a Mendelssohn concerto. It all made absolute, formal sense to him.

When she'd at last deposited her violin case across the wooden arms of the rocker and had taken up the instrument and bow, she turned to him with a toothy grin.

"Tune," he said simply.

First the A for reference, then A and D together. Now D and G, same thing…

He smiled to himself as he sat in the chair farthest from the music stand, pleased that his method for tuning was also hers. *A good start,* he thought. Mr. Grady had known the basics after all, unless she'd figured it out on her own. A certain satisfaction came from knowing that, at only ten years of age, Kelly could recognize and establish a note in perfect pitch. The gift had not come easily to him when he was a child, and he never failed to recognize the accomplishment in young players. Still, this wasn't enough to convince him that she was a prodigy.

Violin tuned, he called out scales for her to play, easy at first just to warm her fingers and loosen her wrists. Then he had her play more advanced scales in different positions before requiring her to delve into a variety of arpeggios. All the while, he listened carefully to even the minutest error in intonation or the slightest scratch from an unaligned bow stroke. Very little, however, constituting a severe defect in her playing caught his attention.

"Good," he said, truly impressed. The ease with which she crossed strings and played the scales and arpeggios sent a rise of excitement up his spine. Her bow hold was almost perfect, save for the irregular spacing of her fingers; her stance adequate, though her shoulders slumped just a degree or two forward. He would have to correct these minor faults.

Perhaps a prodigy, he reflected. He rose from his chair and arranged a piece of sheet music on the Georgian stand.

"Play this."

Kelly spent a few moments looking over the piece, Bach's *Sonata no. 1 in G minor* in *adagio,* or slowly. The work was certainly not out of reach for a girl of her age and ability. He'd seen it in advanced method books for students, and had no doubt that she would play the short piece moderately well. He watched her quietly as she sight read the notes, nodding slightly, and tapping her foot on the hardwood floor.

Yes, he thought, *get a feel for the music; make it yours.*

He had all he could do to keep from standing and embracing a teachable moment, pointing out the nuances and interplays of the piece. But he contained himself and waited patiently for her to start.

At last, she raised the violin to her shoulder, all the while looking at the music, and began to play. Again, he listened carefully, all too committed to finding fault with her performance as the notes climbed the ledger lines and then tumbled down to irregular trills and roughly sustained vibrato, ever so deliberately. By the time she finished, he had identified a few mistakes with intonation, technique, and a shaky bow in some measures. He would have attributed the problems to nervousness if he was not convinced that she was much too confident for anxiety. Then again, he could not lose sight of the idea that Kelly was, after all, only a girl, and one with the weight of the world on her prodigal shoulders. Nonetheless, he had to admit that her playing was almost flawless.

But minor errors aside, he wasn't quite sure what made the performance *almost* flawless. For a moment, he considered whether the issue lay in him and his stony desire to expose her as a fraud, instead of in her ability. Perhaps rather than embracing a teachable moment, he had latched onto the bias of preconceived notions—a kid with a violin and dreams of more than what she was or would ever be. He'd seen this psychosis a hundred times play itself out through the delusions of parents whom themselves were never very good at anything. They all had a prodigy, the next Itzhak Perlman or Maud Powell.

Nodding once to acknowledge the completion of the piece, he pulled a different selection from the back of the stand and presented it to her.

"Now a fast one," he said.

As before, she sight read the score, tapping out the quick time—Bach's *Partita no. 1 in B minor*—double *presto,* or very rapidly. Three or four minutes passed, then, readying herself, she startled him by plunging into the piece so forcefully that at the instant horsehair met strings, the violin seemed to scream and fight to get off her shoulder. Enthralled in the score, she closed her eyes and lived it in every cell of her body. Suddenly, he realized that she didn't need the notes on the page anymore. She had collected each one in her mind and now strung them out, measure by measure, into the air. He stood, finding her place in the music, and followed the score as she played.

Unbelievable, he thought. *She memorized it…No, she knew it beforehand…She—*

"Stop," he commanded her.

Kelly stopped, opened her eyes, and peered at him down the fingerboard and over the scroll of her violin. Bow resting tenuously on the E string, she drew in a quiet breath and waited.

"You already know the piece," he continued, pawing at the sheets of music on the stand. "Let me find something that you're not familiar with."

"I'm not familiar with any of it," she insisted.

He stared at her for a moment, trying to read the sincerity of her words in the rounds of her face. "You mean to tell me that you don't know the partita?"

She shook her head, chin still in the rest, and eyes large and shiny. "I didn't know the first one, either."

"That's not possible," he remarked, turning from her. At the window, he studied the bark of a tree on the other side of the glass. Behind him, he could hear the quiet sounds of the little girl returning her instrument to its pink and silver zippered case.

"Should I come back on Wednesday?"

Alex glanced down at his watch: 12:30 p.m. She had been there over an hour and a half.

"Yes," he answered, but he wouldn't look at her. "Wednesday, same time. Don't be late." He listened to her footsteps sounding softly on the hardwood. "Tune beforehand," he added as she left the room and the noonday sun burned yellow across his forehead.

When at last he heard the screen door click shut, he left the window and looked over the partita sheet music again.

"Maybe," he admitted out loud.

He wouldn't jump to conclusions. Instead, he would find out how she could do what she did. The most likely scenario, he felt, would be that she had memorized the music before as part of Mr. Grady's course, and had simply lied to Alex. But what would it mean if she had not? If she had committed it to memory after a careful read-through? He would have to acknowledge and nurture it; the teacher in him would not act otherwise.

Yet he wouldn't jump to conclusions until he knew better.

~

Midnight found him staring at a dozen different brands of TV dinners in the frozen food aisle of the local supermarket. The last real food he had bought was the salmon for Charlotte's birthday. He thought it best to forget that demented action, and tried to remember where he had hidden that bottle of *Xanax.* For the most part, he ate plain rippled chips with extra sharp cheese or the occasional bowl of flavored rice with buttered wheat bread—coffee, spring water, a beer every now and then. He had decided it was time to cook again, or at least to use the microwave more often and with greater variety, while watching commercials during a break in the eleven o'clock news broadcast. A consumer advertisement for ninety-second beef stroganoff squeezed at his stomach and made his mouth water. Minutes later he was on his way to the grocery store.

Alex soon realized that the age-old adage about shopping on an empty stomach had its roots in hard fact. He had filled his cart with products of all kinds, from lettuce to ground turkey to vanilla ice cream. Why would he buy ice cream? He'd never had a sweet tooth, and he couldn't remember the last time he had actually eaten ice cream. Maybe Kelly would want some, he rationalized. The boring notion of vanilla ice cream prompted him to buy chocolate sauce, as well as butterscotch just in case the girl didn't like chocolate. But the thought of butterscotch topping nauseated him, remembering the candies of the same flavor in the gold foil that his grandmother used to shove into his mouth, so he returned the butterscotch to the shelf and settled on strawberry.

"Every kid loves strawberries," he insisted to himself.

He found an excuse for each item he put into the cart. Milk was necessary for curing heartburn; potatoes and pasta would level his blood sugar; granola bars offered a fine choice for a quick breakfast; Tang was good because NASA said so; at his age, the more fiber the better; and so on. He would have bought dog food if he'd had a dog, or some other mythical reason to make the purchase. The same held true for cat food and birdseed. Birdseed—maybe he would buy a feeder and hang it from a tree branch in the back yard.

"Okay," he said aloud, dropping the plastic bag of birdseed into the display box, "get a grip on yourself."

"If you're trying to convince people that you're not crazy," she quipped in a sassy Southern tone, "talking to yourself in public is a bad start."

The young woman brushed the stray locks of sandy hair from her face and grinned. Her copper complexion betrayed the hours she had spent in the sun, but her tired brown eyes communicated a more diligent existence. She wore hospital scrub-style teal pants and a flowered, V-neck smock that commanded his attention.

"I'm a nurse," she said, as if reading his mind. "I work the second shift, three to eleven, at the hospital."

"I watch the eleven o'clock news," he murmured idiotically.

"What?"

His eyes met hers, and he was sure that they shared the same fatigue. "Nothing," he answered, shaking his head and fixing his eyes on the mound of groceries in his cart. "I don't know why I said that. Free association, maybe. You caught me off guard."

She laughed, showing straight white teeth through parted lips. If he'd had it in him, he would have admitted to himself that she was beautiful, tired eyes and all. Though garbed in the costume of a nurse, her long, slender body managed to express its subtle curves and toned perfection. Immediately, she fulfilled all the stereotypes of young nurses and their inherent attractiveness.

"I'm Grace." She extended a delicate hand to him, and a gold bracelet slid down to her wrist, glittering beneath the store's florescent lights.

"Alex," he said weakly. Her small hand disappeared into his palm as he shook it, and he could feel her rough knuckles and long nails on his skin.

"I know who you are," she said. "You're the violin teacher."

The violin teacher.

"You know me," he declared more than inquired. "I didn't realize that I had such a reputation in this—" The picture in Luella's living room. Suddenly he remembered the photograph, and the pieces came quickly together. The woman standing in front of him looked so much like Clarice, Kelly's mother. Sandy hair, beautiful brown eyes…

"You're—"

"I'm Miss Kelly's aunt," Grace said. "She talks about you all the time. As a matter of fact, she might have a little crush on you. She found a picture of some orchestra that you were in on the computer, printed it out, and hung it on her bedroom wall. She's got you circled in red marker."

Some orchestra that I was in, he mused, almost insulted that she wouldn't know which one. "I was in the New York Philharmonic Orchestra, first violin section."

She looked at him blankly, and he realized that she was not impressed.

"It's a pretty big deal in the city."

"Thank God we're not in the city." Her eyes twinkled mischievously.

"She's a very talented girl," Alex admitted. "We had our first lesson today."

"My mother insists that she's a prodigy. That might be a little over the top. But I agree she's got a thing for the violin. Of course, my sister did, too."

The conversation fell away from them for a handful of seconds, and in its place a cheesy instrumental rendition of Barry Manilow's *Copacabana* eased itself out of the supermarket's ceiling speakers. The avant-garde collision of techno and polka unnerved him.

"What are the chances that we'd run into each other?" he commented for the sake of having something to say. "I mean—"

"You do realize that only about three thousand people live in this town," she said, "so the chances of us eventually bumping into each other are—"

"About one in three thousand," he countered.

She smiled. "Minus the circumstances. Believe me, it's more a case of inevitability than serendipity." She examined his cart. "My, you must have quite an appetite."

Somehow, he was embarrassed. "I don't know what got into me. I haven't been grocery shopping since I moved here. I guess it was just time." He reached into the cart and pulled out the half gallon of vanilla ice cream. "I thought that maybe Kelly would like some ice cream."

Grace was visibly humored, and perhaps keenly aware of his awkwardness. "That was nice of you," she said. She leaned toward him. "Just don't let her grandmother know. She runs a tight ship when it comes to her granddaughter."

He nodded into the subtle scent of a sweet perfume delicately balanced with a signature undertone of coconut tanning lotion. "Luella is a bit overbearing."

She laid a hand on his forearm and he shuddered. "Did she give you the *it-depends-on-which-one-of-my-personalities-wakes-up-in-the-morning* speech?" She chuckled.

"She certainly did," he answered.

Grace pushed her cart away from him. "I'll let you get back to shopping, Alex. I've got my own to do. It was nice to finally meet you. I'm sure I'll see you again. If I don't get home and to bed, I'll never make it through tomorrow."

"You must be very busy," he ventured, "working that shift and then keeping up a house…or whatever." He couldn't have sounded more ridiculous, and he cringed with how the sentence ended, or with what it suggested.

"It's just me and my television," she said patiently, as if one wrong move or barbed word would send him running out of the store. "I haven't been over to Mom's house in a few days, I've been so busy. I'll get over there, though." She shrugged. "I'm sure I'll be working the night they usher her into the emergency department on her last leg. She'd do that sort of thing to me."

He met her eyes again, for an instant stole their glimmer, then unexpectedly broke into laughter. A heartbeat later, she was giggling with him, their eyes wet and cheeks flushed.

"I'm sorry, I didn't mean to laugh."

She raised an open hand to brush off the apology while she wiped her tired eyes with the other. "No, that's quite all right. She's quite a woman."

"Yes," he conceded, "she certainly is."

Grace pulled her hair back, offering him a glimpse of her perfectly angled chin, high cheekbones, and small ears shining with a single golden stud in each lobe. Everything about her seemed fragile, elegant, real.

"I'm sure I'll see you again," she repeated, piloting her cart toward the deli. She glanced back at him, the smile still warm on her lips.

Alex waved, returning the smile as the scent of flowers and coconut lingered and he inhaled them once more. He pushed his cart to checkout aisle ten, the only one with its light on. He stood dazed, the beeping of each item through the infrared scanner ringing in his head, as he watched the middle-aged cashier with wide swatches of blue eye shadow check out the ice cream, canned beans and carrots, sugar, bread, and everything else. *Visa* loaned him the two-hundred and twelve dollars and sixty-four cents to pay for the groceries, and the supermarket thanked him for his patronage by printing out coupons with his receipt that offered discounts on items he had already bought.

In the parking lot, he loaded the plastic bags into the trunk of his car, a pit growing in the depths of his stomach. He knew what was bothering him, but he didn't want to stop long enough to face it. He felt guilty, somehow, for having acknowledged Grace's beauty, for his body shuddering at her touch. It was too soon to be feeling things for strangers, whatever those "things" were. First he had caved to a surreal expression of love from beyond the grave and allowed himself to go back on a personal promise never to play the violin again. To compound the matter, he had taken on a student as well. Charlotte had wanted it that way, hadn't she? She came to him in a dream and made it all right to return to the music; she had sent the monarch to convince him to get over himself and to embrace his passion. But she hadn't freed his heart from hers, and he wouldn't ask her to release it. He tried to bury the ideas among the rubble of his mind, but there were too many vacant pockets into which they could settle and reflect themselves back again in disjointed thoughts.

Driving home, he reviewed the encounter with Grace, shaking his head at the stupidity with which he'd spoken. There was little doubt that he'd handled himself, at the very least, eccentrically, and perhaps even a bit absurdly. But it shouldn't have mattered, since he'd done his best over the past months to shut out the world, no matter how people perceived him. Thankless, graceless, bitter, and indifferent as he fancied himself, Grace had penetrated the shell and stripped him of his walls. He had laughed with her, and now he felt as though he had violated some sacred law of devotion. He felt unclean, unfaithful.

In the driveway, he turned off the car and stared at the side of Kelly's house. The windows were dark and the pair within certainly asleep. In exasperation, he shoved open the car door, insisting to himself that he would have been better off playing professional football.

~

On Wednesday, he called to her from the kitchen to come in and have a seat at the dining room table. She did as she was told, depositing her violin case in the parlor first, then moving suspiciously through the house to the table. She could hear him in the kitchen, the refrigerator door opening and closing, clinks and clanks of silverware, porcelain.

"I thought we'd take a different approach to our lesson today," he said from the other room.

Kelly pulled out the chair at the head of the table and sat in it. While she waited patiently for her teacher to appear, a reunion that since Monday she had no doubt nervously anticipated, she took in the bareness of the room, the stillness of the house. Shadows of loneliness filled the quiet spaces, and she perhaps felt the sickness of something lost nibbling at her stomach. Had she closed her eyes and concentrated, her small heart might have drawn the stories of this place from the walls. She might have learned all its secrets, and the secrets of those who had lived there. She might have, for a single heartbeat, glimpsed Charlotte fading in and out of the sunlight with the butterfly on her shoulder.

"Okay," he announced, at last emerging from the kitchen with his hands behind his back. "I thought we'd set a different kind of tone today."

She smiled up at him, but the slight tremble of her mouth betrayed the wariness of the strangely playful grin on his lips.

"I got you *this*." He produced a large bowl of vanilla ice cream and set it in front of her. Heaping in a great mound, he must have emptied the entire half gallon into the dish, and the little girl gawked at it incredulously, mouth gaping and eyes wide.

"But—"

He slapped a spoon wrapped in a paper napkin down on the table. "I almost forgot," he gasped. He bolted into the kitchen and returned again with a bottle of chocolate syrup and one of strawberry sauce. "I wasn't sure which you'd like more, so I bought them both." He smiled at her, very satisfied with the surprise.

He had lain awake most of the night, dreading lesson two with Kelly. He had behaved badly at the end of the first lesson, communicating to the girl that her talent was in some way his insult. Ironically, his confrontation with Mr. Grady haunted him, like Marley vexing Scrooge, as the tables turned and Alex had in the moment succumbed to the tendencies of a tyrannical instructor rather than to the sound techniques of a progressive teacher. At the flashpoint of his bitterness he'd had a revelation that found him stewing in some negative vortex that slowly picked the life from him. If he stayed the course, the journey would kill him. In the vapors of a new day, he could reinvent himself, he thought. His chance to become whole again hadn't quite passed yet, and he would take steps to finally allow himself to heal. In many ways, the process started with Kelly and a bowl of vanilla ice cream.

"I don't think I can eat all of this," Kelly protested frankly. "That's a lot of ice cream."

He slid into the chair to her left. "Well, have what you want then." He continued to smile, truly happy, almost giddy. As she poured both strawberry and chocolate over the vanilla, he relaxed and crossed his arms.

"Take your time," he offered as she ate, the fleeting notion of a Hansel and Gretel episode apparent only to him. But he didn't intend to eat her; instead, he wanted to learn from her as he edged closer than he had ever been to the prospect of music genius.

"I want to know how you play the way you do," he admitted.

Kelly shrugged. "I don't know."

"Did you actually memorize that partita?"

She nodded, chocolate on her upper lip. "Um-hmm. Most of it."

"It just happens?" he asked. "Just like that?"

She wiped her mouth with the napkin. "It just happens."

He leaned toward her. "I'm interested in knowing how."

Rolling her eyes toward the ceiling, she thought about the idea for a few seconds. "I look at the notes, or I *hear* them," she explained slowly, "and suddenly I know them; they're inside my head. If I close my eyes, I can see the whole thing like it was in front of me on the stand."

"Then why did I hear you struggle so much with Mr. Grady?"

"For the same reason I couldn't memorize the sonata you gave me to play first: I can't do it if I'm nervous.

Everything goes black and I need to look at the paper. I'm not a very good player when I have to play and read the music at the same time."

"How long have you been able to do this?"

"Since my mom showed me how."

"Your mother?"

"Um-hmm." She took another scoop of ice cream oozing with brown and red and swallowed it. "My mom played the violin, too." She shrugged again. "But she's dead."

The candidness of the little girl's words stung him and instantly he considered his own loss. He lowered his head, traced the grain of the tabletop with a single finger.

"Tell me about her," he said.

"I was seven when she died. She had cancer. I can remember her making me learn to read music and telling me that the violin was the most beautiful instrument in the world. Just like a voice box. She said that nothing could sing like it, not even birds."

"It's true," he answered. Years ago, he had embraced its beauty, had let it seduce him to the brink of obsession. "How old were you when you started playing?"

"I don't know. I can't remember *not* playing."

"After your mother died, your grandmother hired Mr. Grady to teach you, I take it?"

Another shovelful of dirty ice cream was in her mouth. "Um-hmm."

He sat back in his chair. "Interesting," he breathed. "It's possible that you could have been reading music and playing the violin since you could walk and talk. Your mother must have been an amazing woman."

"Um-hmm. She loved me very much, and Nana, too." She pushed the bowl toward him. "Done. My belly hurts."

Glancing into the bowl, he frowned at the partially melted mess of brown, red, and white swirls. "You ate almost all of it," he remarked.

"I haven't eaten lunch yet," she quipped, rubbing her slightly distended stomach. "Are we going to play today?"

He rose and took the bowl from the table. "Yes, we are. I wouldn't want your grandmother to accuse me of getting paid to feed you ice cream."

She giggled, the quake of her laughter prematurely interrupted by a loud burp.

"Just let me put this into the sink and we'll get started," he said, trying not to laugh with her. "I have a few things I want you to try."

~

Alex had always participated in Juilliard's Pre-College program as a member of the music faculty. Designed for students ages eight to eighteen, the course of study offered intensive musical instruction on Saturdays for thirty weeks. Natalie, Will's and Monique's daughter, had entered the program at age fifteen, after being accepted on the basis of a performance audition that proved both her technical and artistic merit. She had not been the strongest student he had ever taught, but she showed enormous potential. Consequently, her parents had also paid for her to have private lessons with Alex throughout the course of the year. When Charlotte died, the relationship that Alex and Natalie's family had forged remained strong and proved faithful, until he couldn't take living in the city any longer and made the choice to leave. Nonetheless, he was very familiar with admissions requirements into the program, and he understood the demands to be placed on Kelly, especially at the age of ten.

Luckily for both of them, in terms of ease for the teacher and clarity for the student, Juilliard specifically stated its audition requirements. First, Kelly would have to be able to play all major and minor scales and arpeggios in three octaves. She would have to demonstrate an advanced level étude, as well as a slow and fast movement of a concerto by a classical composer. And to make it all just a bit more difficult, she would lastly be required to play a contrasting piece to the concerto movements already performed.

Alex was certain that the challenges of admission into the program would make little difference to Kelly. Confidence was not a factor in the girl's genetic code, but the backbone of her entire profile. However, before she could even begin to think about receiving an invitation to audition, a sample recording of her ability would have to be made.

In the meantime, bow control was key today. He had her play some elementary pieces with different time signatures, like Mozart's *Waltz* and Bach's *Minuets*. Easy, he knew, but the music would allow him to really study her command of both parts of the violin. Later, she faced Wohlfahrt's études in third position, riddled with double stops which required Kelly to play two notes simultaneously on separate strings. Also, a few of the pieces involved notes sounded in a single bow stroke called a *slur*. Some of the slurs were twelve notes long, others, nine.

He remembered a Russian teacher from college who would assign him one-page pieces to practice the finer aspects of control and technique. At his lessons twice a week, the elderly professor would make him play the pieces over and over again until every beat of it was perfect.

"Now," the old man would begin, dropping his cramped, arthritic body into a folding chair to the right of the music stand, "play it fifty times. I will count."

Alex would play the piece, and each time the professor felt that his student had made a mistake he would stop him, saying, "Start over, and play it thirty-five times more…Start over, and it play it forty more times...Start over, and do it fifteen times more."

He hadn't seen this method of instruction either before or after his experience with Dr. Borechev, and he vowed that he would never employ it as a means to perfection for his students. Still, repetition fostered mastery, and he sensed that Kelly had not fully mastered some of the more demanding aspects of the violin. Regardless, at the age of ten, he had to admit that she was "pretty damn good."

What he had to consider at length was what exactly made a child a prodigy, so he had done some research prior to the second lesson. The dictionary, his first and last source of reliable information, defined "prodigy" as an omen. He'd smiled at the revelation. There were few truths in his life, but this connotation surely ranked among those actualities. If anything, Kelly was a "portentous event" of sorts, a flesh-and-blood incarnation of some incident waiting to happen, good or bad. To this end, she fit the bill, as it was.

However, a prodigy was also something extraordinary or inexplicable. The little girl was indeed extraordinary in many ways, namely in her innate ability to challenge his very existence. She was sincerely far more outspoken than any child of her age should have the right to be, he felt, and her uncanny sense of rhythm and intonation proved to be her most obvious strengths in music. This aside, he absolutely remained at a loss to explain her nature, or at least what made her what she was. Inexplicable might very well have been an understatement, though whenever he considered the idea he quickly realized that he had neither the constitution nor the desire to figure it out.

The dictionary's claim that the word portended an "extraordinary, marvelous, or unusual accomplishment or deed" solidified his belief that Noah Webster had never met the likes of Miss Kelly. Finally, he had decided that "prodigy" in the girl's case indubitably meant that she was simply a highly talented child.

Interestingly enough, further research suggested that prodigies were more likely to be advanced in mathematics than music. He wondered if that was why she had such a strong grasp of rhythm, a talent that lay almost entirely in the ability to count. Then again, he'd seen horses on television that had been trained to tap out numbers in corral dirt in exchange for sugar cubes. Still, science adamantly held that by the age of eleven a child prodigy displayed exceptional proficiency of the fundamentals of a particular field. Apparently, Kelly's "field" was music, and, moreover, the violin.

Afterward, while the spirit of research had still been on him, he'd looked up "lunatic" just to be sure that he wasn't one.

At the conclusion of a particularly difficult étude, he nodded, satisfied, and stood to change the music selection on the stand.

"What's the square root of nine-hundred and ninety-nine," he asked in passing, careful not to look her in the face.

"To what place?" she asked.

Surprised, he faced her squarely. "What?"

The bow dangling from her hand, she reached up and scratched the end of her nose. "To what place?"

"Ah," he shrugged, the tables having been abruptly turned. "Three places…past the decimal point?" He struggled to maintain his composure, for, after all, he was the teacher.

Kelly giggled. "Rounded off?"

"Sure."

"Thirty-one point six-zero-seven." She flashed her teeth at him.

Alex crossed his arms and nodded again. "Good," he answered simply. "Now, look over this piece while I go to the bathroom."

In the kitchen, he dug through a draw beside the refrigerator for his calculator. Slapping it down on the counter, he pressed in the number nine-hundred and ninety-nine, and then found its square root: 31.606961.

"Son of a bitch," he gasped.

"I never understood why people say that."

He spun around to find Kelly standing in the kitchen doorway.

"Was your mama a bitch?"

"Excuse me?"

"I bet she wasn't. So why would you say that?"

He tried to conceal the calculator under an open hand while the thoughts sorted over his brain. "I—it's only an expression. What are you doing in here? I thought I told you to look over that piece."

"I did," she said, rolling her brown eyes. "Easy."

She turned on the balls of her feet and sauntered away from him. At the other end of the living room, she peered down the length of the house, leaning slightly to see him.

"Was I right?" she called.

"About what?" But he knew she had caught him.

"The square root of nine-hundred and ninety-nine."

He could feel the blood rushing into his cheeks. "Yes," he said in resignation.

"That's because I'm a prodigy," she reminded him as she vanished into the foyer.

THIRD MOVEMENT

Because I'm a prodigy…

Specks of light flickered in patterns across the far wall. When Alex realized that he was awake and sitting up in bed, T-shirt and boxers soaked with perspiration, he jerked his head to one side to shake the fog away. Still, across the darkness, the lights glittered in and out of focus. He started from the bed, suddenly overwhelmed, and stumbled through the house, down the stairs, into the parlor. He turned on the desk lamp, eyes stinging with the new brightness, and clawed through the mess of papers and sheet music, until at last he uncovered his composition book.

Shoving himself into the desk chair, he flipped open the book and, pencil in hand, began madly to transcribe the rhythms in his head, the ones dancing on the bedroom wall over staff lines in a dream. He snapped the pages over each time he ran out of space, and as the lead wore down in his pencil, he dropped it onto the floor and dug out another from the middle desk drawer.

"Piano," he spit. He stopped writing and stared wild-eyed through the window and into the fading night. "Keyboard," he mumbled, blinking once to wet his tired eyes. "I need a keyboard," Alex insisted. He stood and skittered around the desk to the Georgian music stand. "I need a keyboard," he said once again, addressing the inanimate stand that seemed to peer back at him inquisitively. He raised a finger and smiled. "Wal-Mart."

Dashing out of the parlor, he returned to the bedroom and pulled on a pair of jeans and a sweatshirt that he'd snatched from a box in his closet. He never stopped long enough to consider that his hair stood on end from the night's restless sleep, that a thin white crust of dried drool had formed on the side of his face, or that the pink sweatshirt he had taken from a box of Charlotte's unpacked clothing read "Queen of Style" in large, curvy, purple letters.

Instead, car keys in hand, he fled the house and raced off to buy a keyboard.

~

The utter focus with which he darted up and down nearly deserted department store aisles betrayed the ignorance of his physical appearance. More than a single stock clerk halted his work at filling shelves to take a second glance at the man who appeared to have stumbled homelessly into the store from the dark underside of a bridge. He barely noticed their stares, though he had made eye contact with one employee while shuffling through the toy section, flashing a tired smile and a nod.

Electronics led him, finally, to a sparse array of piano keyboards. For the first time in months, as he stood musing over which of the items would most closely replicate the sound and full range of an actual piano, he missed the baby Steinway he'd had in his studio at Juilliard. A cup of coffee had seared a milky ring in its shiny, black lacquered finish just above the keys, and on at least two occasions, he'd locked the studio door, closed the grand piano's lid, and made love to Charlotte on top of it. It had been her idea, of course, and a certain heightened climax had come both times. For this he'd jokingly forgiven her for the indiscretion.

"So this is where the infamous Mr. Brogan gives his private lessons to all those pretty little girls," she had said coyly, tracing the lines and curves of the Steinway's sides with the tip of her finger.

He'd been standing by the open door, smiling, while his eyes took in her slender form and the thin, shapely legs extending from beneath her plaid skirt. As always, she was absolutely beautiful.

"This would be the place," he answered.

Charlotte glanced back at him from over her shoulder, green eyes sparkling and delicate lips turned up in a seductive grin. She faced him, one hand on her hip. "Why don't you lock the door and give me a private lesson, handsome?"

The suggestion had been enough to encourage him to push the door closed, lock it, and then put down the lid of the piano. In the next movement, he had swept her off her feet and laid her gently on top of the Steinway while reflections of city lights burned in the dark windows of the studio. Though he never investigated at any great length, he'd hoped that on the first night they had had sex on the piano, Charlotte's intensity had been absorbed into the soundproof walls, or at least drowned in the tenor groans of the rehearsing cellos down the hall.

He shook his head at the memory. At last he pulled down from the shelf a box containing the model of the digital keyboard he'd decided would suit his needs best. He found a stand for the keyboard in a box near the end of the aisle, and with both packages under his arms he made his way to the front of the store. As he walked he thought about Charlotte, the Steinway, the sex. He could feel the desire to cry build behind his eyes, but he subdued it by humming the opening measures of the composition that he had started to write, that he had dreamed.

At checkout number one, he noticed the time on the clock above the exit—5:40 a.m. The hour surprised him, and he considered the idea that he hadn't stopped long enough to find out what time it was. The sun was rising; he had realized that much on the drive across town to the store.

"One-seventy-three and thirteen cents," the cashier sweetly informed him.

Alex looked away from the clock and into the older woman's rouged cheeks. Her name tag read "Hope," and he smiled at her as he dug into his back pocket for his wallet.

"Sorry," he uttered. "I guess I didn't realize that it was so early in the morning."

"It's early, all right," Hope agreed.

He withdrew his credit card from a pocket of the wallet. "You probably thought I'd fallen asleep," he said lightly, for the sake of small talk.

Hope took the credit card from him and swiped it through the cash register. "That's quite all right," she read the bottom of the card, "Alexander."

"You must get a lot of weirdoes in here at this hour."

The cashier, in a quick glance, took in his appearance as the register coughed up a receipt. "You have no idea. If you could just sign here, Alexander."

He declined Hope's offer for bags and left Wal-Mart with the boxes under his arms again. A fat man in green coveralls, buffing the entrance floors with a machine as Alex passed, did a double-take at the sight of the violinist's sweatshirt, and laughed out loud. Alex looked back at him confusedly, but the doors sliding open in front of him drew his attention to the parking lot, to dawn's cool, pink fingers, to—

"What are the chances, Mr. Brogan?"

He snapped his head to the left so fast that his neck cracked in his ears. "Grace," he announced, perhaps a little too loudly for early morning's peace.

The woman approached him, and he instinctively stepped to one side as if her intentions were to tackle him.

"I didn't realize that you were such an early riser," she quipped.

Alex tried not to get lost in the delicate features of her soft face. "Not really," he replied. "I'm working on something, and I needed some things..." He held up the boxes as best he could.

"Some things," she repeated evenly. "Most people need milk or bread the first thing in the morning. Even coffee." She smiled and her teeth seemed to reflect the infant sunlight. "You're definitely one of a kind."

"I've heard that before," he stammered. "I don't usually do this sort of thing, you know. Just an impulse."

Grace nodded, the smile still quivering on her lips. "I usually hope that no one sees me this early in the morning, before I've done my hair and whatever." She rolled her large, glassy brown eyes.

She had pulled her long, sandy hair away from her face and tied it into a ponytail. From the short distance of three or four feet, he could discern the faintest traces of tiny freckles on her clean face. She didn't appear rough in any way even though it was clear that she hadn't put on makeup or eyeliner. Grace wore no jewelry, not diamond earrings or gold bracelets, and yet she glittered. Raw, unmasked, he could hardly believe how beautiful she looked, how easy it seemed to watch her.

"No, you look…"

She leaned toward him slightly, playfully anticipating the words.

"Good." But she looked more than good.

She laughed. "Good? Well, it's too early for me to give a shit about what I look like."

The Southern drawl, subtle but apparent, amused him, not because it was strange, but because it somewhat attracted him to her. Or was it her pretty face, perfect curves, or stinging wit? He tried not to notice how much Grace's mannerisms, the way she walked and gestured, reminded him of—

"Anyway, it's nice to see that I'm not the only one who could care less about her appearance."

"What do you mean?"

She tugged on a fold of his sweatshirt. "The pink looks good, but I wouldn't have taken you for a transvestite."

Alex looked down the length of the sweatshirt as the blood burned in his cheeks. "Yes," he breathed, "it sure does say Queen of Style."

Her hand landed softly on his shoulder as she stepped away from him and toward the store entrance. "To each his own," she said.

"I guess I didn't realize what I'd put on," he spoke after her. "It was dark when I got dressed."

Grace stopped as a bagboy shoved a line of carts through the sliding doors. She turned toward him and crossed her arms. "I like a guy who's in touch with his feminine side."

He couldn't decide if she was being sarcastic. "It's not mine," he said. "I mean, it *is* mine, but—"

She shrugged. "You don't owe me any explanations. What you do on your own time is your business."

Was she kidding? Her eyes shone with the words, but he wondered what lurked behind them.

"The sweatshirt is my fiancée's, or was hers…"

"Was? You're not together anymore?"

He didn't notice, but she'd come closer to him. He met her eyes and thought about what he should say next.

"Maybe you should give it back to her," Grace continued, seizing the hesitation.

The impulse to turn from the woman and simply leave itched in his legs, but his knees wouldn't buckle to any rational desire. Suddenly uncomfortable, he'd begun to perspire.

"She's dead."

Grace stared at him for a moment, then looked off to the east where the sun had broken free of the uneven horizon. When her eyes found his again, her hands were already on her pink cheeks.

"I'm sorry," she uttered. "I guess I should be more careful about what I say."

He ventured a smile while Charlotte pirouetted in his mind.

"You didn't know," he said. "Maybe someday we'll talk about it."

He lingered for a handful of heartbeats, reading the uneasiness on her face. He realized it would be better for her if he just walked away.

At his car, he set the boxes on the pavement and fumbled for the keys. He could have said something else, he thought. He could have been a little easier in the revelation. But hearing himself admit that she was dead made him sick inside, and the shadow of embarrassment that had come over Grace's face only made the feeling worse. He opened the trunk and put the keyboard and stand inside. Closing the trunk, he caught his reflection in the back window and considered the ghost gazing back at him. "Queen of Style," he whispered, though the absurdity of the situation failed to dawn on him. He ran a trembling hand through his messy hair and got into the car.

A dozen notes tiptoed through his head as he turned over the engine and let his disgust flow out of his shoes and into the floor mat. Backing the vehicle out of the parking spot, he watched an elderly couple enter the store by way of the space Grace had occupied when he'd left her there to swallow the words she no doubt regretted saying. He couldn't let it happen, he told himself; he couldn't entertain such feelings at this stage in his life. What would Charlotte say? The love of his life would shift the heavens if she were to discover that in some small, incomprehensible way, he might be falling for the Southern belle.

~

By the time he had unpacked the keyboard and situated it near a wall in the parlor, resting nicely on its black metal stand, he had convinced himself that his unsettling conversation with Grace amounted to nothing less than a mistake in its entirety. As was his custom, he set the issue aside, since mulling it over would only distract him. Regardless of all the things he should have said, he could take nothing back now; the opportunity had passed.

Instead, he took a chair from the dining room table and placed it in front of the piano keyboard. Composition book propped against the fold-up music stand built into the instrument, he slid a pencil behind his ear and pressed out the first few measures that he'd written earlier that morning.

He spent the afternoon sorting it out—erasing, rewriting, adding, and rearranging. Eleven pages later, he realized the potential to edit; in fact, he considered it mandatory. The piece was too long and contained perhaps an excessive amount of repetitions. After all, his objective was to create a single movement for solo violin. If he continued, he might as well have written a full-length symphony, complete with prelude, four movements, and coda. He'd save that feat for someone more adept at musical composition, like a conductor or concertmaster.

Concertmaster…

For the time being, he just had to get it out of his head. Though whatever nebulous corner of dream world the piece had come from wasn't quite clear to him, he felt compelled to record the music swirling in his ears and vibrating in his imagination.

But who would play it?

The effort suddenly seemed futile as he lifted the dulling point of his pencil from the staff lines. Certainly, the answer was as obvious as his attraction to Grace. Lately, everything in his life felt like a B-movie riddled with contrivances and coincidences that even an obsessed soap opera fan wouldn't buy. Then again, he didn't believe that anything happened by accident, and this conviction had become a curse. As it was, he spent more time thinking about the elements of his existence than perhaps any "normal" person should.

He dropped the pencil onto the keys of the piano and stood to stretch the cramped muscles in his lower back. Shadows fell heavily and darkly across the room. The sun, sparkling through the windowpanes hours ago, seemed to have melted into the thickly leaved branches of the trees surrounding the house. Dusk had not formally arrived, but the twitter and peep of the afternoon's birds had already subsided. Alex suddenly became aware of his environment as if he had been sleeping most of the day. He'd been so absorbed in the fluid process of composing the dream song that he never noticed the minutes passing.

On the cusp of early evening, he felt hunger pangs in his stomach and moved stiffly toward the kitchen. Every angle of the Victorian had succumbed to the mellow afterglow of the dying day. He mindlessly turned on the living room lamps as he passed, then pulled open the refrigerator door and took comfort in the cold air rolling up his arms. Nothing on the shelves appealed to him, but he grabbed a loaf of bread and a jar of raspberry jam anyway, at least acknowledging that his body needed food regardless of what his palate expressed.

Peanut butter and jelly in hand, he sat on the couch and summoned the television to life with the remote control. He stared indifferently at a local news broadcast until he couldn't take it any longer. Flipping through the channels, he found a PBS special showcasing a European orchestra in the Netherlands. He followed the movement of the bows as they slid across cello, viola, bass, and violin strings. He watched the conductor's baton move up and down, in circles. When a line of large women in frilly dresses streamed onto the stage and began an operatic rendition of some obscure hymn, he choked down the last bite of the sandwich and tuned into a Red Sox game. Soon he was stretched out on the couch, remote control on his stomach and one arm behind his head.

Baseball, he thought, *is like watching paint dry.*

But it didn't matter; a handful of minutes later he was asleep.

~

He woke up when Kelly knocked at eleven the next morning. The noise drew him from the couch to the foyer where he stopped long enough to rub the kink out of his neck before pulling open the front door. As always, Kelly stood wearing a goofy smile full of straight white teeth, curly hair tamed into pigtails, and round bright brown eyes sparkling with life. She'd obviously been up for hours already, probably rosining her bow and tuning her strings in burning anticipation of her third lesson. He stood in his socked feet, vision slightly blurred, and hair so stiff that his scalp hurt when he scratched it.

"Hi," she chirped, long fingers wrapped uniformly around the handle of her pink and silver violin case. "Nice sweatshirt."

"Yeah," he mumbled, moving aside so she could enter the house.

"Did you just get up?" she asked as she passed.

"I think so," he answered. "Go ahead and get situated and I'll be right in."

He walked a little unsteadily up the stairs and to the bathroom, where he shoved a toothbrush into his mouth, wet down his hair, and refreshed his deodorant. It felt uncomfortable being so idle, barely grasping what day of the week it was, or keeping strange hours that sloughed around something vaguely resembling a schedule. He changed his clothes, careful to double check that everything he wore aligned with his gender, put on a pair of brown shoes, then went downstairs to begin the lesson. Five minutes had transformed him from an oversleeping ruffian to a semi-respectable teacher who'd insisted that he'd only meant to rest his eyes while he awaited his student's arrival.

"Let me see that," he said, reaching for Kelly's violin.

The child relinquished it without a sound.

"Old," he mumbled. "Probably a hundred, hundred and fifty years old. It sounds good when you play it."

She blushed as he turned over the violin and tapped the back. The varnish had worn off its body in many places, especially around the bridge and chin rest. The ebony fingerboard, smooth to the touch, showed streaks and wear from heavy playing, but the peg box retained its oily shine and all the pegs matched. Overall, the violin had been well maintained throughout the course of a century or more, and the fine aging of the maple and spruce construction resonated clearly in the instrument's soft, mellow tone when bowed correctly. Kelly, he knew, could make the violin sing as sweetly or as lively as any student he'd ever instructed. He also realized that she could make it groan and squeal when she wanted to, in those moods when she decided that she didn't want to play something or that she wanted a little more of his attention. He was sure the girl had yet to figure out that he was on to her. Regardless, Kelly had confidently played everything that he'd asked her to play, and well, too, no matter how spontaneous or unconventional the requests had been.

"There," he said at last, releasing the violin into her hands. "I've officially inspected your instrument and your strings. Everything appears to be fine."

"Shouldn't you have done that on our first lesson?" she asked, pigtails jittering as her head bobbed out the question.

"Actually, I just thought of it." He smiled intentionally. "I told you that it's been a long time since I've taught lessons."

Alex shuffled through the sheet music spread across the desk, unaware that the little girl in her persistent curiosity had strayed to the keyboard. In the next breath the violin was at her shoulder and she began to whisper out the first notes of his composition. His back straightened, but he didn't turn around; instead, he stared at the wall behind the desk, where he had hung a reproduction of Monet's *Garden at Giverny*. He lost himself in the pastel shades, in the soft purples and soothing greens. His heart beat with a strong, steady rhythm, in time to the music tattling on him from the other end of the room, unmasking the truth and passion of the everlasting bondage to his art. Charlotte—it made him sick to think that she had been the excuse, the rationale with which he had attempted to abandon his identity. And now, in a blossoming revelation, he felt his body sink into a funk completely foreign to him. The music, heard across a space that finally separated him from his creation, seemed to order the present chaos in his mind. Epiphany might have been an understatement. The pieces of his existence, fractured since the instant of her death, gelled into a cohesive whole, and it began to make sense; the total drama of disjointed acts settled peacefully in his mind. Each step of his life had lead to this moment, when his entire being dawned on humanity's ears in a litany of carefully arranged and universally perfect musical notes bowed ever so gently over the strings of a violin. He had composed himself; she would play it. At last, he would heal. The discovery, overwhelming and exciting, exhausted him, and he braced his body against the desk.

"Stop," he uttered.

The bow halted mid-stroke and the girl lowered her instrument. She turned to him, an expression of fear clouding her eyes and quivering over her lips.

But his smile assured her that she had not offended him.

"Not yet," he said. "You're not ready for that yet."

"When?"

"Soon."

He gestured for her to come closer, to take her position in front of the Georgian stand. Alex checked her posture and bow hold, flipped open Wohlfahrt, and pointed to an étude. She played the piece perfectly and he listened.

The lesson had begun.

~

Kelly left two hours later.

Alex believed that she had sensed a change in him, perhaps noticed that the severity with which he'd originally instructed her eased a little. He would never relent on his demand for perfection, but he would go about it with more subtlety, if in the end he could manage it without his ego usurping his will.

He sat at the dining room table, staring out the window and continuing the thoughts that had begun in the parlor and turned around and around in the bathtub. The afternoon sun had retreated to the other side of the Victorian. As the steam from his microwaveable cheese and broccoli entrée wet the underside of his chin, a weightlessness enveloped him and he felt as if he were not really existing, as if his being—heart and soul—was suspended in the silent space between the ticking of one second to the next. He couldn't get the music out of his head, and he didn't want it gone. The notes had taken on new meaning when played with the violin, a significance he hadn't quite grasped while beating them out on piano keys. And though he'd simply recorded from a dream the lullaby that miraculously defined who and what he was, it no doubt had come to be the perfect piece for the girl to perform. This was perhaps her ticket to Juilliard, and his passage to an awakening he hardly felt happening. Everything had led to this moment.

Stabbing his fork into a chunk of broccoli, a certain part of him, a separate personality, questioned the event. This fraction of his rational mind would have to be convinced if they were to succeed in realizing each other's aspirations. He needed the little girl, now, as much as she needed him. They would study and practice together more closely and precisely than ever before. They had to.

He dumped the partially eaten entrée into the garbage can and stared at the telephone in the kitchen. He wished he'd never thrown his cordless against the wall, but the incident had only given birth to another reason to hate telemarketers. And, of course, it would have been senseless to have purchased a new one while in Wal-Mart buying the piano keyboard. Nonetheless, he scooped the handset from its hook and dialed a familiar number, holding his breath for a moment before pressing the final digit.

But he hung up, fearing the impulsiveness.

Maybe it was too early to know, too soon to flex his influence over the school and its faculty. Surely he could feed from their pity toward him if he was that kind of person. Kelly could gain admission to the Pre-College Division on her own. That much remained certain. He could hold back and let her prove herself, though this course would not fulfill his greater plan—the scene he had built in his own mind. Much planning lay ahead, and against his desire to stay essentially anonymous through it all, he would have to engage the cooperation of not only an estranged conductor, but also of a concertmaster who may have last viewed him as a wolf lying in wait for the coveted position. With any luck, the bridges weren't still engulfed in flames.

~

Clarice had put a shotgun to her chest and pulled the trigger, blowing out her heart. The choice had been balanced tenuously between suicide and suffering; Grace believed that her sister could either let the cancer kill her, or she could beat the disease to the punch. Kelly, only seven years old at the time, had been spared the details. Thinking her mother had died from breast cancer was traumatic enough, let alone compounding it with the truth.

She told him all of this as she sat on the deck and stared into the clean blue sky. Her faded jeans fit snugly over the curves of her lower body, and her pink T-shirt rode just above her thin waistline, enough so that he could tell her belly-button was pierced. Considering the moment, he tried not to let his eyes wander inappropriately over her perfect frame.

The morning sun had tempted him outside with the prospect of catching up on the latest news from the *Times* and of maybe a short nap afterward. But as he'd settled himself into the reclining lawn chair and unfolded the newspaper on his lap, Grace's voice rippled the stillness. She had walked up the steps and onto the deck, smiling, and he'd had no desire to turn her away. Instead, he'd invited her company, offered a drink and a section of the newspaper.

"No, thank you. Just thought I'd pop in," she had explained as the yellow light of a flawless day shimmered in her bangs.

"Mama and I aren't the best of friends," she'd begun shortly after, "so I keep my visits to a minimum. I come mostly to see Kelly, make sure she's okay. It won't be long and she'll need a woman to talk to about things. Somehow, I don't see Mama taking the time to help her with the issues young girls have. Of course, that little girl will probably figure it out all on her own, eventually. She's a lot like her mother—my sister, Clarice."

"She played the violin," Alex stated, as if he'd known it all along and just now recalled the memory.

"God, could she play that thing," Grace confirmed. "She started when she was seven or eight. Daddy played the fiddle, and his daddy played. But when Mama and Daddy only had two girls, I guess the honor went to Clarice. As a matter of fact, Clarice learned on the very same violin that Kelly plays now. It's got to be a hundred years old if it's a day. Supposedly, it was my granddaddy's mother's instrument, Great-grandma Barbara Jean."

"Was Clarice a professional?"

She smiled sadly and rubbed her open hands together. "A professional sales associate," she answered. "She only played for the family and in the community orchestra. There's a picture on Mama's living room wall from a photo shoot for the orchestra's program the same year she died. She put the idea of Juilliard into Mama and Kelly's head. It was a dream she had for her daughter, I guess, so she wouldn't end up in a dead-end job.

Apparently, I had something to do with destroying that dream. You'd think Mama had only had one daughter."

He would have taken the last comment out of her mouth as sarcasm if conviction hadn't ruled the words. But as the conversation turned to a more sensitive subject, he never made a sound, never asked a question, or implored the woman for more. Grace talked and Alex listened, all the while feeling like he was intruding on dark family secrets.

Luella, though she denied it, partly blamed Grace for her daughter's death. Certainly God alone was responsible for the cancer, but Grace knew that Clarice had wanted to kill herself, and still she hadn't done anything to stop it. Later, thoughts like Luella's made Grace question her own innocence.

Maybe if Clarice had lived, she would have overcome the cancer. Maybe if she'd lasted just a few days more...Maybe, maybe, maybe—

Consequently, Grace limited her visits to her mother's house.

Though the method of suicide defied the accepted principles of national statistics concerning women, Clarice nevertheless wielded what she had considered the most reliable means to her own demise.

"She wasn't fooling around," Grace said, almost contemplatively. "She wanted it done with the smallest margin of error. In some small way, I helped to kill her." She met his eyes, perhaps expecting, or even welcoming his criticism.

But he said nothing. He only searched the crystal shards of her irises in the hopes of finding some clue as to what made the woman feel like she could tell him this.

Naturally, any discussion of death and dying folded back on him and Charlotte's memory flared, consuming the better part of his thoughts. The entire conversation wavered contrarily to the plan of moving forward with his life, even if it meant that any gains came proverbially on his hands and knees. Teaching Kelly constituted a small step ahead under the illusory behest of a woman in a dream and the accidental manifestation of her contact across the veil in the brilliant wings of a monarch butterfly. Still, he remained unwilling to acknowledge the excuses his subconscious fabricated so that he'd feel good about doing what he had always wanted to do.

"Anyway…" She looked into her lap, as if realizing that she had said too much. A moment after, her eyes were on him again. "Kelly doesn't know about all that. I just feel like I can talk to you." Grace shrugged her shoulders and smiled half-heartedly.

"What about Kelly's father?"

Summer air shuffled through the tree branches and she looked away from him.

"Clarice's high school sweetheart," she said flatly, but her thoughts seemed somewhere else. "They married shortly after graduation. He worked for a muffler shop in the next town over. Never met a guy who got so much overtime. A few years went by and then he got my sister pregnant about the same time he knocked up a cashier from the convenient store across the street from the muffler shop."

"Ouch," Alex breathed.

"Yeah, ouch. Needless to say, she got rid of the lowlife, and he took off to Nevada or someplace out that way. Kelly hasn't seen or heard from him her whole life. Hell, he never even saw Clarice through her first trimester. That was ten years ago…I wonder if he even knows she's dead."

And he wondered if Charlotte's mother even knew that her daughter was dead, or if she had made it to St. Patrick's cathedral after all. He didn't know, and he couldn't understand the excuse in either case. What made people stop caring, especially if they had once loved someone? Maybe they had never loved them, and perhaps they had never cared—

"…about you?"

He raised his eyebrows, caught off guard by a question he only partially heard.

"What about me?" He studied the fine features of her profile traced in delicate lines of perspiration.

"What's your story?" Their eyes met again, hers wet with sunlight.

Alex laughed self-consciously. "Me? I don't have a story." He couldn't look at her and instead focused on the scarlet maples lining the back of the property. But he knew she was watching him, waiting for a reaction.

Of course he had a story; everybody had a story.

"What makes you think I have a story?"

"We all do," she said.

He nodded, one foot in the trap. "Well, not me."

"Listen," she answered carefully, "I didn't really want to bring this up, but the other morning in the parking lot…I guess I just wanted you to understand that…" She broke off, and birdsong filled the empty space. Then: "Never mind."

He turned his head toward her, but she was already at the steps. "Wait."

Grace stopped, her back to him, and rested a hand on the railing.

"What exactly do you want to know?"

She faced him, jaw set. "Tell me why Kelly thinks you don't like her?"

"Don't like her?" he questioned indignantly. He glanced down at the folded newspaper on his legs.

She crossed her arms and leaned against the railing. "Do you like her?"

The notion seemed ridiculous to him. He liked all of his students, didn't he?

"Of course I like her."

"She doesn't think you like her, if it means anything to you."

He grinned, either paranoid or clever: "So, is this why you came over here?"

"No," she huffed. "Look, I'm sorry I bothered you. I'm sorry that I wasn't smart enough to filter the words that fell out of my mouth. I felt a little foolish the other morning, then I started thinking about you and something that Kelly had told me a couple of weeks ago. I suppose I was wondering if the two were connected." Uncomfortable, she focused on the tips of her shoes.

I started thinking about you…

Whatever irritation boiled inside of him quickly cooled, and in welcome resignation he gestured for her to sit again.

"I like Kelly, I really do," he insisted as Grace sat beside him. "I'm not really sure how we ended up on this subject. If you're asking whether Charlotte's death has anything to do with how I treat Kelly, that's insane. Besides, how the hell would you—"

"Charlotte?"

"That was her name," he countered. "Some scumbag stabbed her to death at Lincoln Center while I played the violin three hundred yards away. How's that for a story? And the fact of the matter is that Kelly in so many ways reminds me of Charlotte." He paused, took a shallow breath. He felt better by degrees, somehow, as if admitting it scared the beast away.

"But that's not Kelly's fault."

"Believe me, I know that. I think I handle her differently," he supposed. "In a lot of ways she's probably affected me more than any student I've ever had. I have a certain kind of respect…or consideration—I swear to God I can guess what she's going to say or do before she even says or does it. Not because I'm psychic, but because I knew Charlotte so well. I don't know…" He studied the scarlet maples once more. "Maybe I've worked with too many kids her age and I'm making more of it than I need to."

"Maybe Kelly came at a wrong time in your life."

He smiled. "Maybe she came just in time."

A pause swelled with the noise of a car passing along the street behind them.

"So what now?"

He felt her eyes on him again. "What do you mean?"

"My niece is your student, you're hiding from the world in this burned-out little town, and—"

"I'm not hiding."

"Then what are you doing here?"

"Teaching."

The corners of Grace's mouth twitched as if she would laugh. "You're hiding."

"From what?"

She closed her eyes and shook her head. "It's not up to me to figure that out. Look at it from my point of view: A successful, young, good-looking violinist from the city suffers through a horrible tragedy and ends up wallowing in small-town America, working for peanuts and hoping the world will forget who he is. Or are you here because you don't want to be forgotten?"

He tried not to become obviously angry with the woman, though he was sure that the color in his cheeks had already unmasked him.

"I'm glad to hear that a woman who doesn't feel like it's her job to figure me out has figured me out."

She stood again and looked down at him. "Everyone has bad days, Alex," she told him. "And, hey, some of us even have downright shitty ones. But we tend to move on, you know, like gazelles even though the tigers are waiting up road to eat them. Then there are those of us whom God chooses to shit on in the worst way, tearing us to pieces in the meantime. Hell, the sun will still rise tomorrow. I learned that after Clarice died, and I learned it again today, here, with you."

"I can see where Kelly gets her candor." The sunburst on her shoulder kept him from seeing her face.

"We're Southern girls, Mr. Brogan. We're in the business of hurting people's feelings. The truth's just destructive like that; it's a great weapon to use against fools."

If he could see her face, he'd know if she were being sarcastic. He struggled with knowing what she really meant every time she spoke to him. He shifted in the reclining lawn chair in an effort to get the glare out of his view so he could see the expression on Grace's face, but she turned away. In a momentary lapse of sunlight as her hips slid through the rays, he caught a glimpse of the butterfly, wings spread open, on her lower back. An instant later, she was at the railing.

"Remember," she said as she descended the steps, "Kelly doesn't know about what really happened to her mama. You'll keep that between us, right?"

Impulsively he stood. "The butterfly."

On the lawn, she looked up at him. "What?"

"The butterfly on your back."

"Oh," she grinned, "my tramp stamp. Got it a while ago, when I decided that I didn't care anymore what the world wanted and started living for myself."

"What does it mean?" he pressed. "Why a butterfly?"

She shrugged. "Ever hear that saying, 'Just when the caterpillar thought her life was over, she turned into a beautiful butterfly?' Well, that's why I chose it. My life never ended when my sister died. It just changed. People do that, Alex. They change."

He stared at her as the impact settled into him.

Then: "Will you go out to dinner with me tomorrow night?"

"No." She started to walk away.

"Why not?" he asked from the middle stair.

She glanced over her shoulder at him as she disappeared between the houses.

"Because you're not ready for that yet."

The words, he thought, had come back to haunt him. Or maybe that was Grace's way of jabbing at him because he felt Kelly wasn't quite talented enough to play his composition. But she would be very soon. Then again, perhaps Grace knew nothing about yesterday's lesson—

I come mostly to see Kelly, make sure she's okay…It won't be long and she'll need a woman to talk to about things…

And what exactly were they talking about? The sudden onset of paranoia unnerved him and he pushed the idea out of his head. He had discovered over the past months that the line between coincidence and serendipity ran blurrily through a weird chasm of suspicion and conspiracy. It was possible, he admitted, that some universal force had not harangued him into an existence of uncanny connections, bizarre happenstances, and dead-on intuition. In the end, things just might have been the way they were supposed to be. Grinding against the Wheel of Fortune most likely proved the wrong approach to his being. He could let life flow, allow it to stream out of him from that sensitive point between his eyes. He could wake the god within and try to understand that the reality he found himself in was the reality that he himself had created. Something inside him struggled to project itself into the world, to realize itself in the scope of his own dreams, fears, faults, loves—music. He understood that he had not surrendered to the sway of the collective unconscious, and in consequence he continually found himself in a cloudy state of emptiness and confusion. What was happening all around him remained proof of this, when he should have accepted each and every event of his life as having led to the next. No coincidences, only twists of fate. But could he really welcome the notion?

Sometimes...They change...

Alex smiled, half expecting Buddha to materialize from the weathered boards of the deck. He didn't need Buddha, after all; he only needed to let life surge as it might. Thinking so much about every image that passed through his brain only hindered his movement toward some higher cause.

"Hamlet," he uttered. "I'm Hamlet."

The difference lay in the fact that Alex had come to realize his tragic flaw, and letting his mind callously rule his hands had done little to make him feel better, to push him on to a fulfilling life where grief, anguish, and guilt held no authority over him.

Consciously, he had figured it out sometime during the conversation with Grace, probably at about the same time he had noticed the tattoo of the butterfly on her lower back.

Taking the next step, however, frightened him.

~

"Start over," he said, tempering his mounting exacerbation.

Kelly began the practice piece again. The expression on her face hadn't changed since she'd first entered the room. He should have known that something was amiss with the girl when he had asked her to tune to the keyboard's A and she had bitterly informed him that she didn't need the reference and could do it by ear. He listened patiently as she tuned, satisfied that she really didn't need the digital note and could do it by ear alone. Next, she wouldn't look at the sheet music he put in front of her, insisting that she could do it by memory. Now, after having attempted the piece twice, the careless mistakes compounded by her ornery attitude were beginning to wear on him.

"Okay, stop."

She stopped, dropped her arms to her sides, and rolled her eyes at him. "I don't need the music."

He faced her squarely. "And I don't need your pissy attitude today, Miss Kelly. Either you do it my way, or you go home and tell your grandmother that you decided you'd be better off acting like a little brat than playing at Juilliard."

"Who cares?" Kelly stared at the floor.

"You don't care anymore?"

She wouldn't look at him. "Why doesn't Grandma try to get into Juilliard if it's that important to her?"

Certainly, he would have loved to have escaped a personal conversation with the little prodigy, but he could feel it coming and he discarded any notion of fighting it.

Instead: "Sit down, Kelly."

Kelly sat in the wooden chair that Alex usually took to watch her play. He pulled the rocking chair toward her and eased himself into it. The girl's chin rested against her chest and she laid her instrument and bow across her lap.

"What's the problem today?"

She shook her head, pigtails swaying back and forth.

"Something's bothering you, and the sooner we can get it out of the way, the sooner we can get back to this lesson."

"Nothing," she mumbled, and he guessed that she had begun to cry.

"Look at me, please."

Kelly hesitated, then lifted her face to him. Sure enough, tear streaks shined over her cheeks.

"If nothing's wrong, then why are you crying?" He wished that he was a little better at relating to young people, or at least had mastered some useful techniques to deal with their errant ways. Then again, he'd never experienced this kind of dilemma while at Juilliard, not to mention, he had never met a kid as truly gifted as Kelly. Maybe the attitude and the talent came hand-in-hand.

"I'm not crying," she huffed, sniffling.

He smiled and she wiped her large eyes.

"Okay, then why are you so nasty today?"

"I don't know," she spit, narrowing her eyes. "Why don't you ask Aunt Gracie?"

The smile faded and instantly he understood the blow to the little girl's crush.

"What about your aunt?"

"You like her, don't you?"

Alex squirmed a bit in the rocking chair. "Of course I like her," he answered. "I like a lot of people."

"She really likes you, and now she's going to ruin everything."

"Ruin everything?"

She didn't answer, but let her chin fall to her chest again.

"Kelly, listen, Aunt Gracie isn't going to ruin everything. We're just friends, that's all, and besides, we barely even know each other. She came over to talk. I think you're probably a little too young to understand this kind of thing, but—"

"Because I'm just a kid?" she fired, hot eyes on him.

His spine tightened as his tolerance thinned. "I am your violin teacher. What happens in my life is really none of your business. I've got a world of shit to work out in my head that has nothing to do with you or your aunt. Do you understand that?"

"Maybe you should have explained that to her. She thinks you're some kind of Mr. Wonderful."

"I tried to explain that to her," he said calmly, "but neither of us is really interested in anything but the weather and you."

"Me?"

"Do you have any idea how much Aunt Gracie loves you? We talked about you most of the time. I want the best for you, and she wants to make sure you don't get hurt. Plain and simple."

Kelly stared at the violin on her lap. "She's always worried about me," she said softly. "Since Mama died, she's tried to protect me. But she can't. Nothing she ever did kept me from knowing what really happened."

He leaned toward her. "What really happened? What does that mean?"

"About Mama," she answered. She looked at him, her eyes deep brown and sad. The temper had subsided, and her cheeks had drained pale. "I was only seven when my mama killed herself, but Aunt Gracie doesn't think I know that. She shot herself, you know, because she was dying of cancer. I'm good at a lot of things, Alex—math, science, music. No one understands that I know when people are lying to me, especially when I've paid enough attention to put the pieces together."

"You're a very special girl, Kelly," he admitted, more to himself than to her. "Sometimes people who love you think they're doing you a favor by pretending things are all right. I know how that feels, too. The difference is, I knew all along and you had to figure it out."

She wiped her nose with an open hand. "Yeah," she whispered, "I guess so."

"I guess so," he repeated absently.

"What happened?"

Alex hesitated, having barely seen the question coming. "You mean, when God shit on me?" Then he told her, word by word, what had taken place, slowly at first, and with rising emotion, perhaps more candidly than he had ever before explained the tragic event. And in many ways, for many reasons, perhaps the little girl had to know the story, had to understand that they shared a similar pain. In the end…

"So, you're afraid of Aunt Gracie."

He frowned, struck. "No, I wouldn't say that I'm afraid of her. I just have a lot to think about."

"Don't you think you've thought enough?"

When his eyes met the child's, he saw in their reflection something sensible that contradicted her age. Suddenly, she was like a mini-adult, scarred and in so many ways alone, already rationalizing a life she had just begun to live. And when she questioned him, for a moment he lost sight of the prodigy and could only see the apparition of Reason taking form in her logic.

"Maybe," he uttered. In the next breath he stood and pointed to the sheet music on the Georgian. "I want you to look at it this time."

Kelly hadn't moved, nor had she gestured in any way to suggest that she intended to get up and begin the lesson again.

"I thought grown-ups were supposed to be smarter than kids," she ventured.

"That's not a claim I've ever made," he replied. "Believe me, I know my faults."

"Still, you walk around in some kind of cloud, when you should already know that you're really not getting anywhere."

He sat again. "You think you understand all of this, don't you? Tell me then, what do you think I should do?"

Kelly stared at him, eyes sharp and focused. She had an answer and he knew it; there was always something else that she had to say, just like Charlotte.

"Well," she drawled, "you could just be yourself, the person you were before God shit on you."

He smiled, her inherited candor amusing him. "I suppose," he answered. "But that's easier said than done. Someday, I'm sure, my life will return to some kind of normalcy."

The little girl stood now, and readied her violin. Over her shoulder, she peered at him. "Aunt Gracie really likes you," she reminded him. "And I guess I think that's pretty cool."

Alex nodded once. "Don't take it personally," he said. "One of these days you'll find someone your own age that will be a lot cooler than me."

She shrugged. "Yeah, but I'm just a kid. What do I know?"

"Start at the beginning," he instructed her. "And look at the music all the way through."

As Kelly began to play, he relaxed his body in the rocking chair and watched the tip of her bow glide back and forth across the strings. If only his life was as perfect as the notes singing out of that hollow body, he thought. His concentration floated away from the lesson and he tried to remember what life had been like before Charlotte's death. If anything, he truly didn't want the life of a concert violinist anymore; his body had yet to miss the exhaustion and general anxiety of such an existence. But there must have been more to who and what he had been back then. He wondered if his life had actually contained anything more than performances, teaching, and sex. Charlotte had captured his heart, no doubt, and locked it up in an iron cage of love and lust. He flowed with her every movement, jibed with her every whim. That sassy, sexy, intelligent woman had proved to be the cornerstone of his being, the anchor that grounded him to what he believed was reality. In her absence, he had fallen apart; he had forgotten that the only heart that had ever beaten inside his chest was his own, and that it was the same heart he had always had, now and forever.

He felt himself letting go already, and, strangely, it felt good.

Quietly, he got up and crossed the room to the keyboard. He took the composition book from the plastic, built-in shelf and brought it over to the Georgian music stand. Kelly didn't stop playing, but her eyes left the music and followed his movements.

"Okay," he said, laying the open composition book over the étude the girl had been practicing. "Let's try this again."

She lowered the violin and bow and looked at him sideways. "This is the piece that you wrote."

"Yes, it is," he answered, his shadow over her. "I want to try something. If you could just play this again, exactly how it's written, I'll listen and we can work together to refine it a little. How's that sound?"

Kelly grinned widely. "You mean, we'll work together to make our own music?"

"Something like that," he said. "I kind of wrote it from…a dream I had. When you played it the other day, I suddenly realized that maybe you should be the one to play it after all. We just need to work on it; it's certainly not finished. Maybe it'll end up being something that you can play in an audition."

"For Juilliard?"

"Let's not get ahead of ourselves," he cautioned her. "Besides, I thought you were having doubts about even going to Juilliard."

"Not any more," Kelly chirped. "I'm so excited that you're going to let me play this."

"We've been through all the basic stuff," he told her. "You can play anything I give to you, more or less. You know it and I know it. Why not do something different, something new? It might just challenge your skill in the long run."

The warmth of the child's enthusiasm inspired him, and he grew anxious to make the composition the most beautiful that it could be. Ironically, he'd never imagined it would be Miss Kelly who would bring to the piece its final polish. Pencil in hand, he sat beside the music stand as the girl pulled out the first few measures of the piece.

Then she stopped and gazed at him. "It's pretty," she whispered, eyes twinkling. "I meant to tell you the other day. Such pretty music."

"From the beginning," he said, the promise tingling in his memory, "and let's see how this goes."

Across the room, the clock read time for the lesson to be over, but steeped in their collaboration, neither noticed the hour. Instead, Kelly bowed the notes and Alex interrupted her here and there to make a correction or to have her try something else. For an hour they worked through the first page, and as the piece took a more solid form, the notes came together in absolute time, sound by sound. One note bled freshly into the next—quarter note, half note, eighth and sixteenth. Rising and falling, the music came to life and the girl tiptoed through it as if it was her own, as if she had always known it.

"I'll have to rewrite it on clean pages," he said at the last measure on the first page. "This part is very strong and we'll repeat some of these phrases here." He pointed to the second page.

"Some of it's really hard," Kelly admitted. She had set down the violin on her chair and was cracking her little knuckles.

"I know," he said, "but you're doing fine. Now, if you just remember that you should be thinking about the rhythm as going something like this..." He tapped his open hand against his thigh to mimic the rhythm as he intended it to be, but a hard rap on the front door broke the cadence.

"I'll be right back," he said to her. "Think about the rhythm while I'm gone."

By the time he had stepped into the dim foyer, he could see the figure in the windowpanes—Grandmother had come calling. He opened the door and greeted her with a smile. Perhaps in her surprise at his uncharacteristic manner, the large old woman stepped back and peered at him through narrow eyes.

"My word, Mr. Brogan," she exclaimed, "those front steps of yours are enough to kill a person with them being all crooked and creaking and whatnot."

"Miss Luella," he replied sweetly, and with an unintended mockery of her Louisiana accent, "I wish I'd known you were coming, I would have called the carpenters to fix them precisely to your orders, ma'am."

"Don't get fresh with me, mister," she retorted. "Come to make sure my granddaughter's all right."

"Why wouldn't she be?"

"It's much past the time that she should be returning home, that's why. We agreed on a certain amount of time three times a week. I'm beginning to think that you've got a big electric bill or something that needs paying and you'd be trying to earn some extra money to make ends meet. But a deal's a deal, Mr. Brogan. We've all got bills to pay." She dug into the front pocket of her apron. "Which reminds me..." She withdrew an envelope with the words *Violin*

Lessons scratched across the front of it. "Here's your payment for the week. It's all there, in cash, but I certainly can wait while you count it."

He took the envelope from her and slid it into his back pocket. "I have no doubt that you're an honest woman, Miss Luella. Why don't you come in and see for yourself that everything's the way it should be?"

She passed by him heavily, the foyer floorboards groaning under the new weight. "A man living on his own, Mr. Brogan, I doubt has everything just the way it should be." Luella paused beneath the light fixture to catch her breath. "Miss Kelly," she called before noticing the girl in the parlor. "Grandma was beginning to worry, honey."

Kelly came to doorway. "Hi, Grandma. Guess what? Alex and I are working on some music that *he* wrote. I'm going to play it."

Luella studied the violin teacher. "Wrote yourself, huh? My, my, my, you must be a talented man." She moved awkwardly into the parlor and found the rocking chair. Settling herself into it, the arm spindles crackling a bit as they spread against their will, she began to move back and forth on the runners. "Well," she announced, "let's hear it. Be nice to know where all my money's going."

"We can't play it yet, Grandma," Kelly insisted. "It's not finished."

The old woman rubbed her chin with a set of thick fingers. "I see," she breathed thoughtfully. "I suppose I'll have to wait a spell then, won't I? In the meantime, you get your stuff together there and head on home. I need to speak with Mr. Brogan about a few matters that aren't suitable to little ears."

Luella waited patiently as Kelly carefully packed her violin and bow into the pink and silver case, and Alex leaned against the parlor casing with his arms crossed, dreading the subject of the impending chat. The little girl slung the case over her shoulder and turned to her teacher.

"See you on Wednesday," she said sadly. "I wish we could work on the music some more."

"We will," he assured her. "I'm thinking that maybe you could come over tomorrow and we can work for a while." He glanced at the old woman. "Free of charge, of course." He winked at Kelly and grinning she ambled into the foyer and out the front door.

"Please," Luella said, "have a seat in your own house. I won't be long."

He positioned the wooden chair across from her and sat with his hands in his lap. "What can I do for you, Miss Luella?"

"It's not so much what you can do for me, Mr. Brogan, but what I can do for you."

Alex leaned toward her. "I don't understand what you're trying tell me."

"Simple," the old woman answered. "Had a little jaw with my daughter about her visit here the other day. Besides sending Miss Kelly into a bit of a tizzy because she's a little sweet on you, I had the opportunity to discuss the matter of Clarice, my oldest."

"I spoke to Kelly about her crush, Miss Luella. I think she's okay now."

Luella frowned. "I don't know how appropriate a conversation like that would be with a child, but if she can get past it, that's good. To the point, I wanted you to hear my side—"

"What difference does it make?" Alex questioned her. "I'm Kelly's violin teacher, not the family therapist. Do you all just sit around talking about what the neighbor needs to know?"

Finally, the large old woman smirked, then laughed aloud. "No, Mr. Brogan, it's nothing like that. You see, Grace and I never really talked much about anything, and after her sister died, God rest her soul, we spoke even less. I was beginning to think that maybe I'd done something wrong by both my children. After all, Clarice was weaker than I told myself she was. Why else would she take her own life? It's definitely a sensitive spot in the family history, one that would have killed her daddy if he had been around to live through it. My word, it's a wonder I got through. Needless to say, I love what's left of my family, Mr. Brogan, with the exception of my sister-in-law from New Orleans. Call it a fault of mine, but the good Lord will deal with it when He's got to."

"What does this have to do with me?"

She took a deep breath and glanced at the sunlight in the window. "I don't blame Grace for a thing," she said evenly. "I never had. And if she'd never come over here and spoken to you about it, we'd never have had the opportunity to get it out in the open. Do you understand what I'm saying to you?"

"Barely," he answered, though he sensed the gratitude in the woman's words.

"That's just the way God works, I suppose," she continued. "There's a reason you're here, after all, Mr.

Brogan. You cleared things up between my daughter and me, somewhat. I owe you something for that."

He held up an open hand and shook his head. "You don't owe me a thing."

"Maybe only a thank you," she said. "I don't really see where the favor would carry any sort of a cash value."

He smiled, either offended or amused, but not sure which. "Do you see me as some kind of a con artist?"

She laughed again. "No, I truly do not. And I apologize for the suggestion. Perhaps both of us could work a little on our bedside manner." She rocked forward and managed to heave herself out of the rocking chair. She stood before him, a massive form blocking the light in the window. "I'll go now, Mr. Brogan," she said. "Just wanted you to know that. And one more thing: Miss Kelly's grown to love you and your lessons. I know it's only been a week, but I've seen more progress in that girl than with the two years she worked with Mr. Grady, God rest his soul. I guess you've done all right by me." She moved cumbersomely into the foyer and he followed her. "You know, Grace seems to like you a lot, too."

"That's what I've heard," he muttered.

She paused and looked back at him. "Oh, have you?"

"That's what brought up the subject when I was trying to get to the bottom of Kelly's poor attitude earlier today."

"Poor attitude, huh? Well, I'll work on that when I get home."

He pulled open the front door for her. "There's no need to address it, really. It's over and we moved on. Actually, we had a good day. And I'll be needing her to help me over the next couple of weeks to get the piece we're working on ready to play, if you don't mind. It might prove useful to Juilliard, but we'll talk more about that when the time comes. Of course, she'll have her regular lessons, too."

Luella nodded and stepped across the threshold. "Good, then. We'll talk about it when it's time to talk. In the meantime, business as usual." She stopped again and faced him. "In the end, only you can take care of yourself, Mr. Brogan. I don't know how much you ever think about that. You've got a nice house here, and you're a decent man. Not that the two go hand-in-hand, but a person's environment says a lot about the kind of person he is. Mess some things up every now and again. Put your rugs on an angle and try not to bring so much order to your life. I'm not saying you should live in complete filth and disarray; I'm only trying to get you to understand that a happy man is a free man, and your environment should speak volumes to your freedom."

He looked into her shining eyes and almost thought he'd hug her. "Thank you, Miss Luella," he said. "You have no idea how much sense that makes to me. I think I'll go mess up the living room right now." He smiled widely at her.

Miss Luella guffawed and touched his wrist. "I'll see you soon, Mr. Brogan, but I'll come to the back door next time. I hear you have a nice deck."

He closed the front door as the old woman left the porch, and peered into the living room. For the first time he noticed that the coffee table, set squarely before the couch, showcased a neatly arranged fan of magazines he hadn't read. The four small pillows on the couch were evenly ordered across the back cushions, and not a speck of lint or fuzz marred the cleanly vacuumed lines on the perpendicular area rug. Impulsively, he marched to the coffee table and haphazardly spread out the magazines. He threw one of the pillows onto the floor and slapped the other three around. He stood back from the disorder and inspected his work. Before he could reconsider, he abandoned the mess and headed for the kitchen to get something to eat.

~

Snapping through the gritty pages of the *Times*, the headline seized him and he stared at it in shock: *ADA Bradley Plans to Seek Maximum.* Stomach knotting, he ventured wearily into the article.

> *Assistant District Attorney William Bradley plans to seek the maximum penalty allowed by criminal law in the State's case against James Cranell.*
>
> *Cranell, 24, was arrested last week in connection with a string of robberies in Manhattan. During a police interrogation, Cranell allegedly admitted to having been involved in at least three assaults and perhaps two murders over the past nine months.*
>
> *"This man is a danger to society," Bradley said in a news conference yesterday. "No citizen will be safe until the law relegates [Cranell] to prison for life," he said.*

The murder case, scheduled to go to trial next month, has become a personal quest for justice, according to Bradley.

"When someone with such despicable intentions as robbery and murder threatens the lives of innocent people, he must be dealt with as severely as the law will allow," Bradley said.

The District Attorney's office assigned Bradley to the case shortly after Cranell's arrest.

Though the murder rate in New York City has dropped somewhat over the past ten years, Cranell's alleged killings strike a nerve with Manhattan's more elite residents. At least two of the assaults occurred in or around Lincoln Center and Broadway, areas known for their security and extensive visitor safety precautions.

"The fact that someone came into our community to feed off of those who have arrived from all over the world to see and support the arts, is incomprehensible," a spokesperson for Lincoln Center said. "What has this world come to?" she asked.

Perhaps one of the most sensitive aspects of the case, however, hinges on the fact that one of Cranell's victims may have been a former Philharmonic member's fiancée who died tragically in Josie Robertson Plaza in October last year. A robbery attempt gone badly, the woman sustained stab wounds that claimed her life hours after the attack.

"This will not go unanswered," Bradley insisted. "This animal will be brought to justice, and I will put him away for life," Bradley promised.

~

"That's a good thing, right?" Grace asked intently.

Alex gazed across the table at her, slightly detached from the activity around them, and considered her fragile face in the candle's soft orange halo. He had decided a week ago that he would acknowledge her beauty, but in light of the present topic of conversation over dinner at *The Oak Leaf,* the damper had been lowered. He had initially reacted to the news story with a contained sense of horror, though the emotion had slowly settled to a numbness that still lingered in him.

"It's a good thing," he answered.

Grace fidgeted with the corners of her napkin. "At least now you can have some kind of closure," she added.

He smiled sadly, nodded. "Yes, the closure's something I've been waiting for, I suppose." He paused to sort the feelings. "I think the strangest thing for me is that I expected to be happier or angrier or…anything but this."

"What does *this* mean?"

He surveyed the customers seated behind Grace, to her left and right. "I'm numb," he admitted. "I guess I just never thought that after they caught him I'd be so…apathetic."

She stared at him, as if mining the brain behind his eyes. "Maybe you haven't decided how you feel yet," she said. "In the hospital we deal with all kinds of grief, in many different stages. I've seen patients laugh at the mention of cancer and cry when they're told it's only a hangnail."

He looked into his lap as the smile twisted through his lips.

"What?"

"A hangnail?" he answered.

"Well…" She smirked. "That's probably an exaggeration, but you know what I'm trying to say."

"I'm sorry; this isn't funny, but a hangnail? That's so ridiculous."

Neither expected to laugh, but they both did. He watched the sparkle in her eyes as her cheeks flushed red. Why was she so beautiful? He feared he was too willingly letting go of the love that had once gripped his heart and torn him away from who and what he was. *I never knew a day…*And it slipped away so easily…*I did not love you.* The smile faded and he wiped his tired eyes.

"What's wrong?" she asked.

"I never thought I'd get over her," he said soberly. "I don't like the way I feel right now."

"And how do you feel right now?"

He met the accidental glance of a young waitress with chestnut hair three tables away. "I feel like she didn't matter."

"Why do you think she didn't matter?"

He breathed deeply and held it. Then: "Because I can't stop thinking about you."

And it had been this way even before she had arrived unannounced at his house an hour or two after Luella had left, sheepishly reconsidering the dinner invitation from yesterday. In the meantime, as he'd waited anxiously to leave the house and pick her up, he had come across the newspaper article. He hadn't expected it; he hadn't expected this.

"I knew you the moment I saw you," Grace said quietly. She fidgeted with the napkin again. "I just had a feeling that night in the supermarket, when I saw you talking to the birdseed. You wear your sophistication so easily I think I was drawn to you."

"I don't think I can handle the fate idea again," he warned her, shaking his head.

"You might have to," she answered, crystal brown eyes on him. "The sooner you realize you can't control everything, Alex, the sooner you might find some peace."

"Believe me," he said, "I think about this stuff all the time. I know what direction I need to move in, and I know in my heart what the right things are to do. I'm not concerned about all that right now, though. It's these feelings that I'm having." He put his elbows on the white tablecloth and leaned toward her, lowering his voice. "Have you ever felt absolutely divided between the two ends of an emotional spectrum? It's so uncomfortable, it overwhelms me. I—"

"She's not coming back, Alex," Grace interrupted. "The best you can do is wait to die if you ever want to see her again. I'm sorry, but is your life so worthless that you'd just jump into the grave and beg us to bury you?"

Blood burned hotly across the back of his neck. "Grace—"

But she was not finished: "Could you love anything else besides yourself?"

"Myself?" He became too angry to be confused.

She set her jaw, brown eyes brilliant. "This is absolutely about you," she insisted. "I figured that out when we talked on the deck. I've been there, and I'll never go back to feeling so horrible again, not with you or with anyone else. I won't let you take me there, and I can't watch you let yourself fade away. So, if this isn't about you, then who else does it affect?"

He didn't have an answer and the sudden defenselessness unarmed him.

"Alex, you can't sit around your house giving violin lessons and waiting to die," Grace continued, less intensely. "How shameful is it that you take the beauty you have the power to create and abuse the God-given talent by letting it rot away in the back of your head?"

He didn't respond; the words were gone.

"I had a friend in high school with perfect pitch who was the best pianist I'd ever heard, but he spent his time wrapped up in petty bullshit. One day he called me because his right ear had started to buzz every time he hit the high notes on his piano. It scared the shit out of him. Two months later he'd gone deaf in that ear because of some kind of bacteria. I saw him shortly after we graduated, and you know what conclusion he'd come to? He believed that because he'd squandered his talent and his ear for music, God took it away from him. It was a hard lesson to learn for him, and one I'll never forget."

"That's quite a story," he said.

"It was quite a wake-up call," she answered. "Maybe it's the kind of story that will make you think about how close you've come to losing yourself."

Though he had only met Grace a short time ago, it turned his stomach to know that she could see through him. He'd spent too many hours, he thought, feeling sorry for himself, struggling with the depression of having had his life turned upside-down. Recently, however, he'd taken glimpses of the world outside his own personal space, had felt the twinge of inspiration, and had rediscovered his marriage to the violin. Maybe that wasn't enough; perhaps popping his head out from under the heavy shell he carried on his back would not be sufficient to reclaim him.

"It amazes me," he said, "that you can look at me and say what you say. I don't mean that in a negative way; only a handful of people have ever been able to read me so well."

She smiled somberly at him as their waiter arrived and slid plates of delicately prepared filet mignon with Julienne vegetables under their chins. The dark young man asked if there was anything else he could get them, and Alex requested a bottle of their best sweet red wine.

"Tell me about Charlotte," Grace said as she turned the plate in front of her and forked through the steaming vegetables.

"What do you want to know?" He laid the napkin across his lap.

"Could she read you so well?"

Unexpectedly, the photograph in his living room crossed his mind, and he remembered how the pearls around her neck had twinkled in the camera's flash, caught forever in a picture like tiny shining stars.

"She was…struggling when I met her," he answered. "She had a hard life, and I don't think she ever really left it behind. Her mother abandoned her when she was just a kid, her father committed suicide. She carried a kind of darkness around with her, and she never expected me to do anything but love her."

He shook his head at the memory of her. "Intense," he continued. "She was the most intense person I have ever met. Everything she did, she did with this overwhelming passion, as if anything less would destroy her. Her heart always beat a hundred miles an hour. She just never stopped. And I think she loved me more than anything she'd ever loved before. Every day she astounded me, and when she was killed, the sudden vacuum created in my life sucked me up. Somewhere along the line, I'd forgotten how to live without her. And then I think back to the three years we had together, and I wonder if I ever really knew her as well as I thought I did." A sense of shame rippled through him. "I wonder if our relationship had been anything else but sex and music."

He looked up at her, realized that she hadn't eaten a thing, but instead had been intently watching him, seemingly enthralled in the words.

"We were together three, maybe four hours a day, between sleeping, my teaching at Juilliard, and my obligations to the orchestra. She worked a more regular shift as a civil engineer with the city, and I can't remember…" He stopped, turned his face away from the candle light.

"Remember what?" she asked softly.

"I can't remember ever asking her how her day had gone." His eyes fell to his plate. "We only ever talked about my job, my life, what I wanted. We'd had discussions about children and marriage. I proposed to her in Paris, on the only vacation we ever had the opportunity to take together. And you know, she never said yes or no. She just cried and slipped the ring onto her finger. I buried her with that ring."

"Your wine," the waiter spoke, chilled bottle in his hands, wrapped in a linen serviette. "Shall I pour it?"

"Yes, please," Grace replied.

"Will there be anything—"

"No," Alex said sharply, raising a hand. "If we need anything, we'll let you know."

The waiter stepped back, and the expression on his dark face betrayed a trace of indignation. He said nothing, but left them.

"Jesus," he breathed. "If people would just leave us alone for a few minutes."

Grace reached across the table and touched his hand. "People don't purposely interfere, Alex," she said gently. "Don't forget that we *are* in a public restaurant. We can talk about something else if you want to."

He lifted his hand and squeezed her fingers into his palm. Her smooth skin, warm and yielding, felt good there, in his hold. He met her shimmering eyes, and for a moment that seemed longer than a moment, he thought he saw the universe shifting across the feathered brown irises.

"I don't think I loved her like two people are supposed to love each other," he uttered. "We thought we loved each other, and in many ways I suppose we did. But I don't think she even knew what my favorite color is, or what kind of ice cream I like."

"What kind of ice cream do you like?"

He smiled half-heartedly. "I don't eat ice cream."

"Then what's your favorite color?"

"Green, emerald green."

"I happen to love ice cream," Grace said lightly. She pulled her hand out of his and raised her knife and fork to cut the filet mignon. "Party Cake is my favorite. Have you ever heard of it?"

He, too, began to cut his meat. "No, I haven't"

"Well, let me tell you, it's so sweet it'll make you sick. But there's something yummy about it. And I love the color purple."

"The movie?"

She laughed her beauty into the room. "The color."

They ate in silence for a while, and then Grace set down her fork. "Did you ever stop to think that maybe Charlotte came into your life only long enough to give you what you needed? I often believe that Clarice stayed just long enough to see me through my younger years, to give Mama and me Kelly. She made some beautiful music, like I'm sure you make beautiful music, but hers is only an echo, now. I'd bet that if she came back for only ten minutes, she'd do two things: Tell us all how much she loves us and play that damn violin." She shrugged. "Maybe things are exactly the way they're supposed to be."

"That's a hard reality to swallow," Alex responded. "I tend to view life a little more skeptically. But I think Charlotte led me here, to this town and to Kelly and to Luella. Maybe she led me to you."

Her smile washed over him.

"Maybe," she said. "Life's full of mysterious circumstances. From my point of view, it certainly feels like

I was meant to find you. And that's not a matter of fate, as you put it, but a truth I hold as real as this table."

"So, what are we doing here? The last time we spoke, you said I wasn't ready for this yet."

She thought a minute, sipped her wine. "I wouldn't willingly put myself in this position," she confessed. "You're a wonderful guy with a lot of baggage. I have my own problems, no doubt, and my mother would be the first to point them out. But there's something about you that I just can't get past. I know that sounds like a line, but it's true. I think I see the life in you, and I see the potential, and in many ways, I can see your heart beating on your sleeve. You're very different from the rest of us, and I'm very much attracted to that."

"Physically?" He grinned. "Because that whole speech sounded like it should have come from a guy in a bar drooling over a pretty girl's shoulder."

"I don't drool," she said simply.

"Fair enough," he answered. "I'm glad we're doing this. It's been a long time since I've thought about much else than how terrible my life's become. You don't make it seem so bad."

"Wasn't it Hamlet who said, 'There is nothing either good or bad, but thinking makes it so'?"

"Hamlet? I'm impressed."

"No, you're Hamlet."

The fact bored into him. "I think so," he conceded.

"So make your life full of good things," she said. "Everything you've been through has made you who you are right now, at this moment. You know what I mean?"

"I know what you mean," he replied. "But sometimes I wonder if, even though I tell myself there's no monster under my bed, there's still a monster under my bed."

"Someday we'll kill that monster, then," she said frankly. "For now, everything on your plate's getting cold." She raised her wine glass. "And you should really try this wine. You might as well; you already know my favorite ice cream *and* my favorite color."

~

They left *The Oak Leaf* around eight-thirty and walked together under the clear night sky, through a deserted park by the lake. Alex kept his hands in his pockets though she stayed closely to him, delicately outlined in moonlight. They sat next to each other in the middle of a wooden bench and silently marveled at heaven's twinkling reflection on the glassy water. He could smell the flowery scent of Grace's perfume, and it bewitched him, made him want to lean into her and kiss her.

"It's pretty here," he spoke instead.

"It's pretty everywhere, if you look hard enough," she whispered.

She reached across his lap and took his hand.

"Don't ever forget her, Alex," she said, laying her head on his shoulder, "but let everything else go. You have to get rid of the anger; you have to."

Though the words from her did little to enlighten him, thoughts he'd had a million times before, hearing them made their possibility seem easier to achieve. Grace, real and compassionate, had fallen over him, and he eagerly welcomed the chance to become whole again.

Some minutes later, she lifted her head from his shoulder.

"Take me home," she whispered into his ear.

He turned his head and looked into eyes that reflected as much starlight as the lake. He leaned toward her, but she shied away from the subtle advance.

"Not yet," she said. She touched his lips with a single, slender finger.

They walked back to the restaurant parking lot and found his car. More than once he had thought about taking her hand, holding it until they reached the car. But she had told him in no uncertain terms that she wasn't ready for that, or at least he wasn't ready to make such contact. He opened the car door for her, waited until she was seated before closing her inside the vehicle. On the driver's side, he glanced one last time into the clear night sky, noticed Cassiopeia winking back at him and decided that she must be right. So he would wait until the feelings grew stronger, until she was surer of him and them.

Grace said little on the drive back to her house. He mentioned the composition and Kelly's tremendous progress in only a handful of lessons. She smiled, proud of the little girl who had become so much like a daughter to her. Clarice would be proud, too.

At the curb in front of Grace's faded white bungalow, he stopped the car, got out, and opened the door for her. She said goodnight, laid her hand on his cheek, and thanked him. He didn't follow her as she walked away from him and disappeared into the house. He waited a moment, as if expecting her to run out the front door and throw her arms around his neck.

Rhett, don't leave me…

Frankly, Scarlett…

He smiled at the thought, at its absurdity. She didn't come back.

~

He sat hunched over the desk, open composition book in front of him, one side of his face washed in orange lamplight. Carefully, he recorded the notes from the page he and Kelly had worked on earlier in the day onto clean, white sheets of music paper. What had formed during the lesson lay nearly perfect across the staff lines, and in the next few days he would finally polish the entire piece.

Since leaving Grace safely at her house across town, he'd begun to feel a buoyancy spread through him, first at his feet, then creeping through his legs and torso. He welcomed the feeling, the weightlessness of it. He imagined his soul unwinding from the twists and knots it had wrapped itself into months ago as it came free of his bones and organs. Ultimately, he accepted the sensation as a bout of relief he hadn't allowed himself to experience in a long time. Being with Grace made him happy, and even if he doubted the elation, certain parts of him offered no room for reconsideration. It was as if some greater part of him that wanted to live, to love and remember, fought to gain control of Alex. Slowly, he surrendered. He wanted to, at last.

The final measure complete, he looked over the partial score in satisfaction before placing it carefully between the back pages of the composition book. As he and Kelly worked through each section of the piece, he would rewrite it in the same manner, and place the pages into the book. The work finished, he would then have to make a decision about what he would do with it. He already had an idea. But he would confront it later, when everything was set.

Alex stretched his fingers over the glossy cover of the composition book. Closing his eyes, he became convinced that he could feel the notes rising through the blank and marked pages like bubbles breaking on the surface of boiling water. They vibrated in his fingertips as the melodies echoed soundlessly through the parlor. And as each measure fell into the next, he could feel the mismatched and irregular pieces of himself come together. The music meant something much more than music; inspired from some source far bigger than himself, he recorded an entity that in so many ways projected an image of Alexander Brogan that no other medium could create. The art had become the man. Lost love, a little girl, a dream, selfishness, guilt, self-contempt, and discovery were the precious ingredients, the keystones of the harmony. The expression lay elsewhere, on the strings and fingerboards of those who could play it, who would play and interpret it and reinterpret it for years to come.

Alex switched off the desk lamp and went into the living room. The *Times* lay folded on the coffee table where he'd left it hours ago. Inside, in the NY/Region section, the story of Will and his crusade to punish Charlotte's alleged killer no doubt still bled through the thin, gray paper. He knew the man's intent, and he knew the personal satisfaction that closing the case would bring to Will and his family. And Alex understood that Will's assignment must certainly have been planned ahead of time, so that eventually the assistant district attorney could balance the scales for his friend. In this regard, he felt relief and gratitude toward Will. Even though the attorney had no idea where Alex was, he would still pursue the mission so that one day his friend would know that Will had made it as right as he possibly could.

"I know it's late," he said into the phone.

"Jesus, I never thought I'd hear from you again."

"I read the paper today."

"So you saw the article? I hoped you would, and I knew you'd understand the suggestions in what I said."

Alex stared at the reflection of the kitchen in the dark window above the sink. "I did," he said. "I wanted to call and say thank you, Will. I know how this is all going to turn out, and I know how hard you'll work to make it right."

"We kind of fell into the whole thing, actually. The dirtbag just can't keep his mouth shut. He's awfully proud of what he's done, and I'm going to need all the help I can get to put him away for good. I was hoping that—"

"No," he said calmly. "I'm not getting involved. I think the circumstances themselves will be enough, Will. Please don't ask me to get involved."

Silence; a pause as two minds worked against each other.

"Okay, Alex. Can I at least get your number so the girls can talk to you? We all miss you a lot."

"Why didn't you recuse yourself from the case? There must be some ethical question here," he said.

"Probably, but I don't consider him a man with rights. I know that's the wrong way to look at it, but his public defender's going to have to dig pretty deeply before he comes across any connection between me and Charlotte. Sometimes we're better off not saying anything and just letting things take their course."

In this case, he agreed with the assistant district attorney completely.

"I know," he answered. "I think you're right. I was only wondering. Tell the girls I'm fine and that I'll be keeping track of the case from where I am."

"Alex, don't do this. I'm not sure what you're thinking, but I only hope that someday you don't need us."

"What are you trying to say?"

"How many times can you turn your back on us before we get the picture and just disappear the way you want us to?"

"I'm not turning my back on you," he insisted. "I'll be in touch with all of you very soon, I promise. Just let this be for now, okay? As far as the court's concerned, you can't find me."

Silence again; a pause as the two minds balanced themselves.

"Okay, but I'm holding you to your word, Alex."

"Good, then hold me to it. I've never let you down before."

"And I don't plan to let *you* down, buddy. This guy will pay for what he's done, and I can promise you that."

"Thank you, Will."

"You don't need to thank me. I'm only doing my job, with a little vengeance, that's all."

"Don't let it eat you up. Take it from me." He could see his wavy form in the window, as if suspended in a mirror.

"I've got it under control, Alex. And remember, I'm expecting to hear from you soon."

"You will," he said, "soon."

Later, laying on the couch and flipping through the television channels, he remembered how good it felt to be with Grace. He glanced at the green numbers on the cable receiver box, saw that it was after midnight and too late to call her. He wanted to call her, to talk to her again about nothing and everything, but he'd have to wait until after the sun had come up. And he'd have to call Kelly, too, so they could work on the composition some more.

Suddenly, there was so much to do and he felt like he was running out of time. Oddly, he welcomed the activity, the preoccupation. Smiling, he chided himself for having slipped back into a lifestyle orbiting music, violins, and a woman. Though far less taxing than his Manhattan existence, he felt like he was where he belonged, doing what he was meant to do.

~

The next morning Alex called the neighbors and asked Miss Luella if Kelly could meet with him to work on the score.

"What's that got to do with her lessons?" Luella demanded.

Alex struggled to comprehend the large old Louisiana lady's multiple personality disorder. "So, I see the nasty one woke up this morning, ma'am," he quipped, exceedingly audacious under the flimsy protection of a telephone line.

Silence, then: "Don't forget a thing, do you Mr. Brogan? Your getting fresh with me won't earn you any favors, mister."

"Is it possible," he asked patiently, "that Kelly could work with me today? The score has everything to do with her eventual audition at Juilliard. We can count the meeting as her required one-hour daily practice session."

"Hmmm," Luella exhaled into the phone. "I was expecting to spend the day with her, Mr. Brogan. Maybe take her to the mall or something. I don't see her much anymore, what with her lessons and constant practicing and all."

He bit his lip with the idea, but: "Why don't you come with her, then? Bring your…knitting, and relax in the rocker. That way you can get a firsthand view of what it is we're doing. I'm sure Kelly and I would both love it if you came. Then we could *all* spend the day together." He grinned with the dig.

"Are you being ironical, Mr. Brogan?"

"Ironical? Not at all, ma'am." His eyes watered, it hurt so much.

"Must be painful being so lonely," she remarked, the edges of her words cleanly sharpened. "Makes me wonder what a man like you does in the dark."

"What does that mean?"

"Oh, not just anything, Mr. Brogan, just something my better half used to say. We'll be over if the notion settles well with Miss Kelly," she said with finality, the line clicking dead.

"Son-of-a-bitch," he sighed. "This should be great."

An hour later, the knock came and he met them graciously at the front door. Their appearance seemed almost cartoonish: Kelly, pink and silver violin case dangling from a tiny hand, in pigtails and a smile full of teeth; Miss Luella, hefty and imposing, wearing a wide-brimmed straw hat and a flowered muumuu, knitting basket hanging from one wrinkled hand.

"Good afternoon, Mr. Brogan," Luella spoke first, her pleasure strained. She had certainly donned her Sunday best for the visit, keeping true to her Southern gentility.

"Ma'am," he replied with a nod. He winked at Miss Kelly and she giggled.

Luella considered her granddaughter indignantly. "You best not be horsing around, young lady."

"Please, come in," Alex said. He stepped onto the porch so that he could hold the screen door for them as they entered the house.

In the parlor, Miss Luella sat crammed into the rocking chair near the window. She swayed slowly as she cast the first stitch with needles and yarn. From time to time, she would glance over at them, Kelly standing beside the Georgian and Alex seated with a pencil behind his ear. And every so often she'd cough, mumble something inaudible, and tap her needles into a new row of stitches.

Alex half expected her to knit the Oriental rug right off the floor. Though he tried not to notice, the sounds of

Luella's craft distracted him, and he suspected that sometimes she worked madly through the yarn spools simply to annoy him. The clicking and ticking needles were in tune to nothing, and their discordant capering challenged the rhythm of Kelly's playing. All the same, he went on. The little girl was either unaware of, or immune to, her grandmother and the monotony so blatantly out of step with any note on the sheet music in front of her.

Alex stood and marked the music. "Let's try it this way," he said.

Kelly began on the measure before the correction and played through the measure after it.

"Liked it better the other way, myself," Miss Luella muttered. She coughed once and kept her eyes on the needles.

He glanced across the room at her, but didn't respond to the comment. Kelly played on until he stopped her and had her repeat a handful of measures once, then twice.

"Now one more time so I can hear how it all works together," he said.

"Lord, I do believe I've heard *that* enough," Luella uttered. Again she stayed focused on her work, as if talking only to herself.

He ignored her, even if the words fed his ever-growing ire. He no doubt felt the gradual effects of a mounting frustration, however. Alex realized that he was not really hearing or registering the notes, but instead obsessing over the noise of the knitting needles. A few times, Kelly played entire groups of measures before he tuned into the piece and discovered that in the distraction he had completely missed them. He erased the wrong notes; fixed parts that didn't need fixing. And through it all, Kelly, patient and obedient, never said a word, pointed out an error, or second-guessed his intentions. Perhaps she stood absolutely clueless to the idea that her grandmother was unhinging the violin teacher.

"Sustain the vibrato here," he said, pointing to a half-note, "and keep it smooth and even. Do the same thing here, in this measure."

"Demanding," Luella breathed.

He gritted his teeth as Kelly vibrated the note, just a little too fast and unevenly.

"No," he said calmly, "slow and even."

The girl tried again, this time almost correctly.

"That's right," he assured her, "but you can get closer than that. I'd have to say that one of the weakest parts of your playing is the vibrato. I want you to relax your left shoulder, arm, and wrist more and *feel* that note from your fingertip to your elbow...slow and even. Think of it as pulling a strand of boiled spaghetti out of a bowl, and you're afraid to pull too hard or too fast because you'll break it. Pull out the noodle in one, full piece without breaking it."

"Spaghetti," Luella murmured. "Hmmm..."

"Miss Luella," he said finally, straightening his back and meeting her stony gaze. "I understand your need to make a comment on everything I say, but—"

"Yes, Mr. Brogan?" She grinned. "I'm sorry, I guess I don't realize when I've even spoken. Please accept my apologies. I thought we were playing the fiddle here and not working on Mama Mia's secret spaghetti recipe." She raised a needle to him. "But, please, go on, go on. I'll just keep working here with my knitting noodles and yarn."

He looked at Kelly who shrugged, her cheeks flushed. He leaned toward the girl.

"Would you like me to ask her to leave?" he whispered.

She shook her head. "She'd have a meltdown if you did," she answered.

When he peered back at Luella, he saw that the old woman had stopped knitting long enough to eavesdrop on the two. Realizing she'd been caught, she coughed once and drew her needles together. An instant later, her hands were kneading at the yarn again.

"Let me try from the beginning," Kelly offered. "I'll play it one time through."

"You go right ahead, sweetie, and you play your little heart out," grandmother declared.

He met her eyes again.

"What, Mr. Brogan?" she questioned. "I'm only offering my support is all."

"Thank you," he said through clenched teeth. He turned to his student. "Okay, take it from the beginning, then, but remember that you're going to get into some parts you haven't even played yet." He sat down and crossed his legs. "Pay attention to everything," he reminded her. "And take your time."

Kelly raised the violin and laid her bow across its strings. She studied the opening measures and waited, the fingers of her left hand, placed lightly on the fingerboard, slightly rising and falling as she read the music. In the next breath she pulled out the opening note in a slow, evenly sustained vibrato. Sliding into the piece, her bow coaxed the melody from its staff lines and lifted it into the room. The needles rested and Alex, coming under the composition's spell, held his breath. The music, singing from the f-holes of the violin, enveloped them in climbing and tumbling scales, extended expressions of pitch and tone, and the raw spirit of passion. Quarter rest to vibrato to trill and back again, Kelly's tiny fingers drew magic from ebony, steel, and spruce. She built methodically to the climax of the piece, entering new and unfamiliar territory, confidently, perfectly, until she dropped a note and scrambled into a vibrato that came too fast to control. Three beats later the music got away from her and in her confusion she repeated a measure, scratching through it as her anxiety forced the bow into a lapse of irritated tones.

"Stop," he insisted, standing. "You lost it halfway into the second page."

She dropped the instrument and bow to her sides. "I'm sorry," she said in exasperation. "This is the hardest thing I've ever played, and I thought I could do it."

He smiled at her. "You'll get there," he assured her. "You have to. You need to push yourself harder than you've ever pushed yourself before. And there are some ètudes I'm going to have you practice that will help you along. I have a feeling that very shortly you'll be a better violinist than me."

"I don't think so," she said softly.

"I do," he countered.

He turned to Luella, who had yet to resume her knitting, and realized that despite the unfortunate demise of the piece, she had been left speechless.

"Miss Luella?"

She blinked once and looked up at him thoughtfully.

"My God, Mr. Brogan," she said evenly, "that is a masterpiece in the making."

"It will be," he answered. "And in time, your granddaughter will bring it to life." He met Kelly's shining brown eyes. "I know she will. But for now, why don't we go into the dining room."

"For ice cream?" Kelly asked.

"I think I have some left," he answered. "You need to step back from the music for a little while. I can take it from here and rewrite the score. We'll get back to it later."

"Ice cream," Luella repeated. "I dare say I haven't had ice cream in at least a week." She tossed the knitting needles, stitches, and yarn into the basket beside the rocker and uncorked herself from the chair. "Lead the way, Mr. Brogan," she instructed, hobbling toward him. "I'll think I'll fade away if you don't get me to that ice cream."

~

He could see where Kelly got the sparkle in her eyes; Luella's gray irises twinkled in the sunlight streaming across the dining room table. He had needed the break more than anyone, if only from the old woman's pointed comments. Trying to refine the score in her presence proved nearly impossible, and he could tell that in her own way, Kelly, too, had been uncomfortable. Not only did she face the stress of performing well for her teacher, but also of appeasing her demanding grandmother. Seated at the table, he saw little stress in the girl's expression now, and even

Luella had relaxed tremendously. The matron smiled at him when she spoke, as if she was truly enjoying herself, and the air about her seemed genuinely congenial. Alex found himself unwinding from the frustration of earlier, and if he'd had to admit it right there and then, he might have conceded to actually enjoying himself.

"And where do we go from here?" Luella asked as she spooned vanilla ice cream from a deep porcelain bowl. She had opted for strawberry sauce.

At the opposite end of the table, Alex sat with his hands laced together and elbows resting on the arms of the wooden chair. To his left, Kelly sat between them, quietly poking at her chocolate covered vanilla ice cream with a spoon. In her grandmother's presence, there was a marked difference in the girl's behavior, as if she had to work extra hard to keep the imp from sneaking out.

"As soon as I think the composition is finished," he answered frankly, "Kelly will practice it for a while and then we'll make a recording."

"And what do we do with the recording?"

"We send it to Juilliard with an application to audition."

Luella licked the strawberry from her lips. "What are her chances?" she inquired. She set her spoon into the bowl and wiped her mouth with a paper napkin. "And don't sugar the biscuits."

He presumed she had asked him to be straight with her. "Let me say this," he said, "Kelly is by far the most gifted student I've ever had. Quite honestly, I think she'll get an audition, and I think the committee will be impressed."

Kelly grinned at him.

"But there's still some work to be done," he added. "Juilliard will challenge her on every level of her ability, especially if they think she's a prodigy."

"*Think* she's a prodigy?" Luella croaked. "What makes you think they won't think she's a prodigy?"

Suddenly he became tense again as he approached a sensitive subject. "I'm not saying that she isn't, nor am I suggesting that the committee won't discover that she is. You know, ma'am, there is a slight possibility that Kelly is simply very gifted, and—"

"Gifted?" the large old woman repeated. "A rat that can snatch cheese from a trap without getting its neck broken is gifted, Mr. Brogan. Kelly's no rat."

He surrendered prematurely. "She possesses all the gifts of a prodigy," he said. "It's obvious to me, and it will be obvious to them. You have nothing to worry about."

Luella was pleased, and relaxed in her chair, adjusting her girth as the wood fibers squeaked.

"Will I be nervous?" Kelly asked with her first words since they had all gathered around the table.

He nodded. "Most likely," he answered. "You know, when I played professionally, I got nervous every single time before a performance. You'll always get nervous. It comes with the territory. Too much confidence opens some people up to failure."

"And what's the good reason why you stopped playing?" Luella questioned.

"I thought we had this conversation before," he said. He looked away from her, uncomfortable. He could feel the sweat form on his forehead.

She chuckled. "Oh, yes," she said. "You're the one who stopped living because God pissed you off. Hmmm, wonder where I'd be right now if I'd done that?" She glanced into her lap.

"I think I'm done," Kelly announced.

He met her round eyes and could see that she feared what was coming. He decided not to fight the battle for her sake.

"Just leave it," he said. "I'll clean up later." He stood. "Thank you, Miss Luella, for letting me work with Kelly today. We're making tremendous headway."

"Why don't you go get your things together, sweetheart?" Luella suggested.

Kelly pushed her chair away from the table and left the room while Alex collected her bowl and spoon and crumpled napkin.

"Mr. Brogan," Luella spoke as he moved toward her to take her bowl and spoon, "I must say that I'm pleased with what you're doing with my little girl."

He stopped beside her and looked down at her. "Thank you," he answered. "I guess I'd like to know why I always feel like you're trying to make me look like an idiot."

She laughed. "An idiot? Oh, no, Mr. Brogan. You've got me all wrong. Have you ever considered that maybe I've got other reasons? You see, my mama was a bitter woman whom the Lord dared not tangle with. It worked out in her favor because she lived to be ninety. I need to live to be ninety, too, Mr. Brogan, because I'm all that little girl's got. So, if I can manage to entertain the Devil from time to time, maybe God will ignore me for a while. I don't know, makes sense to me." She struggled out of the chair and faced him.

"What about Grace?" he asked.

"My Gracie?" she remarked. "Sure, Kelly's got her aunt in the long run, but that woman works too much. Kelly needs someone around all the time, at least for a while more yet. When I'm dead and gone, and Kelly's all grown up, I'll rest peacefully knowing she's got family near her like Gracie. But Gracie's got to get her life together first, and in the meantime I'll tend to Kelly."

He stepped away from the grandmother and took her bowl from the table. "Why do you think Grace has got to get her life together?" he ventured.

Luella peered into the sunlight, her cheeks turned toward the window. "Our misunderstanding over Clarice is all. Seems like maybe she thought more of it than I did."

"How do you mean?"

"Gracie's carried that guilt around a long time, kind of like you, I guess." She glanced at him. "Since Clarice's passing, her life has gradually fallen apart. She's on the upswing now, though, and can't really afford to let anyone bring her down. I'm proud of her. Maybe someday I'll be proud of you, too, Mr. Brogan. Just don't be the one to bring down my Grace."

She walked awkwardly away from him. He could see Kelly waiting for her grandmother at the other end of the living room. He turned away from them, a bowl in each hand, and moved toward the kitchen. When he looked back, they were already gone, and once again he had been left with the solitary company of an empty house.

~

Kelly returned the next morning for her regular lesson. Both seemed more focused than usual and neither had much else to talk about but the practice pieces at hand. She warmed up, moved nimbly through the scales and études, and soon they were at that hour in the session when they normally would go over the composition again.

"I haven't finished rewriting it," he told her. "I meant to last night, but I ended up talking with my parents for a while. I did some grocery shopping and then just went to bed. Why don't we skip the music and wrap things up early today?"

She shrugged, began to pack her violin and bow away quietly.

"What are your parents like?" she asked, case zipped and in her arms.

"They're good people," he answered. "Why do you ask?"

She shrugged again. "I don't know." She looked away from him and stared at nothing in particular on the other side of the room. "I can't really remember Mama as much anymore," she said softly.

He approached her, laid his hand on her bony shoulder. It was the first time he had ever entered her personal space, and the first time he had ever touched her. One of the surest aspects about him was the stinging anxiety that vexed him whenever forced to deal with children on a personal level. As a rule, he didn't understand little people beyond the scope of teaching them to play the violin. He hadn't accepted the idea that being able to teach them meant being able to reach them. Instead, he held true to the conviction that he just could not relate to kids, not matter how much better he had gotten at the practice thanks to the little girl standing in front of him.

"Why don't you put down your case and have a soda with me?" he offered. "Let's sit out back, on the deck."

She laid her violin case across the arms of the rocker and went with him into the kitchen where he took two bottles of orange soda from a middle shelf in the refrigerator. She didn't make a sound, and her silence concerned him. There was something different about her demeanor, something uncharacteristic of the usually energetic, intense ten-year-old. He wondered what had happened to her in the day that had passed between yesterday and this morning.

On the deck, they each held their bottle of orange soda and squinted into the waning morning's brilliant face.

"You know," he began, "I remember sitting out here just after I moved in, and trying to take a nap. I couldn't sleep, though. Do you know why?"

She took a long drink. "Why?"

"Because this old man kept barking at this little girl, and she kept making mistakes because she was so nervous."

"Mr. Grady," she said indifferently.

"What's wrong with you today?"

She didn't answer right away.

"I can't stop thinking about the music," she said at last. She looked at him. "When I play it, it's like I can feel things inside of me moving around."

"In a good way or a bad way?"

"I don't know yet," she replied. "I keep thinking about my mother, but then I realize that I can't really see her that clearly anymore. But the music helps me to remember different parts of her, like her eyes and her mouth and stuff."

He studied the smooth rounds of her face, the expression of absolute gravity swirling in her big, brown eyes.

"For a little girl, you seem to have a profound grasp on life. Do you think it's possible that playing the violin reminds you of your mother because she played it?"

Kelly gazed across the yard. "No," she said, "that's not it. I've been playing for a long time and nothing's ever made me think of her this way before." She paused as if collecting her thoughts while the birds whistled at them. "I think you wrote something that does that to people." She met his eyes once more. "I think there's something in the music."

He stared at her, somewhat struck by the fact that maybe she felt his life in every note of the composition.

"Do you think that maybe you're making more of this than you need to?" he questioned. "After all, you were pretty involved in the whole process. Maybe that's why you're reacting to it the way you are. Music tends to get personal once you get so close to it."

"I know it sounds dumb," she added, "but the music, it's like it's already inside of me and I just need to remember how to play it again."

"And when you've remembered how to play it?" he asked. "What then?"

Her eyes were on the scarlet maples now. "I don't know," she answered. "Maybe I'll see my mama again, the way I used to remember her."

"Maybe," he breathed. A nervous silence descended on them and even the robins, sparrows, and chickadees seemed to be listening to their hearts beat.

"When I finish writing the score over, I'll make you a copy that you can take with you to practice," he said a minute later.

"Okay," she replied.

"If you feel as connected to the piece as I think you are, it's probably the best thing to play for an audition."

"Okay."

"You're going to have to become that music, Kelly."

She stared at her half full soda bottle and nodded.

"Before you audition for anything, you need to know the score on every level," he cautioned her. He knew she was listening, but because he could not see her eyes he leaned forward to get her attention. She must have sensed him closer to her and she finally made eye contact. "You'll have to feel it, breathe it, become it. It has to be yours, Kelly, inside and out, no matter what it seems to do to you."

"Okay," she mumbled.

"Are you going to be all right, kid?"

She smiled, but it was not that toothy, Kelly kind of smile. "Yup," she said. "Guess I'm starting to get a little nervous already."

"One step at a time," he said. "One step at a time."

~

The afternoon sat with him soundlessly as he rewrote the rest of the score at his desk in the parlor. He didn't notice that it had started to rain until the smell of wet summer reached his nostrils and the room grew dim in the shadows of storm clouds. Unaffected, he carefully finished the last measure, took a few minutes to read the music from beginning to end, to consider the changes.

Kelly's words had begun to haunt him as soon as the girl had left a few hours ago, and he wondered if it was possible that the score touched something inside of people, stirred their emotions, and rekindled old memories. Every piece of music did that, didn't it? The seriousness he had seen in her eyes convinced him that maybe this composition inspired the human soul in a different way from all other movements. Crafted from loss and pain, captured and recorded as if from a forgotten recollection, its origins lay in some nether region of his brain. There was no way to know for certain what had been conceived with the music, what had followed it when the notes were finally born. Whatever life it had, whatever presence it made, Kelly felt it. And, like death, he could feel it, too. In this regard, a certain part of him both feared and needed it. Perhaps the music sounding into the air reanimated things within people—deep, dark, buried things once thought lost or gone. He didn't know; he didn't have to know. He had given the score from himself and what the world did with the arrangement was up to it.

He remained satisfied with the result of his work and filled with the lightness of having released something meaningful from his mind and soul. Still, he could not remember the dream from where the notes had come. They had just come in the dark solitude of sleep, finally waking him to their presentation across a wall in his bedroom.

He took a large envelope from the bottom drawer of his desk and slipped the clean pages of the composition into it. Strangely, he felt as if someone else was in the room with him, and when he looked up from the envelope and toward the doorway, he thought he glimpsed a shadow sliding out of the parlor.

Following the illusion, he went into the living room, turned on a lamp near the couch. She was there, with him, somewhere. He could smell her perfume and the hair on his arms tingled.

"Charlotte?" he whispered.

Thunder answered him and he moved through the house to the back door. Every room was empty. He stared out at the deck, watched the rain splash off the treated railings and floor boards.

I can't stop thinking about the music…It's like I can feel things inside of me moving around…

The phone rang and he turned to see her standing in the dining room. He stepped toward her, but she vanished. The phone rang again and he pulled the receiver out of the cradle on the kitchen wall.

"Hello?"

The dial tone didn't register at first and he spoke again into the phone. Realizing that no one was on the other end of the line, he hung up and walked cautiously into the dining room and then into the living room. He was alone, and the weight of that loneliness bore against him. If she had been there, she was gone; he knew it. He lay on the couch and thought about the tree in the dream, about

Charlotte laying on the blanket waiting for him. Closing his eyes, he wished for the vision to come to him, but it, too, was gone. He began to wonder if the music score had been her way of changing him, of pushing him across the chasm that had formed in her absence. Maybe the song bridged his sorrow to his future and in the process he had purged himself of the aching pain. If he could only dream about her again, he could ask her, he could know for sure.

But he was confident that the dream would never come to him again, and as the seconds passed, he could no longer remember the specific images of it. The more time moved forward, the less he could recall. He looked across the room at her picture. The pearls didn't seem so bright anymore, and he wondered what was happening to him. A new feeling fought to reign over him, and he didn't yet understand it, nor could he really identify it. He shuddered to think that his memory of Charlotte got fuzzier every day, no matter how much he didn't want it to. He knew what Kelly meant. Then again, maybe this was all part of the process, part of the journey toward tomorrow.

He took the picture from the table, held it in his hands, and tried to feel her in his arms again. She wasn't there, though, and no matter how hard he imagined her near him, the emptiness of the thought bombarded him. From a shelf in the foyer closet, he pulled down the box containing photographs and fragments of his life with Charlotte. He set the picture and its frame into the box, then returned the box to the shelf. He closed the closet door on the memories, finally.

Don't be the one to bring down my Grace…

Grace. Just when he believed there was nothing left to give, he had created a potential masterpiece, nurtured a little girl to play more sweetly than possibly he ever could, and let a beautiful woman turn his head away from his own wallowing. He had more now than he'd ever had in the past months. It was supposed to be harder than this, he told himself. None of this was supposed to happen. But it did, and he had allowed it. Or maybe the Wheel of Fortune had given him no choice. Caught in the current of life, the only way he could avoid it was not to exist at all, but he did exist in body, heart, and mind. They all did in one way or another. Kelly would play the pretty music and he would try to live again. And he would make Grace believe in him and them. How many hundreds of times had he thought this way?

There was one more piece to be put into place; one more action that he had to take. And he dreaded having to do it.

~

Thursdays in July saw sparse activity within the confines of Lincoln Center. His calendar offered plenty of time for a meeting considering he only taught Kelly on Mondays, Wednesdays, and Fridays. Otherwise, he literally did nothing. With little indication that he had something pressing to do today, however, he stole away from his house, a manila envelope of sheet music stuck under his arm. It had been nine o'clock in the morning and he'd proceeded with all the caution and paranoia of a teenager escaping through a bedroom window after hours to meet his friends at a party down the block. Though he answered to no one presently, the subtle guilt of betraying some other personality weighed on him. Yet the feelings he experienced, he guessed, were more closely tied to the dread of confronting a man he had once despised and considered plotting against; the same man from whom he currently needed a favor.

Then there was the other issue—the one that would bring him so near the scene of Charlotte's attack. He hadn't visited the spot in over nine months, preferring to commune with her at the gravesite instead. Sometimes he wondered if the bloodstains were gone, or if they had simply settled into the cracks of the segmented plaza. He feared hearing the screams he had never heard echoing within the complex, or the rain whisking steam from the concrete into some ghostly recreation of that horrible moment twisted in the powerful notes of a fragile overture.

His sense of predicting morning rush hour traffic had dulled, the precision lapsing with the idle nature of his new life. It had been months since he'd heard the blare of a taxicab horn, or the dissonance of a roaring fleet of emergency vehicles. Children didn't open fire hydrants on the quiet corners of the small town in which he presently lived, and pigeons didn't rule the sidewalks. Nonetheless, he left his car in a parking garage after traveling twice the amount of time he'd anticipated. He had decided not take subway #1 or #9 to the 66th Street station, a stop that would have brought him up just around the corner from Juilliard. Nor did he park his car in the concourse level below Lincoln Center's Damrosch Park on the corner of 10th Avenue and 62nd Street, or in a space anywhere underneath the plaza.

Instead he walked a handful of blocks under the morning sun to Lincoln Center, his senses stinging with the perpetual mayhem of Manhattan's overbearing presence. His spine tightened with the disgust he still harbored for the place. If he hadn't returned, he would never have realized how much he truly hated it here.

Some distance from Josie Robertson Plaza, on the other side of West 65th Street, he arrived at Juilliard. He glanced across the pavement at the rear of Avery Fisher Hall and fought to keep the memories at bay. On the corner, a dozen suited pedestrians waited at the bus stop, and here and there a transient member of the city's workforce brushed by him. Broadway lingered to the east, in the gap that the edges of West 65th made, and he caught glimpses of traffic and bodies moving mindlessly back and forth. The scene reminded him of the lifestyle he had once loved, once breathed as if it had been the very essence of his soul.

Once inside the school, he made his way instinctively to the Music Division. He had taken this journey many times, knew the hallways and offices better than he had his own apartment. He checked in with Kay, the pleasant middle-aged secretary who treated Alex as if she'd said goodnight to him just yesterday, calling him, erroneously, Dr. Brogan, but daring not to ask him how he was or what he had been doing with himself. She handled him delicately, he thought, and when she picked up the phone to let the concertmaster know that his eleven o'clock appointment had shown, she paused before saying his name, as if a curse prohibited her from speaking it out loud.

Alex soon found himself waiting on a padded bench outside Stephen Winslow's office. He could hear the muffled playing of a violin and understood that he was probably being slipped in between private student lessons, the best his esteemed colleague could manage during such a busy time on campus.

A few minutes later the door opened and a young girl emerged with her violin case and music folder. Stephen Winslow appeared in her wake, reminding her of some technique she must practice closely as many times as would cure the "problem" she had. Even tempered, Winslow was a perfectionist, and perhaps one of the most respected violin teachers in the country. His tenure at Juilliard had garnered him recognition worldwide as an authority in technique and a progressive academic in the field of music. His curriculum vitae boasted solo performances from Carnegie Hall to the Paris Conservatoire, with more than two thousand public appearances. He had recorded almost one hundred quartet albums, three of which had received Grammy Awards. The only perceived threat the man had ever known while at Juilliard and as concertmaster of the Philharmonic was Alex, the young, talented, energetic rising star and "Principal Associate Concertmaster," or, as Alex had liked to think of it, "second fiddle." And though no ill words had passed between them, or any discussion other than the purely academic, Alex was certain that Winslow had always known his true intents and desires. Rather than maneuver himself to pull the man's job out from under him, however, Alex had ultimately decided to wait out the months until Winslow retired. In the end, it had been a good decision to avoid hard feelings and professional suicide.

In the soft lighting of the hallway, Winslow looked much older than when Alex had last seen him at Charlotte's funeral in St. Patrick's Cathedral. Tiny shadows collected in the wrinkles under his eyes and drew out his face into the image of an ancient sage. The wisps of what hair remained on his head lay in white streaks just above his ears.

Alex sat patiently, hands folded over the manila envelope on his lap, while Winslow addressed his student as if his former colleague was invisible. Then the young woman flashed her crystal-blue eyes at him and smiled.

"Aren't you Alexander Brogan?" she asked.

"Mr. Brogan," Winslow bellowed, apparently just noticing him. "I'd almost forgotten that you were waiting to speak with me."

Alex stood and shook the concertmaster's strong, steady hand. "Mr. Winslow," he said, "I haven't been waiting long." He returned the student's smile. "I guess I am Alex Brogan," he answered.

"It's such a pleasure to actually meet you," she bubbled. "I was scheduled to have you as my private instructor last semester, but—you know—things didn't work out. I was so excited that I finally got you, I called my parents in Tennessee to tell them. Of course, I had to explain the whole thing to them."

He glanced at Winslow, slightly embarrassed. "Mr. Winslow is a much better choice," he replied. "You should call your parents back and tell them how fortunate you are. Things worked out in your favor, I think."

"Thanks for your faith in me," Winslow laughed, placing an open hand on Alex's back. "Jessica, mind your studies and I'll see you at the end of the week."

The girl departed as Stephen Winslow saw Alex into the office. The concertmaster sat behind his desk and rubbed his chin as he pretended to examine his calendar.

"So," he spoke at last, "I didn't think we'd ever see you again, Alex." He offered a slight grin and sat back in the cushioned chair.

"I didn't think you'd see me again, either." Across the desktop, Alex felt like he sat a mile away from Winslow. He had begun to sweat, and tried to relax in the wooden chair that had been placed out for him.

Stephen Winslow leaned forward and rested his elbows on the desktop. "Alex," he said carefully, "after the funeral—"

"I didn't come here to talk about that," Alex retorted. He steadied his pulse with a deep breath as the admission came: "You must have always known that I wanted your job, Stephen. Being the next in line was never enough." He looked away, at the bookshelves near the window, ashamed.

Winslow sat back again and patiently listened.

"In this careless business, I never stopped to consider the person that you are. But every time the lights came up and my hands touched those strings...I only wanted it more. Charlotte wanted it, too, though she barely understood what it all meant. Let me say that when God yanks the world out from under you, suddenly nothing matters but the will to exist one day at a time. I owe you an apology—"

"Alex—"

He held up his hand. "No, let me do this. I owe you an apology for any negative thought I've ever had, for any desire I may have harbored to be the man that you are. I'm so glad that I've broken free of the life that still surrounds you, and is probably just right for you. I couldn't do it any longer after Charlotte died. It took that event to shake me out of my ego. The more time I had to think about it over the past few months, the more I hated myself for it. I wanted you to know that."

"You came here to apologize?"

"No," he answered. "I came here to admit all of this to you, finally." He clutched the manila envelope. "That's all I wanted. Thanks for your time." He stood and turned toward the door, his conscience lighter by degrees. He was willing to leave the rest unfulfilled, suddenly, for the sake of some fragment of peace.

"What's in your hands?" Winslow asked.

"Nothing," Alex said. "I wanted to…but it wouldn't seem right now."

"You wanted to what?"

Alex faced him. "I discovered this girl," he began. "She may be the finest student I've ever had."

"You're still seeing students?"

He nodded. "Her name is Kelly, and when I heard her play this…" He handed Stephen Winslow the envelope. "When I heard her play that music, suddenly my life made some sort of strange sense."

The concertmaster opened the envelope and pulled out the sheets of handwritten music. He read the notes as Alex went on.

"It came to me in a dream, and I feel compelled to have it performed."

Winslow flipped over each page slowly. "This is brilliant," he muttered. He looked up at him. "You wrote this?"

"For solo violin," Alex said. "It needs work, and accompaniment. I thought that you could help me with all that." He reached for the music. "But like I said, it doesn't seem right now. I came here to ask you to help me round this out, but as soon as I sat down across from you, I realized that I had no right to ask anything from you."

Stephen Winslow put his hands over the music sprawled across the desktop. "Let me study it," he said. "Let me see what I can do. In the meantime, what do you have in mind?" The telephone on the corner of the desk beeped and Winslow pressed the intercom button. "What is it?"

"Your eleven-thirty lesson has arrived," Kay's voice explained through the speaker.

"Tell her the lesson is cancelled and that you'll call later to reschedule."

A long pause filled the quiet office space as Winslow ran his fingers over the staffs of music, then: "Okay…I'll tell her."

"Every year during the Festival of the Arts," Alex reminded him, "the Philharmonic does something special, something different. I was thinking that maybe this work would be something that you and the conductor might consider for your program."

"And the girl?" Winslow asked. "I assume there's something in it for her?"

"She would play the solo."

The concertmaster considered him for a minute, and Alex tried to guess what he was thinking, how tactfully the gentleman would reject the idea.

"She would play the solo," Winslow repeated. He glanced down at the music. "And what would be the role of the Philharmonic?"

"The rest would have to be written," Alex answered. "I could help with that."

"You could be concertmaster for the performance."

Alex shook his head. "No, I want no part in that. I'm her teacher, only. I'll follow her to the wings, then she'll be on her own."

"But it's the job you've always wanted."

In any other time, he might have taken Stephen Winslow's words as arrogant sarcasm. But there was sincerity in the way that the man delivered the syllables, a tone that welcomed the idea of Alex taking the reigns of the orchestra, at least for this performance.

"Maybe I wanted it a year ago, but not now. I only feel comfortable laying this into your hands, Stephen. I've always respected you, regardless of my motives. I believe that whatever muse inspired this movement intended it to work out this way. I can't explain it to you. I don't think it's gelled for me, yet."

"You have to remember, Alex, that there are standards to be upheld," Winslow insisted. "I'd be placing the responsibility of this girl's ability on you. How do I know that she's as good as you say she is?"

"I think I've generated a certain level of respect and competence from my colleagues over the years. You can still trust my opinion. I haven't lost that keen eye for talent, or that sense for true ability. She's the best I've ever instructed, bar none."

Winslow smiled. "Always the prodigy, if I remember correctly. Is there anything else I should expect?"

"There is one other thing that I'd like you to consider."

"What would that be?"

"If Kelly is as good as I say she is, and if you're actually impressed with her performance, then I'd like to secure an invitation for her to audition for entrance into Juilliard's Pre-College Division. She would certainly deserve it, after all."

"You'd stake your reputation on it?"

"I'd stake my life on it," Alex said. "She's the only one who can translate that music into how I need it to sound."

"What happens to you after all of this?"

"I finally find peace of mind. Everything that's ever haunted me goes away."

"Maybe," Winslow commented with a raised eyebrow. "I hope it works that way. There's a meeting next week; I'll bring up the subject then. Of course, the Philharmonic will want to have its say, as well as the board."

"I understand."

"And the music will have to be generated, but we can get graduate students on that. You'd be willing to oversee its production?"

"You can have me twice a week, and on weekends."

Winslow studied his calendar, this time more closely, a bit more genuinely. "We may be able to accomplish this,

Alex." He looked up at him. "What would you consider a feasible rehearsal schedule?"

"For whom?"

"Certainly the orchestra's going to want to play with the girl a few times if this flies."

"Absolutely not," Alex replied.

Stephen Winslow's mouth opened and he uttered a sound, the fragment of a word he decided at the last second not to say.

"You can't be serious," he argued instead.

"If I go home and tell this girl that I've managed to get her a gig with the New York Philharmonic, and that she's scheduled to perform in three months—"

Which would bring him full circle to the moment of Charlotte's death when he marched through the fervent notes of an overture while his fiancée lay dying in Josie Robertson Plaza—

"Alex?"

He blinked. "If I..." He struggled to order his thoughts again. "Kelly would never be able to perform this music if she were aware of the plan ahead of time."

Winslow's eyes grew large. "Are you proposing that the girl just show up on the night of the performance and play with an orchestra she's never even heard?"

"Yes," he answered frankly. "I've designed the work around a follow-the-leader concept. The orchestra rests for the first eight full measures. She'll open, set the pace, and a group as talented as the Philharmonic can adjust to her. It's no different than accommodating the whims of a conductor."

"I understand," Winslow conceded, "but the conductor has authority."

"She won't even realize that the Philharmonic's behind her," Alex added. "You play with your students all the time with little to no preparation, don't you? We can do it; I know we can."

Winslow stared at him blankly.

"I'll make a recording," Alex said. "She's under the impression that she'll have to submit one to the admissions board anyway. I think you can work from a recording. If I remember correctly, we've done it before."

"Yes, once I think," Winslow agreed contemplatively. His eyes had fallen to the music again. "Foreign man, ran into a passport issue in Bosnia. It's a hell of a proposal, Alex. No guarantees. I'll get back to you with the board's decision. This may be somewhat unprecedented."

"Certainly," he replied. "I understand."

Alex thanked the concertmaster, shook his hand again, and left his new telephone number.

"And Alex," Winslow said in parting, "I've always respected you and even admired you. You're an exceptionally gifted violinist, and a talented composer. I never knew you felt the way you did about me before, regardless of your suspicions. Chances are I would have passed the remainder of my life remembering only the tragedy that broke you down. I'm sorry this crazy world took Charlotte from you." He paused as if expecting a response. When none came: "Thanks for coming in; it took a lot of heart. I'll be in touch."

Maybe the plan would come together and he would accomplish the apparent objective of this chapter in his life.

He felt good about the idea, perhaps even a little excited, as he stepped out of Juilliard and into the early afternoon sun warm on his forehead and cheeks. For a short time he stood on the curb with his hands in his pockets, staring toward the plaza. He couldn't quite see the fountain from this angle, could only imagine the front columns of Avery Fisher Hall a stiff, mindless audience to the display of arching and tumbling water. He ground his teeth in the dilemma, but turned away and meandered toward 10th Avenue, passing Walter Reade Theater, the bus stop, and beyond, until any evidence of the morning's affairs had disappeared into ripples behind him.

~

A week later, Stephen Winslow called to inform Alex that the board had approved of his proposal "with reservations," and that he had been able to secure a few graduate students to help him with the venture. Tremendous responsibility, the concertmaster warned, had been placed on Alex's shoulders, and he was advised to be sure that he did not disappoint the board.

Newly focused, summer afternoons slipped by, fading from one lesson to the next as he prodded Kelly ever closer to achieving prodigal perfection. Each meeting he reserved the last hour to work on the technique and intonation of the composition, programming into her pregnant memory every nuance, bowing, and grace note. Eventually, she came to know passages by heart, to love and hate the piece. Still she struggled to remember her mother, whose image, she claimed, grew more pronounced with every new fragment she committed to memory.

He demanded that she isolate difficult measures and play them over and over again. And if ever her rhythm went astray, he would start the metronome, make her listen to the beats, and then play with them sounding in the background. Never, though, did Kelly falter, and the progress she made over the course of July and the better part of August astounded him. He had played the violin for at least ten years before his ability resembled anything like Kelly's did after only two years of Mr. Grady's drills and a month and a half of carefully planned, meaningful lessons.

Miss Luella showed up at his doorstep every Monday, just like clockwork, to pay him cash sorted neatly in an envelope. Each time she told him that she would wait until he counted the money, and each time he assured her that it wasn't necessary. Financially, his resources were gradually dwindling, between mortgage payments and general living expenses. But the money he received from teaching Kelly kept him a step ahead from week to week. Starting his new occupation as a music teacher at the local high school would no doubt offer a steady income, and though he didn't consider the opportunity a dream job, he looked forward to the change of pace. He hadn't even been to the school since his interview, and he knew he would have to make some time to go there, check out his classroom, inventory his materials, speak with other members of the department, and come up with some kind of curriculum in keeping with the district's expectations.

On Tuesday and Thursday evenings he slipped away and drove into the city, to Juilliard, without anyone on the block knowing. There, he met with graduate students and a few eager and curious Philharmonic members as they used the original composition for his solo violin to build parts for the string, woodwind, brass, percussion, and keyboard sections of the orchestra. The conductor appeared on a few occasions after hearing the rumors across campus that Alexander Brogan had returned and was up to something. And Stephen Winslow, the concertmaster, worked with the group, carefully studying each part and piece, watching as the notes played across computer screens, and entire pages of music magically churned out of laser printers. Beethoven might have cringed at the automated production of his beloved medium, but the days of handwritten scores had passed. Nevertheless, the genius remained in form and function, and the human mind alone could realize such melodies. In this regard their spirits lingered—Beethoven, Bach, Mozart, Handel, Schoenburg, and the others now in the deep, dark, whole rest of their lives.

On these two fronts, Alex made great strides throughout the summer. His relationship with Grace, however, moved much more slowly. He saw her from time to time, mostly when she met him on the deck and they talked for an hour or so. They went to *The Oak Leaf* again and spent the evening laughing and avoiding the desire to touch and be touched. They didn't visit the park or sit on the wooden bench together. Grace had said what she'd wanted to say about Alex and his complicated life that first night at dinner. She didn't mention it again, and he remained afraid to relive a conversation about it. Daily he sorted the memories, tried to balance then with now. Each day he felt more alive and inspired, stronger, happier. A certain sadness still floated over him as he approached Lincoln Center, but instead of fighting it, he accepted the feeling as an everlasting connection to the past, to Charlotte. He let it be, and it was. Minutes, hours spent with Grace became episodes in which he discovered who she was, who he was, and what they might be together—without commitment or promises. They talked about Clarice and Kelly, Luella and Charlotte, all the pieces that made them who they were. He explained his misconceptions of Stephen Winslow; she laughed through stories of her father, her sister with tears in her eyes. She told him what scared her; he admitted what did not. And the words passed effortlessly between them, beneath the sun and stars, each the other's book to read and remember.

Mid-August found them laying beside one another on a patchwork quilt his grandmother had made a half century ago. The grassy top of Pilgrim Hill offered the best seat in town for viewing the stars, and they had come to relax, to learn more about each other, far from streetlights, houses, fast food, and strip malls. She met him there because he had called the hospital and asked if she would, just to talk. Some days before he had decided that maybe he should take more control of the situation between them; maybe that was what Grace waited for. She hadn't denied any advances because he had made none since the park. But if he tried again, from this new spot in their friendship…

On his back with his arms behind his head, he tried to count the shimmering lights directly above. He could hear her breathing beside him, wondered if she, too, counted the stars.

"You're right, you know," he said at last.

"About what?" Her voice was soft as if in absolute comfort, her mind was falling to sleep.

"It's pretty everywhere if you look hard enough." He turned his head toward her, saw the smile on her lips.

"Did I say that?" she asked lightly.

"Yes, you did."

"This is one of the most beautiful places in the area," she said. "When Clarice got sick, she asked me to take her and Kelly to Pilgrim Hill to look at the stars. I feel at peace here, humble. And I suddenly understand that I'm just a tiny, tiny part of something infinitely wonderful."

"Something infinitely wonderful," he repeated. He stared up at the stars, breathed in the night, and held it until he was sure his lungs had absorbed at least a fraction of the wonder.

"Just like you," she said.

He turned his head again, into her gaze.

"Just like me?"

"We're both specks in a vast and wonderful universe," she answered. "It's funny how sometimes we mistakenly think that our problems are so important. In the grand scheme of things, we're almost nothing. Our problems don't really matter. I remember reading this poem shortly after Clarice died. It was written by Stephen Crane, you know, the one who wrote—"

"*The Red Badge of Courage,*" he interrupted. "I read it in middle school."

She smiled at him. "Yeah, that guy. Anyway, it's called 'A Man Said to the Universe.' Have you ever heard it?"

"Do you know it?"

She looked away from him and thought a moment. "'A man said to the universe:/"Sir, I exist!"/"However," replied the universe—'"

"'The fact has not created in me…'"

"'A sense of obligation.'" Their eyes met once more. "You do know it," she said.

"I didn't until you reminded me," he replied. "I never paid any attention to the message until now. How many different ways can you continue to amaze me?"

She laughed. "One of my talents, I guess. Besides, anyone who wants to spend time with me at midnight, when I'm still wearing my hospital scrubs, must really enjoy my company. I mean, look at me. I'm a mess."

"I do," he said. "I like being with you. And you're not a mess, you're beautiful. You're always beautiful."

She moved her head closer to his. He shivered with anticipation, rolled slowly onto his side and kissed her gently. He touched her warm cheek, felt her trembling. An electricity streamed down his spine and the passion increased as they kissed more deeply, more intensely. He pulled her body to his and she followed the motion fluidly, letting herself be taken into his arms, into the rhythm of his pounding heart. Her head fell away from him and he felt her lips on his neck. He lifted her face to his and looked into her glassy eyes.

"Charlotte…," he whispered.

Grace closed her eyes, turned away from him. His hands, once gingerly holding her head were now raised to grasp at the night air, empty. She stood, walked slowly off the patchwork quilt. She wouldn't look at him, and he couldn't bring himself to make eye contact with her.

"Someday, Alex," she uttered, and then she was gone, absorbed into the black background of early morning.

He heard her car, parked next to his at the bottom of the hill, start, and the crunching and popping gravel under her tires as she crept away from him. He sat with his arms around his knees and stared absently in the direction of the noise. Why now? He could not understand why, at that very moment, she would cross his mind. Was it him…or her? Could he not let her go, or would she not release him? Either way, he felt ridiculous, ashamed. Certainly the problem lay with him and his subconscious deadlock on Charlotte's memory. The last few weeks, he had managed to convince himself that he could move on, that his love for Charlotte would forever beat in his heart. Maybe he'd been only lying to himself, telling himself an untruth so long that he actually had begun to believe it. Then again, maybe it was too soon to venture into someone else's heart. He had been so unfair to Grace, so inconsiderate. He led her to the hill with every intention of finally kissing her, and instead he violated her trust in him and his feelings.

He just needed more time. Whether Grace would understand had to be left up to her. And how would he know when enough seconds, minutes, hours, days had passed to constitute more time? He shook his head.

"I have to get a grip on myself," he whispered to the stars. "What do I have to do?"

But the fact created in the wonderfully infinite universe no sense of obligation.

~

When Miss Luella got sick, Grace had no choice but to move into the house to take care of both Kelly and her mother. The old woman suffered from pneumonia and the illness had rendered her bed-ridden. Her weight and poor health hindered the body's ability to combat the bacteria, necessitating intravenous drips and formidable doses of antibiotics. The only good fortune keeping Luella from having to endure an extended hospital stay was Grace's willingness and license to provide care at home as a registered nurse. The matron's physical weakness coupled with the slow development of arthritis in her knuckles stole her knitting away and those closest to her suffered because of it.

Alex stood awkwardly at the foot of the automatically adjustable bed that had been wheeled into the living room for the day. *The Price is Right* blared from the floor model television that he hadn't noticed even being there the last time he had been in the house to apologize to Kelly. Clarice hung in portrait as before, and the old woman's rocker and knitting basket, now abandoned to invalidism, absorbed the shadows of a far corner.

He'd brought her a dish garden as a get well token, and he hadn't failed to remember the handful of times he had wished her the worst. Regardless, the gesture had served more to make him feel better about the situation than it had been meant to lift her spirits. After all, discomfort aside, the one thing he feared more than Luella's rebuke was the good chance of running into Grace in her own house, especially after their less-than-ideal parting last week.

"Most men bring flowers, Mr. Brogan," Luella declared sourly.

Just when he thought nothing could make her more abrasive, the limitations and discomfort of pneumonia proved him wrong.

"Flowers die, ma'am. This way you can grow a little garden that could last a while."

"And how do you expect me to grow it, Mr. Brogan? Maybe if you put it there, on the stool next to the bed, it would be in range for me to spit on from time to time to keep it alive."

"I thought I'd come by for you to browbeat me, Miss Luella," he said flatly as he set the plant on the stool beside the bed. "Is that close enough, ma'am? Why don't you try to spit on it from there to make sure? I'd hate for it to die since I spent so much money on it."

She glared at him, huffed once. "Will you be staying long?"

He cocked his head to one side and smiled at her, assumed that this was how Jem Finch must have felt sitting with Mrs. Dubose every day after school in *To Kill a Mockingbird*. He lowered himself onto the end cushion of the couch, and in silence the two of them watched Winona "come on down!" Shortly after Winona bid the closest to a pair of his and her gold watches and bolted hysterically onto the stage, Luella pressed the mute button on the remote and finally spoke to him.

"You must have better things to do than sit with me," she said. "I find it hard to believe that a young man can be so idle."

"It's not a matter of being idle," he replied as pleasantly as possible. "I came because I wanted to see how you are and to wish you well."

"Hmmm," she breathed. "Ladies Auxiliary already wished me well, Mr. Brogan. That's something strangers do to one another."

He was pleased, oddly. "Well, then, look how far we've come," he commented. "I've gone from stranger to neighbor."

"Yes," she agreed half-heartedly. "Can't pick your neighbors, though. They have that in common with relatives."

He laughed and she tried not to.

"Actually, I'm glad I know you, Mr. Brogan," she admitted, pretending to be interested in the contestants soundlessly spinning the wheel on television.

"Why is it that you call me Mr. Brogan?" he questioned. "I know you know my name."

She glanced at him, attempted to blow off the inquiry with the unsteady wave of a swollen hand.

"Why?" he repeated.

"I'm a Southern lady, Mr. Brogan," she answered at last. "It's not proper for a lady to use a gentleman's first name as a matter of respect."

He smiled; her incapacity emboldened him. "Gentleman and respect in the same sentence referring to me," he remarked. "I don't know how I should feel about that, Miss Luella."

"Is it so hard to believe that I might respect you, Mr. Brogan?" She stared an answer out of him.

"I guess not."

She coughed. "Let me ask you this, then: Why is it that you insist on calling me Miss Luella?"

"Because you told me to."

She paused, searched his face for a moment, and then erupted into a labored chortle. "I suppose I did, Mr. Brogan. I suppose I did."

"Yes, ma'am," he responded, "you certainly did. And quite frankly, I'm scared to death of you."

Her amusement increased and she reached for a tissue to wipe her watering eyes. As she struggled for the box, he went to the bedside and pulled a tissue out for her.

"Thank you, Mr. Brogan," she sniffled as she patted her eyes and mouth with the tissue, her flaccid cheeks pink. "I'm pretty vulnerable now, so if you need to take a whack at me, there's no better time than the present."

"I'm not interested in kicking you while you're down," he responded. "I actually came in good faith to see how you are. I am concerned, you know."

She furrowed her brow as if she really didn't believe him. "I think I'm more of a bother than anything else," she said. "What with Gracie having to look after me and little Kelly taking time away from her violin to check on me or to help me get the soup down, I'm sure I'm more unbearable than usual."

He returned to the couch. "Where are the girls?" he asked, though subconsciously his mind had registered their absence half an hour ago.

Her eyes were on the television again as a car commercial flickered across the screen. "Gracie took the little one to the mall for some new clothes and things. I'm sending Miss Kelly to school this year. I suppose I haven't got a choice. I don't think the home schooling is a good idea until I'm well again, and the doctor frankly informed me that at my age—which truly, Mr. Brogan is none of your business—getting the hump on pneumonia could take a while."

He had almost forgotten that the start of the school year was fast approaching.

"Maybe I'll see her in school, then, and be able to help her out if she needs anything," he said.

"That would be a fine idea, and much appreciated," Luella answered. "It'll be quite a change for her. Gracie seems to believe that the socialization would do wonders for her. The last thing I need is sleepovers and school dances. Oh, but I guess in the end it's not about me, is it?"

It's not about me…

"I suppose not," he absently conceded. He gazed at the picture of Clarice, his eyes taking in the smooth features of her face and neck, then settling on the straight lines of her violin's strings and fingerboard. He could see the resemblance to Grace in her cheeks and nose, in the color of her hair. She, like her sister, must have been beautiful in life. And somewhere around the ears and across the forehead, through the chin and into the jaw line, he could see her little girl staring back at him.

"Clarice had a knack for the instrument," Luella cracked through his thoughts. "She picked it up when she was only three, and from the first moment it was like that violin was a part of her in some magical way. She would practice all the time, even though she didn't have a formal teacher. My, what that girl taught herself. So you see, Mr. Brogan, you could say that a great part of our family, hell, maybe even our bloodline, has always revolved around that pretty wooden stringed box. When Clarice first put Kelly's tiny fingers on the violin, I knew that I needed to nurture the talent much more than I did with her mother. We simply didn't have the means to support Clarice the way we should have. But things were different when Kelly started; Papa was dead and I had some money coming in on a regular basis. I found Mr. Grady in the classifieds and he worked with Kelly for a couple of years. I always knew God had a plan for that little girl, and when He brought me you, Mr. Brogan, I felt like some prophecy had been fulfilled. Now you can take it from here and give my little granddaughter the opportunities her mama never had. You're everything she's ever wished for, and I wouldn't be so sure that some of the things you've seen and heard weren't coming from some part of her mother that still lingers here."

He met her eyes.

"Yes," she continued, "I can feel my Clarice here. It's almost as if the sound of the violin gives her life again, and she's able to take a more physical form. I've spent many nights sitting in this living room, in my rocking chair, and talking with my daughter. She sits right there, where you are now, and we chat about the most wonderful things, Mr. Brogan. She knows all about you. I believe that sometimes the hand that has corrected Miss Kelly in your parlor wasn't yours at all, but hers as she comes back to all of us, just to make the dream real."

"You may be right." The photograph had his attention again. "Of course she's with Charlotte," he said slowly, not intending to say the words out loud.

Luella coughed again and took a deep breath. "Charlotte, your lady," she assumed. "Clarice, Charlotte, does it matter? Souls are souls, Mr. Brogan; they all touch us in some way. What difference does it make whose fingers touch your face while you're sleeping, or whose memories weasel their way into your dreams? I think your bitterness has narrowed your focus on life, and you tend to see things only through your own life. We all hurt, Mr. Brogan. We're all weak in one way or another." She shook her head, eyes closed. "Oh, Alex, you've got so much to learn."

He turned toward her, eased his body to the edge of the cushion.

"Ma'am?"

She opened her eyes on him and smiled soberly. "You don't need to think so much about everything," she said. "Why can't you just let it all be? The Lord doesn't give a shit if you understand, nor does He give a rat's ass how you want it all to turn out. He's coming for me, Mr. Brogan. I'll be ready when He shows up, and if He's paid any attention to my prayers, He'll have Elvis with him."

He hadn't expected to, but he laughed, and she chuckled through the distress of a coughing fit.

"You're done dancing with the Devil, then?" he asked carefully.

"I'll leave that to Charlie Daniels," she answered cleverly. "As for me, whatever happens, happens. I don't expect to waste so much time worrying about it or trying to make it make sense. When you're dying, keeping track of the moments you're living becomes the most important thing to you. You might take a lesson from that. For being such a talented and well-minded teacher, you seem to have an awful time learning anything. Make me a promise, Mr. Brogan."

He studied her pale face. "What's that, Miss Luella?"

"Promise me that you'll try to learn something every day, no matter what. Can you do that?"

"I'll try."

She pursed her rough, colorless lips. "You try to make a ringer in horseshoes, sir. Trying isn't something that you take seriously when your life depends on it. You will or you won't, Mr. Brogan. Which will it be?"

He thought for a second as her stony eyes bored into him. What she said made sense, and he knew it.

"I will," he answered. "Every day I'll make it a point to learn something."

She exposed teeth too perfect to be real as she grinned at him in satisfaction. "That makes me glad, Mr. Brogan. And I know you'll keep your word."

"I'll keep my word," he assured her.

He heard the back door open, followed by the sound of footsteps on the kitchen's linoleum floor.

"My girls have returned," Luella muttered. She laid her head back and closed her eyes again.

A heartbeat later, Grace and Kelly appeared in the dining room, bags in their hands. They wore the smiles and warm faces of having had fun on their excursion to the mall.

"Alex!" Kelly exclaimed.

He stood as she dropped her bags and ran to him and wrapped her arms around his waist. Somewhat surprised, he patted her back until she let go.

"I didn't know you were here," she chirped.

"I came to see your grandmother," he said.

"He brought me that dish-whatever," she mumbled. "Something else I'll have to take care of."

Grace had made her way to Luella's bedside and was checking the IV bag. She lifted the dish garden from the stool and placed it on the end table by the couch.

"That was nice of you, Alex," she said.

She didn't look at him, and he wondered if his being there made her uncomfortable, like he had somehow invaded her personal space. Aloof and distracted, she acted as he imagined she behaved at the hospital in a focused and professional manner. Regardless, her inherent beauty didn't go unnoticed and the sight of her, as always, captivated him. But the tension between them dulled his senses, and he found himself suddenly nervous.

"I think I'll be leaving," he announced much to Kelly's distress.

"You don't have to leave," the little girl insisted.

"I'm sure your grandmother would like to rest," he told her. "Besides, I've outstayed my welcome."

Luella set her eyes on him. "The least you could do is wait until I tell you to get lost," she quipped tiredly. "You'd expect that much from me, I hope." She raised an arm and touched Grace's shoulder. "Besides, I'm certain Gracie would like to visit with you for a while."

Grace looked at him, smiled slightly and turned away to change the drip.

"I *am* planning to whip up some chicken and biscuits, maybe some fried green tomatoes," she said, continuing her medical duties with standard efficiency.

Kelly's eyes sparkled in the thought and she beamed up at him. "You could eat over," she declared.

The old woman grunted. "Sure, eat over," she grumbled. "None for me, thanks. I have a hankering for saline and penicillin. Fills me right up."

"It's azithromycin, mother," Grace corrected her.

"Whatever," Luella retorted. "I'll be asleep soon, anyway. It's amazing how hard you work to keep me alive."

"Only because the trade-off is you haunting me," Grace replied. "At least this way I'll know where you are from one minute to the next." The nurse glanced at her watch, and Alex. "You'll stay, won't you?" she asked.

He searched her delicate face, analyzed her expression for traces of sincerity. "If you'd like me to," he responded, content that she might really want him to stay.

"I'd like you to," she said. She passed by him, smiling. "Kelly can get these bags up to her bedroom and you can help me in the kitchen."

The little girl collected as many bags as she could and dragged them through the living room as he followed Grace into the kitchen.

"Chicken's in the bag there on the table."

She stretched her arms up to grab the flour jar from the top of a shelf in the pantry. Through the doorway, he watched her body move, felt his own getting warm, not realizing that she was watching him, too.

"Are you going to clean that chicken?" she inquired coyly.

"That chicken," he mumbled. "Yes, I am going to clean that chicken." He peeled his shoes off the linoleum and took the chicken out of the grocery bag as she milled around behind him, preparing the stove for cooking.

They worked well together, though he didn't have a clue as to how to make chicken and biscuits or any other dish he could just as easily sit down to at a restaurant. He spent most of his time observing, handing her things she asked for. He could measure butter or milk or water in a measuring cup, pinch salt and pepper and spices over the chicken, preheat the oven to 350 degrees, as long as he was told to do it. Beyond these mundane tasks, however, he stood outperformed by the pretty young nurse and her aptitude for fine cuisine prepared with a Southern touch.

They exchanged conversation, mostly concerning Luella's pneumonia or Grace's trip to the mall with Kelly. Alex got the rundown of all the clothes she'd bought her niece, complete with the incredible deals at the different stores. She told him how difficult it was for her to get used to the new styles and fads, though she admitted that some of it reminded her of the eighties and her own high school days. Living alone, Grace rarely spent her money on anything but groceries and utility bills. Having had the opportunity to stash much of her income away into a savings account partly reserved for Kelly's college education, she didn't feel guilty dropping a few hundred dollars on an MP3 player for the little girl, despite the woman's vague understanding of such a device. Kelly, though seemingly sheltered and somewhat unaware of the world of her peers, was all too versed in the latest technology. She did, after all, have a computer in her bedroom and had managed some time ago to convince her grandmother that she needed Internet access. Grace apparently didn't begrudge Kelly a single thing on their shopping trip or on any other occasion. The little girl, prior this afternoon's foray through the material jungle, as a rule, rarely asked for anything, so Grace's benevolence came freely. He couldn't imagine how much money the woman had spent in a single day, and he wasn't about to inquire as to the exact figure. He recalled a time when he, too, willingly gave up countless amounts of money only to see someone whom he loved very much, smile. Ultimately, Charlotte's happiness had been priceless, and he guessed that, in many of the same ways, Kelly's was also.

By the time Grace pulled the chicken out of the oven, the two of them had been able to spend over an hour talking about anything but their feelings and intimate notions. After all, they had both silently agreed that some subjects would only be broached under certain circumstances, and standing in her mother's kitchen baking chicken and biscuits, frying green tomatoes and setting the table, was not one of them. Yet, the urge to say something that had been conceived in his heart was always on the tip of his tongue, and more than once, after an inadvertent touch or an accidental meeting face to face over the placement of silverware or movement around the table, she would open her mouth as if to say something. But she never did. Instead, a new subject would arise or she'd simply continue with what they had been talking about in the seconds before.

Chicken baked and cooling on the stovetop, biscuits browned, and tomatoes steaming in a large bowl, he heeded Grace's request and journeyed upstairs to get Kelly for dinner. He knocked lightly on the door at the end of the long, dark hallway. Lamplight glowing in the fibers of a red shade streamed through the partially opened door and fell softly on the hallway carpet. He felt awkward being on the cusp of the little girl's private world. He hadn't been invited here, though he suspected he would be all too welcome to enter. As he'd thought, she freely allowed him to come in, and he stood with his hands in his pockets, leaning against the door casing.

"It's time to eat," he said, his voice sounding flatly into the cluttered room.

Kelly sat behind her computer, face accented in the blue wash of the monitor and fingers poised over the keyboard. On the bed pushed lengthwise against the side wall, a half dozen shopping bags lay strewn over a ruffled, pink comforter. She hadn't emptied the bags, nor were there signs of her having rustled through them to try something on or to put anything away. The headboard was crowded with thick pillows in fleece pastel covers.

"Okay," she said indifferently.

"What are you doing?" he asked, stepping into the bedroom.

"Chatting," she answered.

The walls were covered with posters of people and bands he didn't recognize. A teddy bear calendar hung over the computer, beside a poster of the New York Philharmonic Orchestra. He could see the red circle drawn on the picture, and remembered what Grace had told him about the poster and Kelly's crush on him that night in the grocery store.

Mounted beside the orchestra spread, a corkboard-turned-collage of glossy photographs displayed still images of the past arranged in scrapbook fashion on paisley and polka-dotted paper, under sticker frames, with decoratively trimmed edges. There were pictures of her mother swimming, laughing, holding a baby, and tickling a little girl; Luella decades younger in a sundress; Grace with a ponytail, shaking pom-poms. Each snapshot captured a moment integral to the backbone of her life, the foundation of her being.

A music stand was to his right, in front of the closet door, and held the open booklet of études she often practiced at her lessons with him. Her violin rested in a small stand beside it and her bow hung from a hook on the wall.

"Chatting?" he repeated.

She looked over her shoulder at him and smirked. "Online," she said. "It's a chat group of kids like me who play the violin."

"How do you know there aren't weirdoes lurking in that chat room?"

She giggled. "I think weirdoes probably hang out in other chat rooms." She bounced out of her chair. "No one's trying to pick up dorks in a young violin players' chat room," she said.

"You never know," he persisted.

In the brief time he'd spent in her room, he already sensed that he had punctured that private space in which the little girl spent so much of her time. He knew as well as anyone that an individual's most personal realm was in his or her own room, and that fact remained true here, within the four walls that framed Kelly's identity. From the stereo in the corner whispering Bach's first movement of *Symphony No. 5* to the pair of porcelain dolls embracing each other on the dresser behind the door, Kelly's entire existence was defined in soft colors, classical music, and girlie stuff. Though the cultured emblems of a string player existed—rosin cakes, peg oil, tack cloth, metronome, music scores, shoulder rest—the elements of a young, naïve, innocent girl reigned obviously throughout the room. It had been so easy for him to forget, many times and in many ways, that Kelly was first and foremost a child viewing the world through a kid's eyes and interpreting its relative dysfunction in terms of misconceptions, ignorance, and innocuous fallacies. Here she was real and unmasked, though she had never hidden her motives or disguised her youth. Had he ever been blessed with such a child, he would have ultimately discovered the same things in his own daughter's bedroom. Sonatas, partitas, canons aside, Kelly was made of finer, more fragile matter bound together by a music box and its twirling ballerina, cotton candy lip balm, shelves of puzzles, board games, and *Goosebumps* books, plastic bead jewelry, colored pencils, diaries, and the friendship of faded, tattered stuffed monkeys named Curious George. So foreign, yet so tangible to him, Alex circled the fringes of a Shirley Temple world whose secrets he could never truly appreciate.

"Your aunt's waiting," he gently urged her. His eyes wandered once more around the room while his senses continued to assimilate the childish atmosphere. He enjoyed the comfort and security of the room, shuddered with the reminder of his own sterile living conditions just next door. "We better get downstairs."

~

"The whole thing is awesome," Kelly exclaimed with her mouth half-full of biscuit. "There's this one part when I have to trill, and oh, my God, I get so nervous when I know it's coming."

"But you're getting the hang of it," Alex assured her.

He sat at the head of the oval oak table, opposite Grace at the other end. Kelly sat between them, chattering; she hadn't stopped talking since they sat down. Grace, conversely, hardly said anything, except for the occasional, "Really?" or "Wow."

"I can't even imagine playing in front of a committee, especially at *Juilliard*," the girl added.

"It's not as scary as you think," he said. "You have to train yourself not to worry so much about your audience. That's easier said than done, though. I can remember playing in Avery Fisher Hall in front of two thousand people, but I was lucky. The lights shining onto the stage were so bright that I couldn't see the crowd if I'd wanted to."

"It must be wonderful there," Grace commented softly in her first real sentence since the start of the meal.

"It was once for me," he answered.

She considered him for a moment as if thinking about what she wanted to say next. "What about when Kelly goes to audition? Will you be with her?"

The little girl's eyes were on him now as well.

"Certainly," he said, even as the reluctance tightened the back of his neck.

"I think I'd feel a lot better if I knew you were there," Kelly admitted. "I've never even been to the city, let alone Juilliard."

He smiled. "You'll be there before you know it."

Grace wiped the corners of her mouth with her napkin. "How do you like the tomatoes?"

"Different," he replied. "I can't say that I've ever had fried green tomatoes before."

"You see, new things won't necessarily hurt you."

He met her perfect eyes and tried not to assume that there had been a double meaning in what she had said. But he gathered there had.

"I guess not," he said. "New things are easier for some to try than for others." The subliminal understanding they shared quickened his pulse.

"More times than not, they won't hurt you," she countered.

"I ate an ant once," Kelly interjected.

"An ant?" he questioned.

"A chocolate covered one," she informed him, "at the county fair. It tasted crunchy and chocolaty. It was pretty good, actually."

"Kelly, why do you have to talk about things like that at the dinner table?" Grace insisted. "I think that's gross."

The little girl giggled contagiously, and soon they were all laughing. Grace's indignant reaction to the story had only made the idea funnier.

"C'mon," Grace said at last to her niece, "let's get these plates into the kitchen."

The mid-summer sun rode low on the horizon, and he had hardly noticed the day fading with the pink sky. They collected the plates and dishes and moved them to the sink in the kitchen. He offered to wash them, but Grace wouldn't hear of it. Instead, she suggested that Kelly head upstairs to the bathtub and get ready for bed. With the little girl gone, the nurse checked on her patient who slept soundlessly in the dusky living room. She turned off the television and returned to the kitchen to find that Alex had already filled the sink with soapy water and was washing the dinner plates.

"I told you that you didn't have to do that," she said lightly. She stood beside him and watched the circular motion of his hand in a dishrag as it scoured the inside of a porcelain bowl.

"Yes, you did," he acknowledged, "but why don't you sit down and let me clean up?"

Hands on her hips, she sighed. In the next breath, she was in a chair at the kitchen table.

"I can't tell you how many times I've done this," he commented as he worked. "My sisters and I were on a rotation growing up. I tried my damnedest to get out of it when it was my turn, but it rarely worked."

Chin in her hand, she pretended to be bothered by her apparent uselessness. "How many sisters do you have?"

"Two," he answered, rinsing a plate. "They're older than me. Marcia and Camille; one married a dentist and the other's a lawyer."

"Wow, successful," she remarked. "Camille, I love that name."

He laughed. "She didn't when we were kids. I'm not sure why, either. Anyway, we all look alike, except that they're beautiful, both of them."

"Like their brother, then."

He looked back at her, surprised. "More like you," he said directly as her cheeks flushed red and she dropped her eyes to the tabletop.

"What kind of lawyer is your sister?"

"Corporate," he answered. He worked at the dishes again, though a warmth spread through his back and he felt his body lighten. "She practices at a firm in DC."

"Do you see her often?" She hadn't looked up from the table yet.

"No, I never really did after she started law school," he said. "She lives for her career. Marcia, on the other hand, is your stereotypical dentist's wife. I'm sure that as soon as they finally have children she'll have a minivan and will be doing the soccer mom thing."

"What's wrong with minivans?" she joked, brave enough to be watching him again.

"Nothing," he replied. "I suppose I can't really comment on things I don't know anything about."

"Did you ever think about having children?"

He stopped scrubbing the tines of a fork and stared out the window above the sink. The sky cooled pink around the tree line and he could just barely see the edge of his deck. The yards loomed silently behind the glass, holding shadows and the promise of a quickly approaching night.

"Not me specifically," he said. Her name lingered on his tongue, but somehow he felt self-conscious saying it. "She did…a long time ago."

"You mean, Charlotte?"

"Yes, Charlotte."

"And I'll bet she wanted a girl."

His cheeks slowly numbed. "Yes, she did," he affirmed the notion. "I suppose that's to be expected."

"Probably," she responded, her voice absolute as if she would force him to talk about the subject. "I always told myself that I would want a girl."

He set a dripping plate into the strainer. "Now you have one."

The silence told him that she thought about the comment.

"Kelly is everything to me," she said. "She came at an awful price, though."

Alex took his hands from the soapy water and turned to her. "I'm sorry, I shouldn't have said that."

She waved off the perceived insult. "No, it's true. She's as good as mine, I suppose, especially if anything happens to Mama." Their eyes met, hers glassy. "You know how sometimes you can feel things, bad things, and you're not sure if they're about to happen or if they already have and you haven't realized it yet?"

He nodded, knowing what she was about to say.

"I feel that way when I'm around my mother," she continued. "It's like I can sense that she's not all right. I don't know, maybe it's because I'm around sickness all the time. I've certainly seen my share of patients pass on."

"How do you get used to that?"

She smiled sadly, studied the tabletop. "You don't," she said frankly. "I don't think anyone can ever truly get over death." She looked at him purposely, but he turned toward the sink.

"It's a hard battle to fight," he commented, finishing the last few pieces of silverware. "I didn't have much experience with it when she died. And it's not like she got sick and went that way. I can't even imagine what went through her head while she lay there dying." He dropped the silverware into the water and let his body lean against the edge of the counter as his knees became weak. "I don't like to think about it."

Her hand touched his back and then the pressure of her body against his.

"You," she whispered. "You're probably the last thing she saw."

He moved away from her, went to the other side of the table. "But I wasn't there for her," he said calmly while the blood rushed through his veins. "Can't you see I was too busy playing my violin? Can you understand why it is that I have such contempt for that goddamn thing laying in its case over there in the parlor?" He ran his hands through his hair and breathed deeply. "I'm sorry, Grace…I didn't mean to…That night on Pilgrim Hill…"

She approached him, her face wearing some reflection of his distress.

"I'm sorry, Grace," he repeated, stepping away. "I should go." And he slipped out the back door, leaving her standing by herself in the kitchen with a mouthful of regret.

He made it as far as his deck before he dropped into a lawn chair and fought to keep the emotion from leaking out of the corners of his eyes. Dark purple had squandered the evening and the dome overhead had begun to twinkle. He held his breath, gazed into the night sky, and cursed the conscience that wouldn't let her go. Though the quest became easier every day, the setbacks hurt as much now as they always had, and his response to her memory continued to twist him into something that he no longer wanted to be. He questioned the price he had set on holding onto someone who was never coming back. What was he willing to sacrifice? And what if in the end there was nothing left for him to live for because he could not bear to let himself live? All the signs had been given, all the words had been spoken. The advice, the admonishment, the support and hope had all passed through him and into oblivion. He had become his worst enemy, he thought. He had become his own demon.

FOURTH MOVEMENT

The late morning sun burned white in a flawless sky as he walked determinedly up Sleepy Hollow Avenue, crossed the bridge, and entered Hillside. He carried his violin case, the Strad covered carefully inside, and he carried the music, too, ordered and neatly arranged in his head.

"Good morning, Charlotte," he said quietly. "I've come to tell you that I'll be coming around a little less, but I suppose you already expected it. I'm not saying good-bye, but that I'll see you later, when the time's right. I really need to move on."

He lowered himself to one knee and touched the flowing script on the headstone.

"You're not really here," he whispered. "You're in my heart where you've always been."

He set the case flatly on the new grass and unzipped it.

"I brought something that you'd recognize."

He flipped open the cover, freed the Strad from its straps and raised it from the coffin.

"I know you never really understood all this, but you pretended to because it was important to me. I guess I'm saying that I could always feel how much you loved me, but there was some bigger plan for me. We were all a part of it in some way or another."

He stood, Strad under his arm as he tightened the hair of the bow.

"I want you to hear the pretty music. It finally came to me; I finally realized it. I'm not exactly sure how it all happened, but I know you had everything to do with it. So I thought you should hear it, that I should play for you like I used to, one last time."

He bowed the open A string and then nimbly tuned the instrument.

"It's called *The Butterfly's Heart.*"

Alex released the notes into the light air in a time and rhythm that seemed to silence the world, hush the rustling leaves, and calm the fleeting river. Whether it was too soon to let go of her was beyond him now; he could no longer consider such setbacks. Instead, the vibrations of a musical universe spread through him and he expressed what he had been, what he was, what he would become, all in the rising melody of a permutating dream-song.

As he coaxed out the final whole note, left hand easing it from the womb in clean vibrato only to lift it from the string and send it fluttering over the gravestones, he drew in his breath and waited. He waited as if expecting the entire piece to echo back to him, but only heard the silence in the trees, the stillness all around him.

When the old man began to clap, Alex lowered the Strad and turned slowly toward the interruption. The stranger stood squinting into the sunlight, hands once poised to pull down heaven now pressed palm to palm. The violinist searched the wrinkled face, and deliberately the old man hooked his thumbs to the blue suspenders. He smiled with crooked teeth and yellow beard.

"Wasn't sure if you were real," the stranger muttered. "Been waiting for you for a long time. Been looking for a sign, at least."

Alex stared at him, body half-turned toward the words, Strad and bow hanging from his fingers.

"I remember the day they brought her here," the ancient one continued. "I sat with her that evening. I get hopeful every time they bring a new one in. Sooner or later there'll be so many folks here, God will have to pay a visit. And I'll be here to greet him." He shrugged. "Maybe you woke him up with the angels in your violin."

"Did you know her?" Alex asked.

The man shook his head. "Nope. Only just met her when they brought her here."

Alex faced the headstone in the pause, traced her name with his eyes. He could feel the stranger still lingering behind him.

"They only disappear when you forget about them," the old man said. "If you always remember, then they'll always be with you…You played a nice piece there, mister. Thought I'd follow the notes and come to see for myself. Wasn't sure if you were real."

But when Alex turned again to question the stranger, the old man had already slipped away, his decrepit form moving awkwardly between the markers a hundred yards down the hill. He smiled absently, considering the irony of himself being a sign to someone that God was coming. After all, he had only come to play for her. Without a word he packed the violin and bow away and held the case grip loosely in his left hand. All the notes remained in his head, as if he hadn't purged himself completely of the memory, or transferred a certain fraction of himself fully to some other dimension.

"I'll see you soon," he said to the mute stone, the indifferent grave. "Somehow, I'll always love you."

He left, wandered with no immediacy through the cemetery and toward the South Gate where he'd parked his car. The old man had made it back to the lawn chair beside the unknown resting place, arms outstretched again, and palms raised to collect whatever pieces of heaven God might graciously toss into them. At last, this part made sense to Alex, as he, too, had been waiting for a sign, perhaps had been searching in the wrong places with some twisted sense of logic. Death in numbers didn't bring God like a free gift. Forty thousand dead were as godless as a lone corpse because, in theory, He had taken them soberly to a different place few living could access. But Alex had never been looking for an omniscient deity; he had only ever sought himself. And whether by Divine Intervention or sublime delusion, it didn't matter anymore. He had discovered the remnants of a checkpoint in his life and he knew the next stop flowed ahead of him down a vein to the future. What he'd left in his wake, each hate and love, had no more substance than exhaust from a muffler—air now, maybe not clean or even undetectable, but formless, nonetheless. The pieces had come together like so many irregular parts of a jigsaw puzzle, and everything seemed right. Everything felt real.

~

The following Monday morning, Kelly arrived for her lesson. The month of August was winding down, and he knew that he would have to take a couple days that week to make an appearance at the local school in order to "get his shit together" before classes started in September. The closer the school year got, the less he wanted to teach music. At least Kelly would be there, he told himself, checking the irony of the idea—at least the little girl would be there for him if he needed something familiar to bolster his security, to reaffirm his authority. A single thought enlightened him abruptly to the notion that three people whom he had come to interact with over the course of the summer constituted a necessary sense of familiarity and comfort for him. The realization strangely awed him, but he could not deny its resounding truth.

The procedure for the morning was routine, save for the fact that Kelly herself brought Luella's envelope of cash in the ill woman's stead. Lately, more time had been devoted to the composition, and with every session, Alex became more convinced that the piece had taken the exact form it should have when he and Kelly finally polished it and he had turned over a copy to Stephen Winslow and the graduate students. Today, however, he needed to take Kelly's performance to a new level.

"I have to make a recording of you playing this piece," he informed her. "That way I can send it to Juilliard and then we can make an application to audition."

She smiled widely, excited.

"I'll have you warm up first and then play through the piece once," he added.

"How will we record it?" she asked.

"On this reel-to-reel recorder," he answered, directing her attention to a square gray box that he had set on the desktop, beside a microphone perched in a little tripod.

"A reel-to-reel recorder?" she questioned, frowning. She stared at the piece of equipment as if it had been beamed down to the parlor by aliens. "What does it do?"

"You've never seen a reel-to-reel recorder? This one is top-of-the-line. It's only about ten years old."

She shook her head. "What's a reel?"

"What's a—" He pointed at the twin reels of magnetic recording tape. "Those are reels and they record through this microphone."

Kelly stared at the circles of brown tape stuck to the face of the gray box. "I've never seen anything like that."

"What? Bing Crosby invested a ton of money to have the reel-to-reel developed, and who'd argue with Bing Crosby?"

She twisted her lips. "Bing?"

"Bing Crosby," he repeated, "the entertainer."

"His name was Bing?"

"Yes," he retorted. He adjusted the microphone on the desktop. "This machine records music and sounds, like a…" He searched for the explanation.

"Podcast?"

"A what?"

"A podcast," she said, "like a midi file you can download or make on a computer."

Confused, he considered the idea. "Okay, like a midi file. Anyway, I'll take the recording to Juilliard and they'll listen to it."

"On a reel-to-reel recorder?"

"Yes."

"Are you sure they have one?"

He suspected that Kelly was not trying to be funny, nor challenging the notion. Her bewilderment appeared genuine, and no doubt fueled by her generation's submergence in the digital age.

"Of course they do," he said as if only partly certain. "Where do you think I got this one?"

"What if they don't?"

"I don't know, do you have a better idea?" He spoke evenly to maintain his patience while she shrugged and examined the strange recording device.

"You don't have a computer with a CD-ROM drive?"

His eyes widened and he looked at her in disbelief. "You're talking to a man who wrote the piece you're playing by hand," he reminded her. "Do you think I even know what a CD-Ram drive is?"

"ROM," she corrected him. "It's a CD-*ROM*."

He'd had enough of the discussion: "Warm up and I'll be back to record the piece." He stepped toward the doorway, but turned back to the little girl. "I'll be in the yard feeding my dinosaurs," he quipped, then rode the wave of her giggling out of the room and walked to the kitchen.

Alex tugged the envelope of money from his back pocket and tossed it onto the counter. He pulled the warm pot from the coffee maker and filled a mug before returning to the parlor to surmise Kelly's progress. From the doorway he watched her leaning over the recorder and examining the foreign piece of equipment and its two round plastic spools of tape. She touched its buttons and toggles, tapped gingerly on the plexiglass covering its needle gauges, and then squeezed the black foam on the tip of the microphone. He noticed that she hadn't even unpacked her violin or bow. He cleared his throat and she spun toward him and blushed.

"When do you think it will be a good time to get going?" he asked. He sipped from his coffee cup.

"Now," she answered simply. She unzipped her violin case and got out her instrument. A moment later she had tuned the violin and had plunged herself into her music scales.

He sat across the room, in the rocking chair, and listened while he drank his coffee. The morning poured itself into the room through the windowpanes, falling evenly over the rough surface of the case he had stashed in the corner behind the desk. He peered at the black case, imagined its contents. Without hesitation, he stood, set the coffee cup on the desktop, and grabbed the case. Laying it across the arms of the rocking chair, he stopped the little girl and asked her to come over to him.

Once at his side, he opened the case and exposed the sleeping Strad within, strapped to the burgundy velvet interior.

"This is a Strad," he said solemnly as he lifted the antique instrument from its bed and placed it into her small hands.

Mouth slightly open, she took it without a sound.

"I want you to start playing on this," he said. "It'll present its own set of new problems for you as you get used to playing it, but the sound it makes might just haunt you forever. I can guarantee that not a single person has ever auditioned for Juilliard playing on a Stradivarius violin."

Had she been holding the Shroud of Turin, the experience would not have been so holy as this minute of extended time. Great brown eyes full of wonder she gazed down at the tired old violin.

"A Stradivarius," she mumbled. She blinked once. "A real Strad?"

"I've had this conversation before," he remembered. "Take my word for it. Tune it to the A on the keyboard," he said. "Warm up and get a feel for it. Maybe today wouldn't be the best time to make the recording, not with me springing a new instrument on you like this."

"I can do it," she whispered, still enveloped in the magic he had come only to barely detect when he played it. "Just let me play it a while."

In the rocker again, he swayed rhythmically as she tuned the violin, played it, became one with it. He had never, not in all the time he had owned the Strad, been an audience to its song. It was a bizarre feeling being detached from an instrument whose voice had always sounded beside his left ear. From this new perspective, he watched the bow glide cleanly over perfectly vibrating strings; he saw fine traces of rosin scatter like dust into the sunlight. He never realized how beautiful it all was until he'd had the opportunity to remove himself from it.

No wonder she loved to hear the pretty music so much…

Forty-five minutes later, she coaxed the Strad into the first few measures of the piece. Whatever minor difficulties the foreign instrument may have posed to Kelly, he could discern none of them. Instead, she played as she had always played. Her violin or the Strad, it seemed to make no difference to her ability, which flowed uninhibited from some place other than her fingers, wrists, or elbows. The music emanated from a fresh heart that beat with innocence and passion like his had so many months ago. She inspired him, renewed him, and he felt his pulse quicken as she journeyed through the composition from beginning to end with hardly a wrinkle. It must have sounded so much like this at her grave, he thought. And his arrogance dared to entertain the claim he had made some time ago that he would one day teach Kelly how to make God himself pay attention.

When she had finished, she let the violin come down gently to her side. "There," she said in a heavy breath. "I think I'm ready to record it, now."

"Do you want something first?" he asked. "A glass of water or something?"

"I want to record it now," she repeated. "I'm ready to record it."

He rubbed his chin. "Okay, check to be sure the instrument is still in tune."

While she played each string against the next and adjusted the fine tuners, he went to the reel-to-reel recorder and pushed the record and pause buttons. He waited until she was ready.

"As soon as I press this button, the machine will start to record," he told her. "Are you sure you're ready?"

Violin under her chin, she nodded and raised the bow.

"Here we go, then," he said, releasing the pause.

The reels clicked into motion and he held up a finger to have her wait. When he lowered the finger, she began to play the piece again, with a different, more intense purpose this time. He settled himself into the rocking chair, but he didn't move while she bowed out the composition in exact movements, fluidly. She didn't need to rely on the written notes, though she glanced at the sheet music once or twice. As was her custom and comfort, she had memorized almost all of it, though for weeks he had been making her sight read pieces she had never seen before in order to increase her proficiency. She would be required to do so in her music education, after all, and so it had become part of his formal instruction of her.

The solo violin piece he had written and they had rewritten took her six minutes to perform, far longer than any piece she had ever played and any piece he had ever been made to play for an audition. The formidable task exhausted her, and he could see the stress on her face as she completed the final delicate measure and at last came to the coda, or end. He was already at the recorder when she vibrated the last note and drew it to a close.

"Well done," he congratulated her after he had stopped the recording. "I'm going to make a copy of this tape and on Wednesday we're going to listen to it and see where we can improve."

Kelly crinkled her brow. "Why can't we listen to it now?"

"Not now," he responded. "I want you to think about how you played, instead. Hear the music that's still in your head and think about it. When I see you again I'll have some things that we'll work on."

She hesitated, opened her mouth as if to speak, but reconsidered.

He smiled at her. "I'll see you on Wednesday, then."

Pouting, she pushed the Strad toward him.

"Take it with you; sleep with it if you want to," he said, refusing the instrument. "You're going to have to rely on it for a while until you're able to get a professional instrument of your own."

She let a smile slip across her face as the pouting vanished. "Thank you, Alex," she said, wrapping her arms around him, the violin bouncing off the back of his legs.

"Be careful with that," he said lightly. "Treat it like you would a puppy, except don't feed it anything but music."

Proudly, she set the Strad into her pink and silver violin case, secured her bow, and zipped the cover closed. "I'll see you on Wednesday," she sang, bounding out of the parlor and into the foyer.

"Remember what I said," he called after her. "Take care of that violin!"

And she was gone, having flown out the front door. He could hear her feet pounding off the concrete sidewalk, then her quick steps onto the porch next door.

He stood silently in the parlor for a few minutes, feeling as though he had given away his own child. He picked up Kelly's violin that she had left behind and laid it into the Strad's case. Ultimately, he knew he had done the right thing; he had done the only thing that made sense to him at this point in his life. He hadn't gotten rid of the Strad, but loaned it to what might be the greatest performance of its life if it all worked out the way he had planned, the way the Philharmonic was hoping it would.

In the kitchen again, he rinsed his coffee mug and left it upside down on a dishtowel beside the sink. Noticing the envelope on the counter, he picked it up and went into the living room to relax and flip through the *Times* he had tossed onto the end table. As he had always done, he waited until he was alone after the lesson every Monday to count the cash in the envelope and to tuck it into his front pocket. He wasn't sure why he continued weekly to count the money, especially since he had always made it a point to assure Luella that he trusted her. Besides, what would he do if the amount in the envelope was ever wrong? Certainly, he wouldn't say anything. He couldn't imagine how that conversation with the old Bayou matron would unfold, so he had decided many Mondays ago that he would never broach the subject even in a time of need.

Nonetheless, he unsealed the envelope that had, as usual, *Violin Lessons* scrawled across its front, and reached in to withdraw the payment. But there was something else in the envelope besides the money, a sheet of paper folded neatly around the fistful of crisp twenty dollar bills. It was not like Luella to leave anything but money inside the envelope, and with caution, he set the twenties aside and unfolded the paper.

The note from Grace read:

Dear Alex,

I suppose we all watch the same sky and wish upon the same stars. There is a lot to be said about the stars—they will never leave you. They will always be there. We share our memories, our thoughts, our dreams, and our love with them. They are our silent healers.

I know I'm not Charlotte, nor will I ever be. I never want to replace her because I know I can't. Sometimes, we get caught in the moment. I know and understand how much you loved her. I will never hold that against you. She is gone, Alex. You need to move on. You need to realize that this universe has other plans for you.

I'm not sure how or why you have come into our lives, but you have. You have given all of us hope for a future. We have all had unfortunate losses, but we need to get past them. I feel that in many ways we have. I can't imagine you not being a part of our lives. Kelly needs you, Luella needs you, and, yes, I need you. I notice the stars more, Alex—you have taught me that's where love is and grows, in those beautiful sparkles of light in the sky. I notice them more now, because of you.

And so, as I dream each night, you are there. I think I've fallen for you, Alex. I have never experienced this before. My only regret is that you might be gone someday and I pray to the life of the universe to keep you here. Not just for Kelly, but for me, too.

Dream on, and notice what can be. Let the journey to your soul be your pathway to the stars. Realize what's there. It's me, Alex. It's me. We can either find a way or make one.

There is always a someday. There are always stars.

Love,

Grace

He felt strangely whole, like the part of him that was missing had been there since the beginning, ignored, perhaps neglected. Thoughts of Grace had always occupied a certain sector of his mind, but apparently he had never stopped to acknowledge that she was there because she loved him. She loved him? The idea had fallen away from him because maybe he was unable to fully comprehend the notion. No, he had been selfish, self-absorbed, and incapable of embracing what he still had, even after Charlotte's death—his family, his vitality, his violin, his command of the music. He hadn't thought any of that was important anymore, so like the egotistical machine he had become, he simply left it on the fibers of his brain to rot. Fortunately, God hadn't taken it all away and plunged him into oblivion.

Why would she love such a man? Her explanation lay in his hands, in the note Grace had written. Truth be known, he loved her, too. He could even pinpoint the moment when she had captivated his heart. The time to let Charlotte go had come weeks ago, though he had continued to fight it. Letting her go didn't have to mean forgetting her. And if Grace's wisdom later revealed itself as a misconception, a fallacy, what then? He would have to wait and see. He would have to discover the way back to her, collecting the remnants of their first moments together along the way, facing, finally, his own foolishness.

In the minutes following the first, second, third reading of the note, as he lay back on the couch, heart pounding in a measured thump like a funeral march, it finally came. In the dream, she waited for him under the tree, patchwork blanket spread out for him, blossoms falling in pink and white flecks…

It's me Alex…It's me…

She gazed up at him, her face familiar and foreign, reached for him to take her hands. Warm, her palms felt so real to him, her eyes knew him all too well. The taste of her lips on his…he remembered the feeling, the desire. He lay down beside her, and as her arms wrapped around him, the pretty music whispered through the tree branches, the sunlight faded and every star in the life of the universe poked through the new night's black film…

It's me Alex…It's me…

It was her, and she had been there all along.

~

He hadn't intended to get so busy, so suddenly. Every morning he read Grace's note, kept it hanging from a magnet on the refrigerator, to remind him of what was important, what really mattered. It motivated him, focused him, but what it could not do was give him the time he needed to meet with her, to talk with her, the way he knew he must. The morning after he had read the note, he called Luella's house. Kelly answered, told him that Aunt Gracie was working and that she would leave a message for her to call him. Tuesday passed and she never returned his call. Wednesday came and Kelly, thankfully oblivious to the situation between Alex and Grace, arrived for her lesson. Business as usual from beginning to end. On the two days opposite her lessons, he went again to Juilliard, oversaw the final steps of the project, delivered the recording on the reel-to-reel and watched as they miraculously turned it into a compact disc instead, a copy of which he brought back to the house so he and the girl could use it in their lessons. The Philharmonic, he gathered, met to review the recording, to read the new music and to rehearse. Everything but his "relationship" with Grace proceeded as planned.

The week passed, he called again. Grace was working and Luella assured him she would send the woman over the next day. No Grace, no call. On Saturday, he had to convince a custodian that he really worked at the local school so that he could get into his classroom and poke around. Finally, he sat behind the old desk in the large, open chorus room, grand piano to his right, risers straight ahead, and dug through the drawers of six filing cabinets in search of anything that would direct him to some course of study in keeping with the district's objectives. He had a curriculum outline, but it didn't mean anything to him. If Mrs. Hurley hadn't popped her head into his room, he might have self-destructed all over the white tiled floor.

Somewhat flighty and a little too much of a hippie for him, Dawn Hurley, six years away from retirement, was gracious enough to sit down with Alex and, over the course of ninety minutes, walk him through what had been taught in the past. Slowly he began to grasp what was expected of him, and with the speed and efficiency of a career teacher and musician, he pulled together his resources and began to sketch out his school year. He would make mistakes from one semester to the next, he knew. But he also hadn't forgotten that he'd made plenty of mistakes in the last few weeks alone. A stack of file folders under his arm, he left the school just before five o'clock and went home, sat at the coffee table in his living room and poured over the hundreds of papers. He figured out the photocopying procedure for the school, mixed and matched different activities with others, flipped through music selections for the choral program, decided what he should order, and anticipated what the district wouldn't allow him to have.

By Sunday morning, he'd had enough of lesson plans and trying to discern what would work and what wouldn't. At the dining room table he stared indifferently out the window at the sunshine accenting the blue clapboards of the house beside his. The knock didn't register right away, just soft enough not to disturb the placid silence of the room. He turned his head, peered through the kitchen, and saw her standing on the other side of the screen door.

"Hi," she said faintly.

He blinked once, recognized her again, and all at once realized she was there, smiling at him. He stood, went to the door to let her in.

"You looked deep in thought," she said lightly as she stepped past him.

Caught in the wake of her sweet perfume, he closed his eyes for a moment and absorbed her presence. He moved as if in a dream, leading her into the living room where they sat together on the couch, in the midst of papers and folders and writing pads sprawled across the coffee table and floor.

"You've been busy," she remarked.

"School," he said. "I'm trying to get a handle on what it is I need to teach." She was beautiful, and, having been away from her for who knew how many days, he found himself looking at her perhaps more than he normally would. "I read your note," he admitted. "Actually, I've read it a dozen times."

She glanced away from him. "And?"

He hesitated. "And...I love you, Grace."

Her eyes met his, and the tears had already begun to well on her lower lashes.

"I know," she uttered.

He reached for her, took her into his arms. "I'm sorry I..."

But her lips were on his before the words could escape, pouring herself into him. He accepted every part of her as his hands slid over her body and she trembled with the touch. He carefully undressed her, blindly felt for each button of her shirt and freed it from its hole, then pulled the shirt away from her soft, delicately sculpted shoulders. She responded in kind, unzipped his pants, ran her hands under the waistline and into his boxer shorts. Moments later, she lay naked on the couch while he raised her leg slightly to enter a space that took him in freely, unconditionally. And when he moved over her, their rhythms synchronized until they flowed as one body, until he felt the pressure begin to build in his legs, in his head. It had been so long since he had felt this love, this—Her back arched and he held her steady, one hand on her side, the other pressed against the ridge of her backbone. Sweat beaded on his forehead and ran in warm streaks down the sides of his face, falling drop by drop onto her bare breasts. She pushed her fingers through his hair as she rose to kiss him, but his mouth found her neck instead, wet and salty, and he slipped more deeply into her. The air from her lungs came in a labored sigh. His name leaked out with the breath; he turned his head toward hers and accepted her lips and tongue. Her body relaxed and he braced his arms against the cushions of the couch. He looked down at her, caught shards of brown gazing back at him through partially closed eyelids. The earth shifted and the climax came, thrusting out of him and into her in an explosion of life and love, hot and concentrated. Instantly, her thighs tightened around his hips as her back arched a second time, bringing with it a wincing culmination of passion suddenly released, quick and satisfying. His body fell against hers, both slick with perspiration, and he tried to catch his breath as her lips closed on his burning cheek.

"Grace," he gasped. "Grace…"

~

Alex barely noticed the passing days rolling into one another. The academic year began, he brought Kelly to and from school, and during the day she would visit him on certain periods, just to say hello or to ask for help with homework. Sometimes in the evening, he would eat dinner with the little girl and her aunt. As September came to a gradual close, Luella's health had improved somewhat, enough for her to join them from time to time over red beans and rice, chicken and shrimp Creole, jambalaya, or muffuletta sandwiches. Later, when the table had been cleared and the candles lit, they might savor Doberge cake, pecan pie, beignets, or bananas Foster. If a dish even vaguely resembled Louisiana, Grace could cook it or Luella could tell her how. Consequently, he came to ingest foods he never knew existed, all along learning something new almost every day about people whom he came to love more and more with each passing week. And on those nights when he found himself alone because of a backlog of school work or a conductor's meeting at Juilliard, he missed them, all of them, even the abrasive old woman.

What force of nature had brought him here? What line of fate had drawn him so close to something he had needed for so long? He thought about these questions from time to time, counted himself fortunate in so many ways. Sometimes he would lay awake at night, Grace's naked body pressed against him as she lay sleeping peacefully, and wonder what life might have been like if Charlotte had never been killed. These weren't thoughts that oppressed him, but rather musings that continued to liberate him. He acknowledged and Grace agreed that Charlotte had been a necessary part of his life once, a being so precious and fragile that she enhanced who he was on multiple fronts. As tragic as her life had been, as terrible as the end had come, the love he had felt for her only later endowed him with the capacity to love all the more passionately. Charlotte had led to Grace, no matter what the circumstances. One level had risen to the next. Nothing, he came to realize, had ever been anyone's fault. The world, the universe, unfolded to a design far larger than any of them. How arrogant he had been to believe otherwise. What Charlotte had given him in physical, raw love, Grace had returned with a tenderness he had never experienced before. The ebb flowed, and the flowing ebbed, forever connected, forever the same.

Since the inception of the school year, Alex had had to move Kelly's lesson time to six o'clock, and he modified his approach to her ongoing development by strictly confining the lessons to an hour so that the girl could get her homework done. She absolutely hated having to do homework. If Kelly had had her way, she would have gone back to her home schooling and spent the majority of her time playing the Strad Alex had loaned her. Still, they made time to precisely work on different parts of the solo without neglecting other parts of her violin studies. The more she played the piece, the better she got, the more she remembered and committed to memory. Her mind seemed to expand infinitely, and he had some time ago conceded to the idea that she was, indeed, a prodigy. Not to mention she was a good girl, a sweet, loving, thoughtful little person who proved to be very much like Aunt Gracie. But the feisty, indignant, insistent, impish part of her personality continued to frustrate and amuse him. In this regard, she was so very much like Charlotte had been.

On one particular Wednesday evening in September, as the lesson came to a close successfully and both student and teacher felt satisfied with the progress achieved on all sides, Alex suggested that Kelly leave the Strad at his house for the night.

"Leave it here?" she had whined, frowning.

"Just for tonight."

"Just for tonight?"

"Just for tonight," he insisted.

"Why?"

"I want you to go home and do your homework, then go to bed, and get up tomorrow morning and go to school. All of which I want you to do without playing or so much as touching a violin," he explained.

"What are you talking about?" Her eyes were dark and blazing through him. "I can't do that."

He sat her down and pulled his chair up to hers. "Listen," he began, "you are by far the number one best student I have ever had at any age. I don't think I've ever played with anyone as devoted and talented as you are. But you need to get a life."

She wrinkled her brow as the temper tantrum threatened to erupt right there in the parlor. "Get a life?" she retorted.

"Try it," he said, smiling. The entire conversation perversely entertained him. "Try spending one whole day without touching the violin."

"I can't."

He stood. "You will. Now go home." He pretended to be stern, but the twinkle in his eyes betrayed him.

"No." She crossed her arms and pouted.

"Do I have to call your grandmother?"

She grinned wickedly. "Go ahead," she challenged.

He reached for the phone on his desk. "Okay, you asked for it." He picked up the receiver and pressed it to his ear.

Kelly waited for a second, and he could see that she was anxiously holding her breath.

"Okay," she surrendered. She pushed herself out of the chair and stomped into the foyer. She spun around and snapped out a single finger. "One night," she said forcefully.

"One night," he agreed. He hung up the telephone. "It'll be good for you. Hey, you might like being normal for a little while."

"I doubt it," she spat at him.

As she left the house, he laughed to himself and went to the window to make sure that she made it safely to her front porch. Once the pigtails and pucker had disappeared, he approached the Strad resting soundlessly in the stand beside the desk. He lifted the instrument by the top of the scroll and laid it on his shoulder. He moved his fingers up and down the fingerboard, loosening his knuckles and wrist. Crossing the room, he took his bow from the case behind the rocking chair and tightened the horsehair while he held the violin snugly between his chin and shoulder. He tuned the Strad, his ear still remarkably accurate as he adjusted the fine tuners. He pulled out a few scales, an étude or two, and then set the violin back onto its stand. He loosened the horsehair and laid the bow on the desktop.

A handful of hours later, Grace arrived with a bag of apples. Her hair shimmered under the full moon as she stood shivering on the deck. If he hadn't known better, he might have fancied her a goddess visiting him from some other world. Not only was she beautiful, he thought, but sexy. There wasn't a moment that passed when he didn't want her, anywhere, anytime. And here she was—tight shirt, form-fitting jeans, sandy brown hair tied back into a ponytail, holding a brown paper bag full of apples.

"Apples?"

She giggled as she glided into the kitchen. "Yes, apples," she answered. "A woman at work has an apple tree. I happened to mention that I like apples, and lo and behold, she shows up for the afternoon shift with a bazillion apples."

When Luella's health began to fail in August, Grace had requested and gotten a shift change. Since then, she had continued to work the day shift so that she could be at home during the night just in case something went wrong. Besides, she reasoned, Kelly and Alex were at school all day and Luella slept most of the afternoon, so it all worked out in the end. Slowly, Luella was getting better, gaining strength, forcing herself out of pneumonia's heavy grip. Grace had saved her life, no doubt, whether the large old woman would ever have admitted it. Yet Miss Luella still hadn't left the house, nor was she allowed to. Not yet; not until she could go an entire day without antibiotics.

"Horse balls," she'd exclaim. "Goddamn quacks have indoctrinated you, Gracie. You can only save someone's life by killing them. What kind of medical mumbo is that?"

But it didn't matter. Luella, much to her own dismay, had given birth to a daughter fit to take on the Devil and win, just like her mama.

"And what are we supposed to do with these apples?" he asked very close to her.

She pushed herself up on her tiptoes and kissed him. "I don't think you need the apples, Mr. Brogan," she whispered.

"Are you staying?"

She turned away from him and put the bag of apples into the refrigerator. "For a little while," she answered. "Mother gets her meds at midnight. I don't know how you can stay up all night with me and then get up so early and go to work."

His arms were around her waist. "The same way you can, Aunt Gracie."

"Don't call me that," she said playfully.

"Why not?"

"It's creepy. I don't want to be thinking about my niece when I'm with you, doing, you know."

"Doing what?" he teased.

"This…"

Later, in bed, she lay on his arm and he ran a hand through her long hair.

"I know something that we haven't done yet," he said.

She snuggled up to him. "I can't imagine that," she responded.

"What's one thing I've never done for you?"

She thought a minute as he listened to the clock ticking somewhere on the other side of the dark room. If he concentrated on the opposite wall, he could still see the ghostly vestiges of the notes that had yanked him out of the forgotten dream and inspired the composition.

"I've never heard you play the violin," she finally answered.

He smiled into the darkness. She had said what he'd hoped she'd say. He rolled out of bed and pulled on a pair of pajama bottoms. He turned on the lamp next to her and asked her to wait, he had a surprise. Disappearing from the bedroom, he returned a minute later with Strad and bow. She sat up, beaming with anticipation.

"You're going to play for me?" she asked incredulously. Her eyes glimmered in the pale lamplight.

"What do you want to hear?"

Her smile widened. "Anything," she breathed.

"Then let me play you anything..."

And next he relived a scene that had occurred over and over again in the past few years of his life. This time, however, something different possessed him; something within him that made him want to play, need to play for her. He had wagered, even though he performed cold, that all the music inside of him would come back. It had to, for Grace. It did, more freely and openly than ever, and he consciously settled into its spell, once more allowed it to charm his senses as the notes rolled uninhibited over the crumbling walls breaking down all across his mind. With each mood the music inspired, his fingers reacted instinctively, and the expression on her face changed as every theme presented itself and drew her into its passion.

On he played in requiem to the vanishing moments. The symphonic tapestry, bits and pieces of new and old, original and classic, floated through the open windows and fell softly into the neighborhood, into the waxing night.

~

The answering machine came on after the third ring. Alex had planned it that way by calling in the middle of the afternoon, not wanting yet to talk to the girls until he had the time and desire to say everything that he probably should say to them. He knew that they would have questions, possibly many. If he'd been in their position, he'd want the blanks filled in as well. However, he wasn't exactly sure that he could answer their questions right now. He'd need more time to get it straight in his own mind.

"Hello, Bradleys," he said into the telephone receiver as brightly as he could manage. "This is Alex. I know it's been a while since we've talked, and I'm sorry for that."

But he didn't feel the remorse like he had expected he might.

"You may have already heard something about the Festival of the Arts that's coming up. If not, I wanted to let you know myself that I'm returning to Lincoln Center, sort of."

Sort of…

"I'll be there, and I was hoping that all of you would be, too. Maybe we can catch up with each other afterward."

He paused, trying to discern whether he should tell them more, but: "There have been a lot of changes since Charlotte was killed. I'd like you to meet some of them."

He smiled with the notion.

"Anyway, check the posters or the website or whatever and you'll see my name. You know the show routine."

Was there anything else left to say at that moment? Anything that he could—

"So, I guess that's it until then. I hope to see you soon."

He extended the silence, as if offering one last opportunity for someone to pick up the phone on the other end.

But no one did.

"Okay," he said at last, "bye."

~

He remembered the autumn smell of burning leaves as a kid growing up in Massachusetts. He remembered the October air biting at his cheeks, at the tips of his fingers after the sun had set early and he had delivered the last few copies of the local newspaper to his customers.

He stood in front of Kelly's house, the orange glow of an ancient streetlight frosting the front of his body, the lapels and sleeves of his black tuxedo coat, the glossy tips of his dress shoes. The atmosphere around him, the darkness of a chilly fall evening, recalled the memories of his childhood, images of his New England youth.

He waited for the others to come out of the house—Kelly, Luella, Aunt Gracie. He waited for the car to arrive that would bring them to Lincoln Center. He couldn't sit in the living room while Kelly paced. She made him more nervous than he wanted to be, so he removed himself from the stress and ventured out into the night to stand alone, to wait, under the old streetlight.

Two weeks before the scheduled performance, he had sat Kelly down at the dining room table with her aunt. He held in his hands a letter from Stephen Winslow, printed on Juilliard stationary, that outlined the events of the community performance. Kelly, unbeknownst to her, would be listed in the program as "an exceptionally gifted young student of the violin whose innate ability could earn her a place among the most talented violinists of her time…At ten years old, her prodigal nature presents itself in stunning clarity and overwhelming passion."

He, of course, had much to do with the brief biography, but he met no resistance in wording it so from either the conductor or the concertmaster, both of whom had been impressed with her recording. He had no intention of telling her any of this, however. In fact, he downplayed the event, explaining to her that she had received an invitation to audition at Juilliard, but the format in which she would play was a little different from the usual. Actually, the agreement between himself and members of the Juilliard Pre-College Division Board, who happened to be affiliated in one way or another with the Philharmonic, dictated that her performance would constitute a kind of "pre-audition audition." The little girl would ultimately be asked to play at Juilliard regardless.

"Here's the deal," he'd begun: "I received this letter from Mr. Winslow. He's a teacher at Juilliard, the one I sent the recording to. They want you to play at a public performance. You should think of it as a pre-audition."

"Okay," Kelly said suspiciously. "What kind of public performance?"

He purposely avoided her stare and had seated her at the opposite end of the table so he could get through the story more easily.

"At Lincoln Center."

Her back stiffened. "Lincoln Center?"

"In the city?" Grace interjected from her spot between them at the table.

"Yes, at Avery Fisher Hall, to be exact."

"No way," Kelly gasped. "Like where the Philharmonic plays?"

"The very stage," he answered matter-of-factly.

"Why?" The idea hardly seemed to make sense to her.

"Every year," he explained, "the Philharmonic hosts a concert that showcases the city and the proven talent of the area. They call it the Festival of the Arts. I pulled some strings, so to speak, and got you a gig for that night."

"What will I have to do?"

"Play the solo piece," he replied. "Some members of Juilliard will be there and I know they're quite anxious to hear you live. I figure that by playing at this concert, you can get some exposure to performing publicly without the pressure of trying out for Juilliard. Believe me, that will come later."

"Without the pressure of trying out for Juilliard?" Grace repeated. "Are you kidding? How is playing at Lincoln Center in front of thousands of people less pressure than trying out for Juilliard? Couldn't she just take part in a recital down the street or something?"

He smiled, undeterred. "She's too good for a local recital," he said. "This will be fine; there's nothing to worry about. Besides, at her age this is an opportunity of a lifetime."

"I'll be by myself?" Kelly asked timidly.

"I'll be in the wings, watching, but otherwise the stage will be all yours," he lied.

The surprise would come when Kelly finished the first dozen measures or so of the solo and the Philharmonic began to play behind her. He had already decided that if he told her the whole truth it might be too much for her to take. The risk of her collapsing on him, considering her relative inexperience in the public forum, would be too great knowing the involvement of the orchestra beforehand. As the most talented young student he'd ever instructed, his confidence soared in the fact that she could and would pull it off. After the initial reaction when the orchestra began its part, she would coast into the performance like a professional. He knew it. Yet he hadn't exactly had the conversation with Grace ahead of time. No, the entire plan, save for the little girl's "solo" performance, remained under wraps.

He explained to Kelly that a limousine would drive them to Lincoln Center where she would be assigned to a private warm-up room. Alex would help her loosen her fingers and practice for a while, and then she would be escorted to the stage where she would perform her magic.

"You'll be going on first," he told her. "You'll be the opening act."

"The opening act?"

The expression on her face—brilliantly ripe eyes, quivering lips, and flushed cheeks—betrayed both fear and excitement. Just thinking about the position she would be put into thrilled and stressed him, and he anticipated the event more than he had ever looked forward to anything in his life. What she didn't know wouldn't hurt her, he inwardly surmised, and in the end she, they, he would all be changed by it. Kelly would get her audition and Luella would get her wish. Grace would realize her own sister's spirit celebrated more grandly than she could have ever imagined through the fingers and soul of Clarice's daughter.

And the heart of the butterfly, fluttering through the minds of over two and half thousand spectators, would beat out a new hope, a new beginning from the f-holes of the Strad as he at last released the vestiges of his passion and the spiraling memory of Charlotte into the world. He liked to think of it as a rebirth destined to affect far more people than he had initially considered when the score had come to him months ago. Now, the music was larger than any of them, and waited in its cocoon until the moment it would break free and spread its beautiful wings.

The following weekend, per his request, Grace and Kelly arrived at his house on a Saturday afternoon with a pile of dresses that the girl was made to model, one at a time, in front of her aunt and teacher. Alex insisted that what she wore be right for the occasion, formal but in no way restricting the movements that playing the violin required. Grace, on the other hand, was not really sure what Kelly should wear to such a function, and in the end liked all the dresses. Finally, they agreed on a black, sleeveless dress that exposed her bony shoulders but flowed in straight, even lines down her body to her ankles. Of course, she would need shoes to match, but that task would be an easy one to accomplish. Ultimately, Kelly seemed satisfied. She wasn't elated about having to don such formal garments, and he couldn't remember a time when he'd seen her in anything but shorts or jeans and t-shirts, save for the morning of Mr. Grady's funeral. Culture did not come easily to the young, stubborn, and overly-confident girl, primarily thanks to her simple yet genuine ancestry. Nonetheless, he knew she could play the part, and soon her life would continually revolve around such notions.

Later that same evening, after Kelly had gone home to bed and Luella had fallen fast asleep in her own room since her health had vastly improved, Grace sat with Alex on his couch as they watched a black-and-white love story on the classic movie channel. The title of the movie could have been anything because he wasn't paying attention to it. Instead, he stole glances at the woman beside him, so beautiful, natural, and real. At last she met his eyes and smirked.

"What?" she asked playfully.

He could not contain it: "I have something for you."

She leaned into him. "Not that line again," she whispered.

"I'm serious," he said. "Wait here."

And with that he fled the room and went upstairs. He returned to the living room with a large white box tied with thick silver ribbons.

"What's this?" she questioned as he set the box on her lap.

"Open it."

Carefully she untied the shining ribbon and lifted the top off the box as he sat beside her again. She pulled open the white tissue paper inside and revealed a black velvet evening gown with satin accents and spaghetti straps.

"It's beautiful," she uttered, holding up the dress. "It's beautiful, Alex." She dropped the gown into the box and wrapped her arms around his neck. "Thank you."

"For the concert," he said. "You'll be the prettiest woman there."

"Just like a princess…"

"Just like a princess."

Luella demanded that she could wear her mother's flowered knit dress. After all, it was black with white daisies, and she could wear a nice coat sweater with it.

"Is it in one piece?" he asked gently on Sunday morning as the old woman sat for tea in her rocking chair.

Still unable to ply her trade with yarn and needles because of the cramping arthritis, she had become somewhat more ornery since the pneumonia let go. Boredom contributed to the greater part of her salty personality, though no one doubted that Luella had always had the sourness in her.

"In one piece?" she coughed out. "What are you suggesting, Mr. Brogan, that my mother was some kind of country bumpkin that wore rags on her back? I'll have you know that—"

"Mother," Grace intervened while Kelly giggled from the kitchen, "we all know how sweet and proper Grandma Adder was, but—"

"Adder—like the snake?" Alex pressed.

"Shhh," Grace shot at him as she tried not to smile. Luella grew evermore indignant. "No one is saying that your mother wore rags," she began again. "This is a very special occasion for Kelly and we want you to feel special, too."

Luella glared at the pair. "That's bullshit," she said. "I will wear Mother's dress, end of story. And if Mr. Brogan doesn't like it, then I'll take a cab and make my own way to the place."

Alex sighed, sure enough that he had raised her blood pressure simply for his own enjoyment. "Okay," he conceded, "I'm sure your dress will be fine. Go ahead, wear it."

The large old woman grinned at him. "I'm not asking for your permission, Mr. Important. You just got a load of matter-of-fact, and I'd kindly like you to swallow it like any gentleman would."

Grace put her hand to her mouth to hold in the laugh tickling at the back of her throat.

"Yes, ma'am," he replied, "I'll go ahead and do that…whatever it is."

And out came Luella to the idling limousine in her black dress with white daisies all over it, and a black coat sweater draped over her broad shoulders. Her pocketbook dangled from a pudgy arm, though he had already insisted that there was nothing for which they needed money. He had to explain that one didn't "tip" a limousine driver, since many worked on commission by the hour of service. Regardless, she brought along her pocketbook.

At the old woman's elbow came Grace, the striking picture of beauty. She held herself as if she had always been a princess and had only recently tossed off her everyday disguise to assume her role as Southern belle once more. Her hair was pulled back, away from her perfectly painted face and glossy lips, and set into a bun at the top of her head. Flowing strands fell down her thin neck and onto the upper back of her long dark coat. In the gown she moved as if on air, every step deliberate, the click of one heel in rhythm with the other. Delicate and shining, he took her in one ounce at a time as a stream of heat crept up his spine.

He led them both to the curb where the driver stood holding open the back door. The women passed into the limousine, and he turned to see Miss Kelly emerge from the house looking as uncomfortable as she possibly could, struggling to shove an arm into her coat while awkwardly carrying the violin case holding the Strad in the opposite hand. Aunt Gracie had straightened the girl's hair and clipped her bangs back from her eyes. Suddenly, she was a young woman whose cute face had become pretty in the atmosphere of the evening. She looked so much like Grace, so much like her mother.

"If it's that hard to put on your coat, how are you ever going to squeak out a note on that violin of yours?" he called up to her.

"I'm trying," she whined.

When she had finally made it to the sidewalk, she'd managed to fully pull the coat over her shoulders. Her dress poked crookedly out of the bottom of the jacket, hung up with static and crackling at her calves.

"You're a mess," he said lightly. "We'll fix you up when we get there."

"I can't believe how nervous I am," she admitted as they walked to the limousine.

"You'll be fine," he assured her. "As soon as you play the first note, you'll forget about everything else. And when it's over, you'll feel like you're on top of the world. That's the best part."

The four sat quietly in the spacious cabin of the limousine, Alex and Grace on one end, Luella and Kelly on the other. Six feet of emptiness separated one couple from the other and tiny round lights overhead glowed yellow into the void.

"Are you nervous?" Grace asked him softly.

He watched Kelly stare blankly at the violin case on her lap. "I feel like throwing up," he answered.

She patted his knee and laid her head on his shoulder as the limousine rolled quickly toward Manhattan.

~

Grace and Luella had been given reserved seats in the 1st Tier Box of Avery Fisher Hall, overlooking the expansive stage and the crowd buzzing below. The women were on their own with respect to finding the seats, but soon learned how helpful the Lincoln Center staff could be in directing patrons to the correct areas. Alex and Kelly had accompanied them from the parking garage to the building via the concourse level, never once having to walk beneath the night sky flushed pale with city lights.

Backstage, in a small warm-up room, Kelly stood with the Strad tuned and on her shoulder. He called out scales and she played them, loosening her fingers and wrists. She also played some pieces she knew by heart, like Bach's *Minuets,* warming her joints and adjusting her intonation. When she had finished, a sheen of sweat had formed on her forehead. She laid down the Strad and bow and dropped into a steel chair by the door.

"I know you're nervous, but do you remember what I said about the lights and not being able to see anybody in the audience?" he asked, seated across from her.

She nodded and kicked her feet into the air.

"Kelly?"

She looked up at him and he could see the anxiety in her round brown eyes.

"When I was your age I performed my first concerto in the auditorium of my elementary school," he said.

"Were you scared?"

"I was scared as hell," he admitted. "But there was a difference when I walked out onto that stage to play my violin. You see, I had to practice really, really hard in order to get my teacher to believe that I could do it. Sure, I may have been naturally gifted or ahead of my time or whatever, but I was no prodigy. I was no Miss Kelly. Instead, I stood in front of all those people and tried to remember the first notes of that concerto. I must have been gawking into the crowd for a good thirty seconds before it finally came back to me."

"What happened?"

He smiled, remembering the incident so clearly so many years later that it still made him shiver. "I played the concerto probably better than I ever had in any lesson. But the interesting thing is that about a minute into the performance I had forgotten all about the crowd, my teacher, my two sisters making faces at me from the front row. It was like the whole world disappeared and only my violin and I existed. I became a part of that music and it took me away to some other place far from the hundreds of eyes glued to me. Do you understand what I'm trying to say, Kelly?"

She gazed at him, her body still. "Do you love my Aunt Gracie?" she asked.

The question broadsided him. "What does that have to do with what I'm trying to get you to understand?" he questioned. "Are you listening to me?"

She nodded. "I heard what you said," she answered. "I want to know if you love Aunt Gracie."

"Yes," he said. "Yes, I do love Grace." He felt good saying it out loud, confessing it to the little girl.

She flashed him that toothy smile that had become over the past months her signature reaction to almost everything. "Good," she chirped. "That's all I need to know."

"What do you mean?"

She rolled her big eyes and he remembered the little girl he had met on the front steps of her grandmother's house at the beginning of the summer.

"I was wondering why I was so nervous today when I woke up," she explained, "and then it came to me, just now. I'm not worried about performing tonight. I think that I've been worried all these weeks because I wasn't sure if you'd always be in my life."

He left his seat and knelt on one knee beside her. "That's a silly thing to worry about," he said gently. "Even if I didn't love Aunt Gracie I'd be in your life for as long as I could."

"But if grandma would have died, and I would have had to go and live with Aunt Gracie, how would I know that you'd find me? How would I know that you'd even try to look for me? It wouldn't be as easy as just going next door. Then you met Aunt Gracie and I hoped you'd fall in love with her, for all of us."

He studied her innocent face, the eyes that saw the world so much more clearly than he could. "I love you, too, Kelly," he said. "I want you to be in my life as much as I want to be in yours. And I want you to make your mother happy tonight because I know she's out there, waiting to hear you play."

"With Charlotte," she whispered as if perhaps she shouldn't say her name. "Mama and Charlotte are here for both of us, Alex." She threaded her tiny fingers into his. "You make us all happy."

He slid his arm around the little girl and pulled her into his chest. He didn't have to say anything, only hold her while her body relaxed and he felt her heart beat evenly against him. A tapping on the warm-up room door disrupted the moment and he released her, turned his head toward the door, and tried to hide the tears that had snuck into the corners of his eyes.

"It's time," he uttered. "I'll walk you to the stage." He pulled open the door and spoke to the woman standing outside in the hallway, telling her that Kelly was ready. Behind him he heard her tune the Strad one last time, then he felt her beside him, her hand in his.

"Let's go play for them," she said confidently.

Alex walked with Kelly to the wing of the stage. From where they stood, the Philharmonic's position at the back of the stage was obscured by heavy black curtains. Stephen Winslow was speaking to the crowd.

"Almost a year ago today," he revealed to the attentive audience, "a respected, talented, wonderful member of our Philharmonic family endured a tragedy beyond what many of us fortunately will ever have to live through. He left us shortly after, and went out in search of the peace of mind and heart that had so suddenly abandoned him on that cool October night. Much to my own dismay and joy, Alexander Brogan came to see me some months ago, and what he offered us is what we offer you this evening."

Kelly looked up at him and smiled, Strad and bow in her right hand. He slid his arm around her shoulders as Stephen Winslow continued.

"Alex came back to Juilliard with an idea, a composition, and a story of a prodigy named Kelly. We talked, cleared the air, and then he inspired me the way he always had inspired me when he sat in the first violin section next to me for each and every concert the Philharmonic performed since the time he was twenty-one years old and himself somewhat of a prodigy. Tonight, all three of these things come together here, on this stage, as that little girl named Kelly performs for us Alexander Brogan's original composition, *The Butterfly's Heart*."

"*The Butterfly's Heart*?" she mumbled.

He glanced down at her as the audience began to clap for her appearance. "*The Butterfly's Heart*," he breathed easily. "Good Luck."

The stage darkened and the little girl walked out in the sterile glow of a spot light. He stood in the wings as he had promised and watched her curtsy, shake Stephen Winslow's hand—like Alex and Kelly had practiced the night before in the parlor—and wait until the man faded into the darkness behind her. She glanced back at him, and nodded once. Composing herself before the crowd that he knew she couldn't see in the glare of the spotlight, he watched her take a deep breath and raise the Strad to her shoulder. She laid the bow softly onto the strings, paused another moment, then drew out the first note of the composition.

The muscles across his shoulder blades tightened through the difficult technique of the first measures. He didn't realize that he'd shifted the weight of his body onto the tips of his toes as he listened carefully to each note, anticipated those to come, and held his breath as the music rose and fell in perfect pitch. Soon, with her eyes closed, she appeared absorbed in the music, a part of it, in it and of it. She didn't notice the stand lights come on silently behind her as the members of the New York Philharmonic Orchestra readied their instruments to play the full score that he, the graduate students, Stephen Winslow, the conductor, and all the other members of the orchestra had spent months creating collaboratively on Tuesday and Thursday of every week throughout the course of the summer.

When she fluttered into the final measure that she would play alone, he balled his hands into fists as he waited for the orchestra to enter the piece. On cue, the first and second violin sections eased into their part of the score. Her eyes opened briefly as she became aware of the other sounds. The lights rose on the stage, flushing into clear view the little girl swaying at the edge of the apron and the full orchestra behind her. In unison, Kelly and the more than one hundred members of the Philharmonic freed the composition, sent it pulsing out into the audience and echoing into the ceiling. The climax seized him and he felt himself become increasingly overwhelmed with the music, the pretty music. A tear slid down his cheek as he realized his creation, his life, his love for Charlotte, the little girl, Grace…all of them.

He looked into the tier boxes directly ahead of him, the only ones he could see from his vantage point on the side of the stage. As if subconsciously drawn to her, he saw Grace patting the corners of her eyes with a tissue. Luella sat like a stone beside her, captivated, her aged face soft with pride and colored with emotion. He knew that Grace could see him standing there, and he wondered if she could tell that he was trembling, if she would follow him when he left.

The end of the score was coming, but he didn't have to hear it. He already felt it. Instead, he turned away from the girl, from the orchestra and the thousands who had come to see them play. He passed out of the wings and into the hallway, through the lobby and out into the night. She had come to hear the pretty music. He could sense her there, watching, listening, and breathing again, one more time for him and her. She had brought someone with her, someone who also needed to hear the music lifted from the tiny fingers of her little girl. It all came together so perfectly, so absolutely, and he could still hear her playing as he walked soundlessly into Josie Robertson Plaza.

CODA

Hands in his pockets, he stared up at a dozen stars strong enough to pierce the city's artificial glow with evanescent twinkles. From the fragile black void overhead he found a semblance of peace while all around him the earth shifted restlessly. A certain part of Alexander Brogan did not belong here anymore, hazy through magical fountain spray, teetering at the fringes of orange radiance casting pillar shadows across the segmented plaza. Something not real, forgotten. Yet, another fraction would live on in this space, entwined in the fragile melody of a dream.

Not so much had changed, he feared, on the very spot that had changed him. To his relief, the stains were gone, washed cleanly away in November's rain. He suspected October bore them as long as it could. Surrounding stone absorbed the screams, held them silently in mortar seams, brick, steel, and glass. It felt too strange to stay. But she laced her arm in his, laid her head gently on his shoulder, kept him there a moment more, heartbeats longer, so the part of him that did belong would never forget their story.

About the Author

Brian L. Doe was born in Ogdensburg, New York, and grew up on the shores of the St. Lawrence River. From a young age, he recognized a passion for the written word and committed himself to the pursuit of writing. He received a Bachelor's Degree in writing from St. Lawrence University in Canton, New York, and a Master's Degree in secondary education from the State University of New York at Potsdam College. He is an English teacher and amateur violinist in Upstate New York where he lives with his wife and children.

Visit www.Inkslingernotes.com for more on Brian L. Doe and *The Grace Note.*

ALL THINGS THAT MATTER PRESS ™

FOR MORE INFORMATION ON TITLES AVAILABLE FROM ALL THINGS THAT MATTER PRESS, GO TO
http://allthingsthatmatterpress.com
or contact us at
allthingsthatmatterpress@gmail.com

www.ingramcontent.com/pod-product-compliance
Lightning Source LLC
LaVergne TN
LVHW091026080826
845145LV00002B/368

* 9 7 8 0 9 8 2 2 0 5 6 7 9 *